Playing with Fire

By

Desiree Holt

Playing with Fire
Copyright © 2015 by Desiree Holt
ISBN: 978-1-68361-216-2
Cover art by Fiona Jayde

Published by Decadent Publishing Company, LLC
Look for us online at:
www.decadentpublishing.com

From Desiree

People ask me all the time if I always wanted to be a writer. I don't know if "always" is the word but certainly for all the years I can remember. I was a voracious reads, as were my mother and sister and books held a royal place in our home. The funny thing is I always thought I would write mysteries because that's what we all read. I didn't read my first romance until 2004, when I was sitting with the same three chapters of a mystery on my computer that had been there for three months. But then my eyes were opened and they never closed.

Submitting that first book was scary, but after a lot of rejections you stop being scared and become determined I'm glad I never gave up, because I am having the most fun in my life I have ever had. (Well, maybe not *ever!* LOL!) So here I am, with all these titles under my belt.
Writing a book is a solitary experience but it never comes to the bookshelves, virtual or other, alone. For me it starts my treasured friend and beta reader extraordinaire, Margie Hager, who has the best eagle eye in the world. Thank you, Margie my love, for all the hours you put in to help me bring my stories to life. And for your friendship, which is a highlight of my life.

Thanks to the ladies of Belle Femme authors—Cerise Deland, Brenna Zinn, Dalton Diaz, Regina Carlysle and Samantha Cayto who are my BFFs. Guys, you make me smile on the very worst days.

Then there is my family. Do they read my books? Absolutely not! But they are the best public relations team in the world. From my daughter Amy who tells all her clients about me to my son Steve who makes sure he lets everyone he knows when I have a book released to my younger daughter Suzanne who is my good right hand and my granddaughter Kayla who is my wonderful left hand. Guys, I could not do it without you. If you see me at a convention, Suzanne will not be far from my side.

My cats, of course, keep me company while I write. And you all have seen pictures of Bast at the keyboard with me. She thinks she should get co-author credit!

Thanks to all the people who let me pester them for information, on all the different topics I tackle, from SEALs to Force Recon Marines to Delta Force soldiers to the local sheriff to the people at Beretta and the folks at the San Antonio Stock Show and Rodeo. I'm sure I've forgotten someone and if I have, I am so sorry because the time you continue to give me is very special.

Last but very far from least are all of you, my wonderful readers, who send me such great emails and posts and are so faithful. A special shoutout to Phuong Phen, Fedora Chen, Shirley Long and Patricia Sager who have been with me since my journey started and in frustrating times give me the inspiration to push ahead.

I love you so much. You are my extended family and I send you all many hugs.

There are a lot more stories to come. Please stay tuned.

Where can you find me?
You can write to me at *desireeholt@desireeholt.com* and I hope you will do that.

Where else can you find me?
www.desireeholt.com
www.desireeholttellsall.com
Facebook: www.facebook.com/desireeholtauthor
Twitter: @desireeholt
Pinterest: www.pinterest.com/desiree02holt
https://plus.google.com/desiree02holt
http://www.tsu.co/desireeholt

Also by Desiree Holt

Joy Ride
Aftershock
Night Mission
He Came Upon a Midnight Clear
Flyover
Lust Becomes You
Overnight Sensation
Soul Dreams
Dark Secrets
Knockin' Boots
Hard Lovin'
Playing with Fire
Coming Soon

Wolf Moon
Venus Moon
Blood Moon

Playing with Fire

One hot summer, Cassie Fitzgerald gave her virginity and her heart to Griffin Hunter. When he married her sister, Diane, she fled Stoneham, and, for six years, nothing could make her return. Not her sister's murder, for which Griffin was and continues to be the only suspect. Not her father's suicide, which the police chief wants to sweep under the rug.

But when her mother dies, Cassie has no choice. As the sole surviving family member, she must return to Stoneham, Texas. She plans to meet her responsibilities and get the hell out. But Stoneham doesn't let go so easily.

And then there is Griff, the man whose hold on her heart has never slackened or eased. She wants to hold her hatred for him close to her, but he wants to hold her body close to his. And the fire between them flares to life.

Together, they unravel the mysteries surrounding her sister's murder. With each layer they peel back, more secrets are revealed. Can she uncover the secret Stoneham's hiding, the riddle of Diane's murder, and the answer to her relationship with Griff without destroying herself in the process?

Dedication

To my faithful beta reader Margie Hager who makes all of this possible. Margie, without you there would be no Desiree Holt. Thank you from the bottom of my heart.

And to Sharon Slick Reads, who keeps me honest and whose support means so very much to me.

Chapter One

The call came at seven thirty in the morning, as Cassie Fitzgerald was getting ready for work. She was hardly prepared for either the sound of Harley Graham's voice or the information he was delivering. She hadn't spoken to him in years, and his announcement hit her like a blast of cold air.

"I'm sorry to be the bearer of sad news, Cassie, honey, but your mother passed away just after dawn this morning."

She clenched the receiver to stop the shaking in her hand, processing his words. Her heart felt as if a fist was squeezing it, and tears for a woman she'd wiped out of her life were like grains of sand behind her eyelids. Memories she'd kept barricaded in the closet of her mind sprang loose to assault her.

"Cassie? You still there?" Harley prodded, as the silence extended.

She swallowed hard against the sudden tightness in her throat." "Yes, I'm here."

How did he expect her to react? She and her mother had never been close, and the six years since she'd left home had stretched their relationship to a thread past the breaking point. Months had passed since they had spoken. Not even Diane's death had brought her back. *Especially* Diane's death, No, Diane's *murder*.

Say it, Cassie. Your sister was murdered.

"I didn't know she was ill," she managed, wetting her lips with her tongue. She could picture Harley on the other end of the call, holding the receiver with infinite patience. As a young doctor, he had delivered both her and Diane, helped them through their father's suicide, and now it seemed had tended the last of the Fitzgeralds who lived in Stoneham.

"She hadn't been doing too well the last few months," he said. "I wouldn't exactly say she was sick, but it was obvious she'd been failing. I've been treating her for some heart problems, but, last night, I guess she just gave up the ghost."

His words were edged with reproach, and his silent criticism hummed across the long-distance connection. Well, too bad. He wasn't the one who'd had to flee to save himself. For six years, she'd been able to shut Stoneham right out of her mind—the only way she could save herself from emotional destruction. Now, damn it, everything was back and pouring hot saltwater into open wounds.

"I'll have to make arrangements to take some leave from the office," she told him. "But I can't take more than a couple days. Let me give you my cell number."

She would let them know right away she wouldn't be gone for long. She had no desire to linger in Stoneham. The town held so many agonizing memories for her, had left so many emotional scars, that even a brief visit would strain all her emotional resources.

"I understand," Harley assured her. "I sent the body to the funeral home, and Neil McCloud is handling all the paperwork for the estate. Your mother had him helping her with everything the last few months."

"Handling? Estate?" Cassie puzzled. "What on earth could there be for Neil to take care of? My mother had nothing but the house and a small income."

"I guess she just wanted to make sure everything was tied up nice and neat. She knew her health was bad. I'm guessing she didn't want you to have any trouble with anything after she was gone." He cleared his throat. "He left the funeral arrangements until you got there. Thought you'd like to take care of that yourself. That okay, Cassie?"

"All right." There it was again, that slight accusatory tone. She pressed her fist to her forehead, trying to think. God, going back to Stoneham was like walking into the fires of Hell for her. But there was no way she could explain that to anyone without dragging all of her secrets out of the closet where she kept them hidden. "I'll fly in to San Antonio and rent a car at the airport. Otherwise, it would take me two days to drive to Stoneham from here. I still have a key to the house, Harley, so I'll go straight there."

"You call me when you get in, honey. Okay?" He gave her his office and pager numbers, extended his condolences again, and she was left to her thoughts.

She hung up, her head pounding as she tried to assess her situation. If there was one place she did not want to be, it was Stoneham, Texas, a small town with big memories, none of them pleasant. Well, almost none of them. When she fled the town and her family, she left with the intention of never returning. She hadn't even gone back for her sister Diane's funeral. Or her father's. She couldn't. There was too much pain. Now, she had no choice. There was no one left now except her.

So, here she was, thrust into it again. She would have to arrange for the funeral and burial, have Neil take care of probating whatever estate there was. Sell the house, that was a definite. Putting it in the hands of a realtor would be the smartest thing to do. Maybe Neil could help with that, too. She didn't want to hang around and deal with it. In fact, her preference would be to take care of everything she could from a distance.

She couldn't stay, and that was that. Along with all the other memories she'd have to contend with, staying meant coming face to face with Griffin Hunter.

Just thinking his name made the heavy weight of memories slam into her. Yet, beneath the anger and pain that were still fresh after all this time, she felt the familiar stirring in her loins, the heat igniting low in her belly, and her nipples tightening. The mere thought of his name brought it all back.

No! She banged her hand on the counter. Griffin was out of her life, and he'd stay that way. No erotic memories were going to change that. She would do everything possible to avoid him, slipping in and out of town before he even knew she was there.

Cassie swallowed two aspirins, trying to take the edge off the headache, and called her editor. She already knew it wasn't a good time for her to take leave.

After a year of struggle, *The Sports Weekly* had at last turned a corner. Florida was filled with sports teams. The Tampa Bay area, squarely in the middle of the state and with its own major league and college teams, was an ideal place for a sports publication. It had been a real coup to be hired on as the sole female reporter, a job she worked twice as hard as anyone else to keep.

They were approaching their next crunch in the schedule. Since they were two months into baseball season, with football looming, everyone would be working nonstop. Well, too bad but it couldn't be helped. Death didn't leave you many options.

Mike Rivard, her editor, listened without saying a word while she told him what happened.

"I'm sorry," she said. "I know this is a busy time. I feel like I'm finking out."

4

"Cassie, it's always a busy time around here." He sounded as if he was speaking from the bottom of a barrel. "Sometimes other things have to take precedence. This is one of them. Go and do whatever you have to. Your job will still be here. Just call me when you get there and give me a read, okay?"

"Thank you, Mike. I will. And you can always reach me on my cell if you need me."

"No sweat, kiddo."

She hung up, enormous relief sweeping over her. She and Mike had an excellent working relationship, but she knew how tough he was on people. He'd surprised her with his understanding.

It took most of the hour she'd predicted to take care of packing and give all her plants a good soaking. Last, she called her closest friend, Claire, who promised to keep an eye on her place, take in the mail, and field any questions.

"Do you want me to come with you, Cassie?" she asked. "Dealing with this stuff can be very stressful."

She and Claire had been roommates in college. The friendship had gotten even stronger as they fought to establish themselves after graduation. Claire was now a paralegal for an attorney who did a great deal of estate work. When Cassie's life had come unraveled so long ago, it was Claire who saved her, who talked her into moving to Tampa after graduation and looking for a job.

"No, thanks just the same. I plan to be there and gone before anyone realizes I was even in town."

"Well, at least let me drive you to the airport," Claire insisted. "Parking costs an arm and a leg there. Just because you say you'll only be gone for a few days, doesn't mean something won't come up where you'll need to be gone longer."

"Okay, I'll take you up on that. Let me go do my stuff."

Grateful for the offer, she was packed and ready by the time Claire arrived.

"One suitcase?" Her friend raised an eyebrow.

"I meant what I said, Claire. I don't plan on making this a long visit."

By lunchtime, she was on a nonstop flight to San Antonio, Texas. Closing her eyes, she fought back the nausea at the thought of what faced her. *Stoneham*. The scene of so much pleasure, yet so much pain. And Griffin Hunter, who, despite her most determined efforts, had lived in her dreams every night for the past six years.

Chapter Two

Six years before....

Summer in Central Texas. Hot, sultry nights beckoning with unspoken promise. The air redolent with the mingled scents of phlox and hyacinth and forsythia.

Cassie strolled along the sidewalk. Why did she decide to walk to the movies in this unbearable heat? Already, her skin was sticky with the humidity and her clothes hung limp against her body. It occurred to her that leaving an air-conditioned house might not have been the wisest thing to do.

But the house had closed around her, suffocating her. Diane, her older sister, was out living up to her wild reputation. Their parents, with Diane out of the house, were too engrossed in watching television to remember they had another daughter. No wonder she sometimes she felt as if she didn't exist in their eyes.

They were such a study in contrast, she and Diane. Two years apart, they might have been two worlds apart. Her sister blasted through life like a comet, her wild gypsy looks beckoning to every man who laid eyes on her.

Cassie was so rigidly proper, so bright and self-sufficient, her parents had long ago decided she required no supervision on their part. Cassie won the awards and gold stars while Diane accumulated detention slips for her deliberate violations of rules. Cassie went to college. Diane stayed home to work and live life in the raw.

Diane was a flame, drawing unwary moths and burning those that got too close. To her parents, she was a bright star, vivacious, full of life, lighting up their universe. They were fascinated they could have produced such a child, captivated by the colorful aura surrounding her.

So, while Cassie labored in bland anonymity, Diane did as she pleased and made her parents love her for it. Cassie had long ago stopped raging about the unfairness of the situation. She was focused on two things: graduating and getting as far away from Stoneham, her parents, and Diane as she could.

Even if she hadn't wanted company tonight and wasn't in the mood for socializing, she still had the fidgets. Sitting shut up in her room didn't appeal to her. A movie by herself seemed a good solution. Anything to get out of the house that felt more like a prison with every passing day.

The lone theater in Stoneham was just twenty minutes away; walking had seemed like a good idea when she started out. Now, as the moisture-laden air lay heavy on her skin and sucked at her breath, she wondered if she should just go back home and hole up in her room.

"Taking the night air, Cassie?"

The voice came out of nowhere, low, seductive, flowing over her like warm honey.

Cassie jerked her head around. Lost in her own thoughts, she hadn't realized she was in front of Griffin Hunter's house. "Griffin? Is that you?"

"It's me, sugar. Come on up and have a beer."

Griffin Hunter. Stoneham's resident bad boy. Ten years ago, his mother had died and forever altered life in the Hunter household.

"I don't know what you see in that boy," Mrs. Fitzgerald whined, every time Diane flew out the door with him and the rest of the "wild bunch."

"Griff Hunter's got it all, Mother," Diane would say with a laugh. "And he sure knows what to do with it."

"When that boy's mother died, his father fell into a bottle and never came out," she said in a waspish tone.

"If it hadn't been for Griffin, their landscaping business would have gone straight to hell," Diane shot back. "That says something about him."

No one argued he wasn't an excellent landscape gardener, a hard and dependable worker. But when he wasn't working, he was the acknowledged leader of the wildest crowd in the county, the ones who drank to excess and held wild parties. They were considered trouble. The police always had them on their radar.

If there was trouble to be had, Griffin was square in the middle of it. Although very bright, he barely managed to graduate high school with his class. He didn't consider studying a high priority, finding himself in one scrape after another, always angry, always ready to brawl. His mother's death and his father's collapse into alcoholism seemed to give him more license to thumb his nose at society.

Nowadays, only the business made him focus. He balanced his time between landscaping, hauling his father home from some bar, and running at night with the crowd that made a hobby out of seeking trouble. A crowd Diane fit in far too well.

He was the guilty pleasure of every female in Stoneham. Like a forbidden prize, his wicked smile and sexy body charmed every one of them. Prepubescent teenagers, ripening adolescents, women both repressed and lusty—they all harbored secret dark fantasies about Griffin Hunter.

Say good-bye and keep walking, Cassie told herself, even as her feet ignored her silent direction and carried her along the path and up the steps to the wide front porch. Buried in her mind were her own secret fantasies about Griffin Hunter. The boys she dated, even in college, lacked any semblance of finesse, instead viewing sex as a competitive sport. How many nights had she lain in bed, wishing for Griffin's hands on her body instead of on Diane's, the pulse throbbing between her legs where heat pooled like liquid silver, her heart racing, her skin flushed?

"How come you're not out with Diane and the others tonight?" she asked.

"Didn't feel like it. How come you never come out with us?" He flashed a quick grin. "I'd show you a good time, sugar."

"I'm not Diane."

"No kidding."

He lounged in the glider, a beer can in his hand, one foot rocking himself back and forth. Skintight jeans molded his muscular body, outlining a bulge at his crotch from which Cassie averted her eyes. His half-buttoned shirt exposed the crisp curls on his chest. Sun-bleached hair, worn just a little long and casually disarrayed, brushed his collar. Cassie couldn't see his eyes, but she knew they were a piercing electric blue.

Griffin looked like an Adonis come to life. Except Adonis never had such a rough-carved look to his face or exuded such a sense of the dark side. She could see what Diane saw in him.

Her heartbeat accelerated, and faint heat gathered in her stomach. *Danger!* her uptight self shouted at her. *Go to the movies. Go home. Go anywhere. Leave.* But here she stood, her feet planted on the porch. She peered through the fading light at him, her breath quickening just at the sight of his dark angelic face.

"Is that a slam?" She leaned against the porch railing.

"Come on over here and sit with me." He patted the section of the vinyl seat next to him. "Take a chance with the town bad boy. Come on, Cassie. I don't bite."

As if drawn by an invisible thread, she walked over and sat down at the other end of the glider. In the dim light of the street lamp, she could see Griffin's wicked grin.

"Keeping your distance?" He laughed, a rich, deep sound. "No, you're nothing like your sister."

"I think this is a bad idea." She started to get up, but his long fingers clamped on one arm.

"Don't leave yet, sugar. We've had practically no time to get acquainted." He reached to the table beside him and handed her a cold metal can. "Have a beer, Cassie. Just one beer. I don't think that will ruin your reputation."

"Well...all right. Maybe one beer would be okay."

She sat stiff as a board, clutching the icy can in her hands, sipping from it, wondering what she was doing there anyway. And trying to ignore the tension coiling within her.

"Home for the summer?" Griffin asked, his tone of voice casual.

"Sort of."

She'd just finished her sophomore year at college. In two days, she would be meeting her roommate, Claire, and four other friends for a week of whitewater rafting in Georgia. Then she would find a summer job that would keep her as far away from her parents and Diane as possible.

"How can you be sort of home?"

"Where's your father?" she asked, changing the subject.

"Where else would he be?" His voice flattened to a monotone.

"The Winter Garden, waiting for closing time and someone to haul his ass home."

"So, you're just whiling away the night, here alone on your porch?"

"Maybe I was waiting for you, Squirt," he said, his tone soft and seductive, whispering to her of forbidden pleasures.

"Why do you always call me that?"

"Squirt? I guess because you seemed so much younger than Diane."

"Because I'm not wild like she is? Because I'm dull and boring?"

Griffin chuckled. "Anyone who calls you dull and boring hasn't bothered to take a good look."

He was Diane's lover. One of her many lovers. All the times Cassie had seen him waiting for her sister to come flying down the stairs, smiling that wicked sexy smile, exuding an unconsciously erotic air, she'd fantasized he was waiting for her.

Her shameful, dark desire for him, hidden in the deepest recesses of her mind, leaped to the surface. Cassie, the virgin, the ice queen, the nobody, hungered to have Griffin's arms around her, molding her to him, touching her in all the mysterious places of her body. She ached to feel his penis inside her, his mouth on her breasts, his fingers tantalizing her clitoris that was swollen just from her fantasies.

All of a sudden, she realized she was no longer in her isolated corner. Somehow she'd moved across the glider—or Griffin had—and his arm draped around her shoulders, his face dangerously close to hers.

"What do think, Squirt?" His words slid out like hot molasses. His mouth was inches from hers. "Want to take a walk on the wild side?"

"Don't tease me, Griffin." The nickname made her feel small and unattractive.

"Oh, sugar, I'm for sure not teasing. Maybe I should call you Dewdrop."

She blinked. "Dewdrop?"

"Mmhmm. Fresh as the early morning dew on a blade of grass. I'd love to pluck you and lick you all up."

He bent his head, and she knew he was going to kiss her. Common sense told her to push him away, but she couldn't make herself move.

He waited the space of a heartbeat for her to move away or object then his mouth came down on hers, hard, his tongue forcing her to open for him. She felt it sweeping into the dark recesses of her mouth, tasting her like a sweet dessert, flicking at nerves she didn't even know she had. Tentative, she let her tongue meet his, twist with his, duel with his—and she was lost.

Chapter Three

The present....

The plane landed in midafternoon. Cassie hadn't called ahead for a rental car, so, by the time she retrieved her luggage and arranged for transportation, she hit the interstate at the beginning of rush hour. The Texas heat had enfolded her as soon as she walked outside, plastering her clothes to her body. Once inside the rental car, she turned the air conditioner on full blast, praying for icy relief.

Her neck ached with tension, her head throbbed, and the clogged highway didn't add to her mood. Stoneham was still a good hour's drive away once she hit the outskirts of San Antonio, and she didn't relish spending all this time in gridlock. She fiddled with the radio, trying to find a station with soothing music while traffic inched along.

At last, *at last*, she moved beyond the city limits. Traffic thinned, and she increased her speed. As she drove along I-10, she noticed changes since the last time she'd made this trip. Signs of progress were everywhere. New housing developments, strip centers, office buildings.

But not in Stoneham, I'm sure. Nothing ever changes there.

She was hot, tired, and hungry by the time she pulled into the small town. It was just after six o'clock, and daylight was fading. The exit road from the interstate had dumped her off at the edge of downtown, and she skirted it, following familiar side streets.

As she drove, she scanned for any sign of Griffin, though she didn't expect to see him just because he was in her thoughts. But he was out there, somewhere, and, sooner or later, they'd run into each other. Her stomach knotted at the thought. What could they even say to each other after all this time?

At last, she pulled up in front of the house she'd lived in most of her life. The giant oak trees still guarded the front yard and shaded the porch, but they couldn't hide the sad, neglected look the house now wore. The lawn and bushes needed tending. The wooden trim around the limestone had faded and, in some spots, peeled. Shades pulled down at every window added to the look of despair.

Her stomach tightened as she took out her key, long unused, and opened the front door. A dank, musty odor hit her at once. Her mother may have been existing here, but she hadn't been living.

She snapped up the old-fashioned window shades, hoping a little light in the room would improve things, but it just made them more dismal. A thin film of dust covered everything, accenting the worn look of the furniture that had served them well for so many years. She walked through the rooms, mentally taking stock. It was obvious that, after her father's death, her mother had spent her life in as few rooms as possible.

Guilt reached out to touch Cassie, but she chased it away. It was not her fault. None of it. For twenty years, she had labored for her parents' love and approval. She was the forgotten child hidden in the shadow of Diane's brighter light. They probably hadn't even missed her when she left, and now, she was the one remaining.

Sighing, she trudged up the stairs, lugging her suitcase. The bedrooms looked like relics from an old movie. The heavy furniture in the room her parents had shared seemed so austere, the coldness broken by the rumpled look of the bed, which no one had thought to straighten after they'd taken her mother away. *Well, and who would do that, missy?*

Nothing in Diane's room had changed. Her parents had turned it into some kind of shrine, with pictures of her sister on every available surface. A pink sundress still lay tossed across the bed, pink sandals tumbled onto each other on the floor as if the wearer had just slipped them off. If she strained her ears, Cassie could almost hear Diane's laughter, and a chill washed over her.

For six years, she had pushed the circumstances of Diane's death away. Standing in this house again, everything popped back into her brain, bringing familiar memories and emotions. Diane might have been wild, but what could there have been about her to drive someone to commit murder? An unwelcome need to find answers wormed its way into her system.

With determination, she backed out of the room and went to her own, another site of little change, but not for the same reason. Looking around, she could have been the young Cassie again, dressing for high school classes or home from college between semesters. The same yellow-and-white wallpaper, the white ruffled bedspread with the daffodil sprays across the surface, the little vanity with the yellow skirt where she'd applied her makeup. Except, everything was old and faded. No nostalgia involved, just a sad memory.

Opening her suitcase, she hung up the few things she'd brought that needed wrinkles to fall out then pulled on a pair of shorts and a T-shirt. Thank goodness someone'd had the sense to leave the air conditioning on, albeit at a high temperature, and she bumped the indicator down as she passed the thermostat in the hall.

The kitchen yielded little in the way of food. No surprise there. She had no idea how or when her mother ate. The freezer held a half gallon of vanilla ice cream that she decided would do as her dinner.

16

Standing at the counter, spooning the creamy confection from the container, she called Claire to let her know she was okay. Afterward, she dialed Harley Graham's home number.

"I'm so glad you got here safe and sound, Cassie." That warm voice had soothed her since she was a toddler. "I was beginning to worry about you. Have you eaten? Would you like to come by the house for a bite? Your mother ate such strange meals of late, I can't imagine you'll find much there."

No kidding. "Thanks, Harley, but I'm okay. I can get stuff tomorrow. I guess I just wanted to let you know I'm here and ask what happens next."

"The body's at Stoneham Mortuary. Still the only one in town. They're just waiting to hear from you about final arrangements."

"Will there need to be a big funeral?" She frowned, thinking of the unpleasant possibility, of half the town showing up from morbid curiosity.

"I think a small service at the mortuary would be appropriate," he assured her.

Cassie realized there was a great deal left unsaid in that simple sentence. "I'll talk to them tomorrow," she told him.

"And Neil McLeod said to catch him in the morning. You know, he still handled all the legal work for your folks. He'll make time for you to go over your mother's papers."

"I'd like to wrap this up by Monday. Do you think that's possible? I need to get back to work, and there isn't much to hold me here anymore."

"I know this is hard for you, Cassie. Stoneham hasn't been what you'd call kind to your family." He sighed. "We'll make this as easy on you as possible, but I think a lot depends on what you want to do.

Talk to Neil first. Then, if you want to chew anything over, give me a call."

"I can't tell you how much I appreciate this, Harley. You're a good friend as well as our doctor."

"You thinking of calling any of your old friends while you're here?" Like everyone else, he knew her leave-taking had been anything but pleasant, and he had no idea who she'd kept in touch with. "Tonight's Thursday. In another hour, they'll all be at Pete's Pizza."

"I think I'll pass. Thanks just the same." She was already battling too many old memories she felt were better left tucked away.

"Well, you know where to find them. Or me. Nothing ever changes in Stoneham, you know."

I know. Nothing except my life.

Chapter Four

Six years before....

They were in Griffin's bedroom, a room that reflected his masculinity in the stark oak furniture and the walls bare of adornment. The only relief was a framed photo of his mother on his dresser. The pale golden light from the street lamps poured in through the window, casting shadows on their bodies.

Cassie had no recollection of how they got there. One minute, he was kissing her and wiping out all her brain cells. The next, they were upstairs next to his bed, his eyes burning into hers, his hands hot on her face.

He undressed her with exquisite care, peeling away her blouse, sliding her skirt down to her ankles then tossing it to the side. With a deft movement he unclasped her bra and disposed of it with an ease born of long practice. When her breasts sprang free, he cupped them in his palms, his thumbs rasping against the nipples. He bent and licked the hardened points—just a brief swipe of his tongue—and electricity jolted through her.

She barely felt him remove her panties, her last line of defense. Shivers chased themselves along her spine as his hands roamed her body, and he murmured in her ear, his words seductive and reassuring. He touched her everywhere—her shoulders, her back, her hips. One finger teased at her navel before his hand descended to the nest of curls between her thighs. With exquisite gentleness, he combed his fingers through them, sliding down to the lips guarding her virgin sheath.

Then she lay on his bed, in his arms, and he whispered naughty things, erotic words that made her skin burn. His mouth locked to hers, his tongue probing and tasting. Tentative at first, she met his challenge, and as their tongues tangled together, fire shot through her. Fear and desire mingled in a potent combination, fueled by the unexpected intensity of her response. This was unsafe, uncharted waters for her, and she had no idea how to act. She only knew whatever Griffin was doing, she never wanted him to stop.

Her body trembled as his gaze swept over her, his eyes taking in every detail of her naked quivering body. The streetlight shining through the window highlighted the planes and shadows of his face, giving it an even stronger, more sensuous look. The earthy scent of whatever aftershave he used invaded her nostrils.

"Griffin," she breathed.

"Griff," he corrected. "Call me Griff. Say it, Cassie."

"Griff." The name came out on a sigh.

He stroked his hand over her body, exploring in earnest, his touch igniting little nerve endings. He cupped one breast with his warm palm and abraded one nipple with slow strokes of his thumb. Every touch set off another explosion of electricity inside her. The heat of his mouth as he sucked one tip scorched her then he bit down gently, and she was sure she'd explode from the cascade of sensations.

He took a long time teasing and tantalizing, paying careful attention to each breast in turn, kissing and licking the skin, suckling at the nipple swelling in response to his touch. Her nerves fired, and she couldn't seem to draw enough air into her lungs.

"Griffin— Griff, I...." She worked to clear the fog from her brain.

"Sssh, sugar. Don't talk," he murmured. "Such sweet little

breasts, just waiting for the right mouth to suckle them."

His hand drifted lower, lower, trailing across her navel down to her abdomen, the tips of his fingers just touching the beckoning triangle of curls. When he ran his fingers through them with a possessive caress, Cassie reached out a hand to touch him as well and encountered hot, naked skin. When had he shed his clothes? Her hand jerked back, but Griffin captured it with one of his and placed it on his chest, trapping it between them.

"Relax, Cassie," he crooned. "Let me make you feel good. Let me love you."

He cupped her feminine mound and touched the inside of her thighs. Nervous, Cassie clamped her legs tight together.

"Open for me," he whispered. "Come on, sugar. It will all be worth it."

She was powerless to do anything but obey. She felt hot all over, inside and out. A slow throbbing at the entrance to her vagina grew stronger, like a primitive drum beat. She resisted only a little as he nudged her thighs apart. Then she felt that same feathery caress as he toyed with the curls covering her mound, just skimming the tips of his fingers over them. No one had ever touched her there before, but letting Griff do it seemed the most natural thing in the world.

"Okay, sugar?" he whispered, the sound of his words hypnotizing her. "Don't be scared, all right?"

Her mouth wouldn't work, so she just nodded.

"Good. You're gonna love this even more, I promise."

One finger parted the folds at her entrance and slid between them. She jerked, but the arm cradling her held her in place.

"God," he breathed. "You are so damn wet. And hot."

He eased one finger inside her, its passage moistened by her own lubrication. He paused, watching her with an intent look then inserted a second finger. After a moment, he moved his thumb to the nub of her sex, rubbing the tip of her clitoris back and forth.

Sparks shot through her body. "Oh, God, Griff. Oh my God."

Sensations swept over her, rousing her. She was frightened, terrified of the unfamiliar feelings he'd awakened in her. She should pull back, but her body wouldn't let her. She wanted this. Wanted him. Without any further thought, she parted her legs for him even more.

"That's it, Cassie," he breathed. "Open wide for me."

He kept up the soft murmurs, coaxing her, soothing her. With his thumb and forefinger, he gave her clit a gentle pinch, tugged on it. She almost exploded out of his arms, arching off the bed. Then, shocked, she realized he had stopped all caresses, all those delicious strokes of his talented, clever fingers. She forced her eyes open.

"Griff? W-what's wrong?"

"Were you waiting for me, Cassie?" he whispered, staring into her eyes. "Saving your sweet body for me?"

"What?" Should she tell him he was right? Let her dark secret out of its hiding place?

"I don't know whether to feel guilt or beat my chest, darlin'." He pressed soft kisses on the corner of her mouth. "You didn't tell me you're a virgin, sweet thing. Did you want me to be your first lover? Tell me. Was that it?"

The answer bubbled up in her throat with a mind of its own, and her lips barely formed the word. "Yes."

She didn't dare tell him how many nights she had lain in her virginal bed dreaming of just this moment. She was eager and ashamed at the same time, but, more than anything, she was so aroused she couldn't think.

"I won't disappoint you," he breathed in her ear. "I'll make sure you're good and hot and ready for me. A little bit of pain, but the pleasure, oh, sugar, the pleasure. I'll make you feel so good. Just close your eyes and feel, sugar."

She felt suspended in space. Her heart beat so loud she was sure he could hear it. He stroked her inner sheath, his fingertips rasping the sensitive skin, reaching far inside to stimulate every muscle and nerve. All the while, his thumb kept up its unbearable torment, back and forth, back and forth, on that hot, swollen nub. She clutched at the sheet beneath her, moving her body, wondering if she would go mad with the pleasure. Every sense was vibrant and alive. Then the first flutterings began inside her virgin sex. She was torn between fighting it and embracing it.

"Open your eyes and look at me," he demanded. "Let go, Cassie. Just let go. Come for me, sugar. Let it happen."

A mountain in her path couldn't have stopped her. Her body was beyond her control, betraying her with every response.

All of a sudden, spasms raced through her. The intensity was too much, so much it frightened her. She had to stop it. And then she convulsed, her head coming off the pillow, her thighs clamping around his hand. She was over the edge as her orgasm racked her body, wave after wave of pleasure beating at her, consuming her, liquid pouring from her into his hand.

Griff pressed his mouth to hers, forcing it open, swallowing her moans as he pressed his fingers into her hard. Then it was over, and she lay panting on the bed. Her heart raced, and her sheath still contracted around his fingers with aftershocks. She almost cried out in protest when he withdrew his hand, cupping her mound with a gentle touch.

"Felt good, didn't it, sugar?"

His deep voice was like a caress itself.

"Yes." She could barely speak the word.

"That's just the beginning, darlin'. Trust me, Cassie. I'll take you to the top of the world."

Before she could catch another breath, he slid down her body in a slow, languorous movement until his head rested between her thighs. He blew a soft puff of air on the entrance to her still quivering sex, his breath a hot breeze against her heated flesh, then stroked her with his tongue. With just the tip, he traced the line of her folds and the pink skin guarding her sex. Light as a feather, he teased and tasted, lapping up the slick moisture from her orgasm.

She might have thought she was finished already, undone, but at the first lick of his tongue, Cassie almost came off the bed. Strangled moans came from her throat as he held her thrashing body in place with his strong hands. He showed her no mercy, gave her no room to draw back as he used his tongue with relentless intent. Back and forth, around and around, until she was crying, begging, pleading for more.

Just as she thought she couldn't bear the exquisite pain for another moment, he thrust his tongue into her and she came once more, pushing at him, pulling at him, her hands holding his head. He gripped her thighs as she rode out the storm and the quivering in her muscles subsided.

She was still waiting for her pulse to slow when he moved back up and took her hand.

"Touch me, Cassie. I want you to know what you'll feel inside your body."

His shaft was enormous and almost shocked her out of her fog of sensation. The silky skin, the hard thickness was like nothing she'd ever touched before. The tip was wet, and she used one finger to slide the moisture back and forth over the petal-soft skin. "All right, sugar. You are wide and wet for me." He put his mouth close to her ear. "I'm glad you saved it for me, Cassie. Did you know you were always the one I wanted? The one I dreamed of at night?"

He shifted to reach into the nightstand drawer. Cassie heard the tearing of foil and opened her eyes to see Griff sheathing himself in a condom. Then he moved over her, positioning himself, the head of his shaft at the entrance to her sheath. Slowly, inch by inch he slid into her until he reached the membrane waiting to yield to him at any minute.

"Look at me, Cassie," he commanded. "Open your eyes and look at me."

She opened them. His eyes bored into her, glittering with deep desire. "A tiny pinch, darlin,'" he whispered. "That's all. There."

She recoiled a little at the pain, but he held her in place.

"Okay?" he asked in that low rumbling tone?

Was she? Oh, yeah. As the pain ebbed, hunger and craving took its place.

She nodded.

He thrust with his hips again, one strong push and then he was in all the way.

"All right, sugar," he ground out. "Here we go."

He slid his hands beneath her hips and lifted her to meet him. With a slow and steady movement, he thrust into her, forward and retreat, his gaze locked with hers.

Her tissues stretched around his thick, hard cock. She reached for him, clutching at him, drawing him deeper yet. When she lifted her hips to him in a silent signal, crying, "More", he increased the tempo. Harder, faster, he held her tight against him so he could reach her deepest recesses, rocking her with the motion. When he slipped his fingers into the cleft of her buttocks, pressing his fingertips against the tight opening, that was all it took.

They came like the cataclysmic eruption of a volcano, falling over the edge together. Cassie felt as if she were shattering into a thousand pieces. She was flying; she was floating. Her body shook with the force of her orgasm, and colors swirled behind her eyelids. Through the thinness of the latex, she could feel Griff's hot liquid jetting into her, his iron maleness throbbing as his release came with tremendous force. She never wanted it to end.

At last he collapsed on her chest, his heartbeat thudding against her, panting for breath. They lay in each other's arms for a long time, neither of them speaking.

Cassie twined her fingers in his long, wheat-colored hair, trying to get her brain working again. She had just given her virginity that she'd guarded with such care to the town hooligan, her sister's lover, and she didn't even regret it. She didn't know what had made her do it, but at the moment, she didn't care.

She roused herself. "Griff?"

"Yeah, sugar?"

"I have to go. It's very late."

He sat up, taking her with him, searching her eyes. "Are you all right, Dewdrop?"

She smiled in the darkness. The nickname tickled her heart. "Yes, Griff. I'm fine. Better than fine."

"I didn't hurt you?" He smoothed the hair back from her face.

"God, you were so tight."

"And you're so...large." She smiled again. "No, I'm okay. Really."

"I want to see you again, Cassie."

"I-I'm going away day after tomorrow. I'll be gone for a week. Then I'll be heading back to the university."

"Come back tomorrow night? Please? If that's all the time we have, give us one more night. I'll make it even better for you. I promise."

She wanted to tell him if he made it any better she might die. But her sister intruded in the moment they shared. "What about Diane?"

"What about her? She's got more fish to fry than she has a pan to put them in. It's you I want, darlin'." He put his lips close to her ear. "It's always been you I've wanted. In my story, the bad boy gets the good girl."

He stroked her ear with the tip of his tongue, and she shivered. She nodded, knowing she'd regret it.

She fought with herself all the next day and almost stayed away from him, calling herself all kinds of a fool, ashamed of her wantonness. But when the next night rolled around, there she was, lured by the Siren call of the most erotic experience of her life.

And Griff was right. The second night was better. He taught her things she'd never dreamed of, helped her to scale new heights of sexuality with him. She was in a constant state of arousal, never getting quite enough of him.

For two nights, cocooned in the secrecy of his room, away from unsuspecting eyes, Cassie learned about love and sensuality from Griffin Hunter. She reveled in it, gloried in it, celebrated life and loving in the big king-sized bed with the street light pouring in on them.

When she was dressing to leave the second night, he pulled open the drawer of the nightstand and handed her a little box. He seemed hesitant, almost embarrassed.

"For me?" she asked widening her eyes.

"It's not much, Cassie, but it's all I have to give you."

"You don't have to give me anything," she protested.

"Yes," he insisted. "I want you to have something that will always make you think of me."

She opened it and drew in her breath. Nestled inside laid a tiny silver heart on a chain. She looked at him, questioning.

"I don't give my heart that easy, sugar. But it belongs to you. Always. Take good care of it."

She was so full of unexpected emotion her heart almost stopped. She clasped the gift to her breasts, treasuring it, moved almost to tears by his words. He helped her fasten the chain around her neck and gave her a soft kiss on the lips.

"I'll see you when you get back," he said. "Let's not waste a minute before you have to go back to school."

She nodded, already counting the days, visions of wedding dresses floating in her head.

But when she saw him a week later, he was already married. To Diane.

Chapter Five

The present....

Cassie asleep was restless, and she woke often from the troubled dreams that plagued her. Being back in this house did nothing for her peace of mind. Giving up, she trudged downstairs, found some instant coffee in a cupboard, boiled some water, and made a cup. Sitting on the barstool at the end of the counter, she set the telephone book in front of her and made the calls she'd been dreading.

The people at the Stoneham Mortuary would be happy to meet with her any time she could make it during the day. Donald Brandon, under his father's tutelage, tried to engage her in conversation, but his unctuous tones made her skin crawl. She planned to be in and out of that place as fast as she could.

"Oh, let me give you my cell number, since there's no service here at the house. I guess someone had it disconnected."

"I believe Neil did that," he said. "No sense wasting money."

It's mine to waste, she wanted to tell him.

Her next call was to Neil himself. Along with his father, he handled most of the town's legal work, and he also took her call right away.

"I've been waiting to hear from you, Cassie." His tone was warm and sympathetic. "I'm sorry we have to meet again under these circumstances, but it will be a real pleasure to see you. I'm happy to take care of things for you."

"I have no idea what there is to do, Neil," she told him, "but Harley says you've handled everything for my mother."

"There's a small estate," he explained, "and, of course, the house to deal with. Why don't you come by around noon, and I'll take you to lunch?"

No social engagements. Get it done and get out. "I'm really only here for a short time. If we could meet this morning, that would help me a lot."

"How about ten?" he asked, his voice barely concealing his disappointment. "Then maybe I can talk you into dinner."

"Ten is fine," she said, ignoring his other comment. "See you then. Oh, and let me give you my cell."

She hadn't brought much of a wardrobe with her, but she had packed her brand new summer pantsuit that would take her just about anywhere. She'd bought it because Claire told her the soft rose color was perfect with her light-blonde hair and deep-brown eyes, and Claire was definitely the fashion maven. At least she'd project an appearance of success with the people she'd be seeing. That was important to her. She showered, applied her makeup, and pulled her hair back into a gold clip to keep it away from her face in a neat style. Gold hoops at her ears completed the outfit.

She examined herself in the mirror. Yes, she'd face the town in style.

Before she left the house, she added some cleaning supplies to the list of groceries she needed. If she planned to sell the house, it couldn't be shown as it was, and her mother didn't seem to have much in the way of household items. She might as well buy enough groceries to get her through the weekend, too. Public places like restaurants, where she might run into Griffin, were to be avoided at all costs.

Her watch said ten sharp when she walked into Neil McLeod's

law office. Six years ago, when she was a junior in college, he'd been graduating from law school. He'd been tall and handsome then, athletic, with dark hair and deep-black eyes. Maturity agreed with him, improving on those good looks. Not that he was her type or anything. Too smooth, too polished.

I like them rough around the edges.

She shook off the thought and focused on the moment at hand. *What does Neil know about Diane's death? Did he keep up with her wild activities?*

Gazing around the office, she spotted two framed photos on the credenza behind the desk. Neil had married Leslie Walters, daughter of his father's partner, right after graduation. One photo showed the two of them laughing on the deck of a sailboat; the other included two small children, boys, carbon copies of their father.

"Good to see you, Cassie." Neil stood to shake her hand, and indicated a chair across the desk from him.

"You're looking well, Neil." She nodded at the photos. "Life must be good for you."

"Yes, it is. Dad and I share the practice," he told her, "and there's plenty to keep us busy. Leslie's father retired about three years ago. Heart attack. He keeps his hand in with a few cases, but the doctors don't want him working full-time."

"I hope he's feeling well," she said. "You know, I was always surprised you stayed in Stoneham."

"Never wanted to leave, believe it or not. Leslie and I have made a wonderful life for ourselves here, and it's a terrific place for kids to grow up. None of the city problems." He grinned at her. "How about you? Anything on the horizon? Maybe coming back here to settle down? Or is there a marriage coming up to keep you in Tampa?"

"Not if I can help it," she said. "Besides, I love my job, and it keeps me busy enough. Listen, I'd love to exchange pleasantries, but I'm trying to keep my time here as short as possible. Can you tell me what papers I have to sign, or what I have to do?"

He opened a file on his desk. "I'm sure you know the estate is not extensive. However, your father had been a real saver and made wise investments. Your mother had a good income and never touched the principal, so there's about two hundred thousand in annuities."

Cassie stared at him, astonished. Had she heard right? "You're kidding!"

"Nope. Dead serious. You're the beneficiary, so transferring the assets should be quite simple. There's just one form to sign. They'll cash it out if you want. Just tell them where you bank, and they'll do a direct deposit." He flipped over a sheet of paper. "There's also the house, which is now yours. I guess you'll be wanting to sell it?"

She nodded. "Still just one real estate agency here?"

"Just the one," he agreed. "Jesse Markham, and now his daughters. Jesse does the commercial, and they do the residential. Want me to have one of them call you?"

"To tell you the truth, if you could have someone come by this afternoon, that would be great. I'll be home doing some work in the house. What else?"

"There's a small life insurance policy, about twenty five thousand. It will cover funeral and other immediate expenses. I've called the insurance company and asked for the paperwork to be faxed, but this is Friday, so I'm not too optimistic about getting it until next week. Also, I need to file the will for probate, and I can't do that until Monday. You'll need to pick up a copy of the papers when I'm done so you can take care of things at the bank. I have copies of the death certificate for you, so there shouldn't be any holdup."

"The bank?" She frowned.

"Sure. Well, really, just the checking account. Howard Cook will take care of you when you get there. I already talked to him. Course, he's gone for the weekend, too."

She huffed a sigh. *Damn it all, anyway.* "Neil, I don't mean to sound pushy or ungrateful, but I was hoping to leave here on Monday. Do you think that's possible?"

He leaned back in his chair, looking at her. "Well, now, Cassie, I know it's been a long time since you've set foot in this town, but things haven't changed a bit. I don't think you can get anything done in a hurry here."

She ground her teeth in frustration. "Let's just see how fast we can move things along, okay? If I have to, I'll call my boss and tell him I need a day or two more."

He checked his watch. "Why don't you give me a holler this afternoon, and I'll see how far I can get. Been to the funeral home yet?"

"No." She shook her head. "That's my next stop."

"Well, shouldn't be too much of a hassle there. Your mother made all the plans and left instructions."

Cassie stared at him. "She did?"

"Yes, ma'am. Said she didn't want anything big or fancy. You can tell Don Brandon he'll get paid as soon as the paperwork's done on the insurance policy. If he has any questions, have him give me a ring."

Cassie breathed a small sigh of relief, grateful to have at least those decisions taken out of her hands.

"What do you know about Diane's death?" The words popped out of her mouth before she even realized she'd said them, startling both her and Neil. Why had she said that? She hadn't faced the issue in six years, hadn't thought about it, so why had she brought it up now out of the blue? When had Diane's death become a subject for her curiosity? Why did she even care? It seemed being back in that house was doing weird things to her mind.

Neil looked at her, sadness in his eyes. "Aw, Cassie, what do you want to bring all that up for?"

"To tell you the truth, I don't really know." She shook her head. "I couldn't get home for her funeral, so I guess I'm just a little curious. All I ever knew was there was some kind of violence...." She stopped. "I don't know why I even asked. Forget it, okay?"

Neil seemed to weigh his next words. "You know they thought for sure Griffin had killed her, don't you? But it seems he had an airtight alibi."

"Griffin?" Not the man she fell in love with all those years ago. Not possible. "I read that he was a suspect, but I never believed it."

"Well, there was a lot of speculation going on there." Neil shifted in his chair as if he found it uncomfortable. "I hate to speak ill of the dead, but your sister pushed the envelope hard, as they say."

Cassie stared at him. "They never found out who did it, did they?"

"No, never." He twisted his mouth in a sour expression. "And Griffin Hunter just walks around town, big as you please, still running his business. I guess if we had another landscaper around here, folks wouldn't be putting up with him." Neil shook his head. "Anyway, if I were you, I'd just leave things alone. No sense raking up past history."

She stood up in a hurry then, gathering her purse and keys. She had no intention of discussing Griffin with anyone. She'd worked very hard to keep him tucked away in a secret corner of her mind.

"I have to go, Neil. Please see what you can do about the paperwork on everything, and I'll call you later."

"I'll do my best," he assured her. "But you know this town. Even tomorrow is too soon for everyone." He came around the desk and placed a kiss on her cheek. "Sure I can't talk you into lunch? Or how about dinner? I'd love to have you come out to the house and meet the family."

"I'm not exactly here socializing." *No, that sounded too rude.* "I mean, I'm just here to take care of business. To make sure things get done the way my mother wanted them. I appreciate the offer of dinner, and everything else you're doing for me. I'll expect to hear from you."

She fled the office, her brain rattling. How could she get through this? With all the rage and pain bottled up inside her, socializing in Stoneham was impossible. She just wanted to escape without too much damage to her emotional state.

Chapter Six

Cassie had kept Diane's death pigeonholed in the back of her mind for six years. She hated the fact it was swimming to the forefront of her consciousness with such suddenness. She had refused to discuss it with her parents, instead learning what she could from articles on the Internet. But whatever details she managed to find were sketchy. Nobody seemed to know anything.

The stories had offered little more than the bare facts. Three months after Diane's marriage to Griffin her battered body was found in a ravine at Stoneham Municipal Park. Suspicion had first fallen on the husband, always a prime suspect in cases like this. The problem was he had an airtight alibi and three witnesses to back it up. Besides, she could imagine Griffin doing a lot of things, but committing murder wasn't one of them.

After that, the case just languished until at last it fell off the radar. Cassie had simply put it out of her mind. At the time, she had been so angry with Diane she could have killed her herself. Being in Stoneham after all this time had brought all of the unpleasantness to mind.

Donald Brandon was oily obsequiousness itself when he greeted her at the mortuary. His impeccable black suit blended into the dark wood paneling on the walls. His hair looked as if he glued it in place, every strand arranged with perfection. Cassie almost expected to hear organ and harp music drift in from the walls.

Donald held onto her hand so long she had to yank it away from him. As distasteful and unappealing as he had been in school, he had gotten worse as he'd aged.

"I understand my mother left instructions for her funeral," she told him right away, wanting to get this over with. "If you could just tell me what they are, I'll sign off on everything, and we can get this done."

"I hoped we might have a moment to chat," he said, somewhat petulant. "It's been a long time since you've been home, Cassie. We have a lot to catch up on."

She tugged her hand free and took a step back. "I'm trying to get this done and get out of here by Monday, so if we can just get to it?"

"I'm sorry, but I don't think that will be possible." A little frown creased his forehead, and there was no mistaking the definitely disapproving tone of his voice, as if she'd committed some cardinal sin of funeral procedure.

"Neil told me my mother had made all the arrangements ahead of time." She put every inch of authority into her words. "According to him, all I have to do is go over the details with you. I don't understand what the holdup could be. What could be taking so long?"

The judgmental frown remained in place. "Today is Friday, Cassie. I have to confirm the arrangements with the cemetery, place the notices in the paper, arrange for a service, and prepare the body for burial."

"Well, just how long will this take?" She was fast becoming impatient with the whole situation. This was getting worse by the minute.

"Your mother wanted a small service," he explained in even tones. "We can do it in the chapel here. But I'd say, with everything, Tuesday would be the earliest we can finish up."

"Tuesday!" She wanted to smack him and wipe that holier-than-thou look off his face. "Donald, we're not burying the president."

His lips thinned in disapproval. "Cassie, I must say, I'm a little disappointed in you. This is your mother we're talking about. I know the two of you had issues these past few years, but we in Stoneham still believe in showing the proper respect for the dead."

She gave up. The deck was stacked against her, Stoneham style, and fighting it would be a losing battle. "All right. Just do whatever you have to and call me when everything's finalized. I'm staying at the house." She paused. "By the way, what can you tell me about Diane's death?"

"Diane's death?" He kept his face blank.

"Yes. I wasn't here at the time, and it just seems strange no one was ever arrested for it."

"I'm sure I wouldn't know anything about it except it was a dreadful tragedy. Have you checked with Chief Dangler?"

"No, but thanks for the suggestion." The sarcasm in her words seemed to be lost on him.

Dangler would be just someone else to stonewall her, she was sure. Why wouldn't anyone talk about her sister's death?

Back in her car, she wanted to bang her head on the steering wheel. Her quick trip in and out of town was looking longer and longer. She wanted—no, needed—to shake the dust of Stoneham once and for all, but the town kept reaching out its tentacles to trap her in its own special hell.

Pulling out her cell phone, she called Mike and gave him an update.

"Don't worry, Cassie." *At last, kindness.* "Take however long you need. I'm sure this is a tough time for you, and I don't want to add to your stress. Take all of next week. And don't worry about your paycheck."

This was more sympathy than she ever would have expected from this man. If she could just tell him that the toughest time was having to be here at all.

She passed the police station on the way to the grocery store, and her car seemed to turn in on its own and park without her doing a thing. In the next minute, she shook hands with Barry Dangler, the chief of police, telling him she was fine, and yes, it was too bad about her mother. She thanked him for his condolences.

"I wonder if I could see the file on Diane's death," she said, social niceties out of the way.

"Now, Cassie," he admonished. "Why bring all that up now? It's been six years since it happened."

"I guess because I ignored it at the time and now I'm feeling some latent guilt." She uncrossed her legs and re-crossed them. "And maybe a little bit of the reporter in me."

"That's right." He nodded. "I heard you were working for a newspaper in Florida. But, honey, there's just nothing to tell. Honest. I wish there was. I felt it in my bones that Griffin Hunter did it, but he was covered up with witnesses."

"And he was the only suspect?" She could never believe Griffin killed her

He looked uncomfortable with his next words. "No disrespect, Cassie, but your sister walked a lot on the wild side. Speculation was that marriage didn't change her social habits, and Griffin had had enough. If he didn't do it, it could have been some guy she met that night, someone she provoked into a rage. She was pretty good at pushing people's buttons, you know."

Yes, especially mine. "So are you saying I can't see the police report? Why?"

Dangler was silent for a long moment. "The law says you can go to court to get this if you want, so I guess I'll just save us all that trouble. I think this is a big mistake, and it won't make you happy, but I'll do it."

"Thank you, Chief. When can you have it ready for me?"

"I'll have to get it from the dead files. All the old cases are in the archives. Give me until the first of the week."

Cassie tamped down her frustration. Everything was "the first of the week." She was ready to just blow the whole thing off, but her reporter's nose was twitching. Both people she had brought this up with wanted her to forget it, which just made her more determined to pursue it. She was stuck in town anyway, so she might as well get what information she could.

Just maybe she could at last shut the door on Griffin Hunter.

"Call me Monday afternoon if you haven't heard from me by then," Dangler told her. They shook hands, and he ushered her out.

Everything today served to remind her more and more why she hated this place so much.

Next, she stopped at the grocery store. Cleaning supplies. More food than she first planned on since it appeared she was going to be stuck here for a few days. She rushed along the aisles, pushing herself to be home by early afternoon. She needed to call Neil and check on his progress and also see what he had been able to do about arranging a real estate agent to come out to see the house. She'd been in Stoneham less than a day, and already she could feel it suffocating her.

She wheeled her cart out the door to the parking lot, and stopped, frozen in place. Griff Hunter leaned casually against her car, watching her.

Chapter Seven

Her breath was trapped in her chest. Swallowing hard, she made her feet move, one in front of the other, doing her best to ignore him, her gaze still drawn to him. This was a different Griff than the daredevil who lived in her darkest dreams. He was not only older but harder, less yielding. His hair was still sun-bleached and too long, but his body was fuller, though still tanned and muscular. Aviator sunglasses hid the remembered blue of his eyes, but his mouth that had pressed such passionate kisses on every part of her body was set in an expression of bitterness. There was something almost lethal about him now. If she hadn't known him so well, she might have been afraid of him and thought people were right about him.

Something else defined his posture. Anger? Sadness? She didn't want to know. More than anything she didn't want to feel the quickening of her heartbeat, the tightening of her breasts, the instant hardening of her nipples, and the primal beat throbbing between her legs. The heat had burned her once—scorched her—and she wasn't about to play with fire again.

But her brain seemed to have taken a vacation, along with her ability to make a sensible decision and stick to it. All these years, all that pain, and it only took seconds for her body to leap to life in the once familiar response. She detoured to the trunk of the car, her keys in a hand that trembled despite her best efforts.

Griff reached out one arm and pressed against the lid of the trunk so she couldn't open it. "I heard you were in town. I came to see for myself."

"Please let me open my trunk." She tried to make her voice as flat as his.

"We have things to talk about, Cassie."

"You're wrong. We have nothing to say to each other." *Not anymore, anyway.*

"Oh, but we do." He moved until he stood right next to her, crowding her. "We have a lot to say. We have unfinished business between us."

She looked up at him, anger heating her blood. She hated him for what he'd done to her, and even more for the memories he'd left her with. Every one of her failed relationships could be traced back to her inability to get Griffin Hunter out of her system. No one's kisses sparked such passion, no one saw into her soul the way he did. She wanted to kill him for destroying her life.

"Our business was finished a long time ago," she spit out. "We're done."

He lifted his hand, and she opened the trunk, stowing the groceries inside.

"I was sorry to hear about your mother."

"Thank you."

She slammed the trunk lid shut, but when she moved to get into the car, he blocked her path. She forced herself to stare up at him, hoping her face gave nothing away of the turmoil inside her. "Please let me by. I have things to do."

"This is far from over, Cassie." A muscle twitched in his jaw. "You won't be able to run away from me this time."

"Run away?" She met his gaze. "I wasn't the one who ran off and married someone else. I wasn't the one who made false promises that I didn't keep."

His face remained expressionless, everything hidden behind the dark glasses. "There's a lot you don't know."

Fury blazed inside her. "Did you have a good laugh, Griff? Seducing the baby sister of your lover, taking a naïve virgin to your bed then dumping her? Did you all have a good chuckle over that?" She drew a deep breath and fought for control. She hadn't meant to let him provoke her this way, and her anger was directed as much at herself as at him.

Griffin yanked off his sunglasses and gripped her arms with his strong hands. His blue eyes flashed in the sunlight. "You have no idea what you're talking about," he said, each word clipped and sharp. "And you're wrong. We aren't done. Not by a long shot."

As fast as he had grabbed her, he released her and stepped back. "We will be seeing each other, Cassie. Make no mistake."

Then, like smoke in the wind, he was gone.

She sat in the driver's seat, shaking uncontrollably, unable even to fit the key in the ignition. The feeling was still there, that flash of intense sexual tension between them, and he could still crack her shell with just a few words. She had to get out of town, had to get away from Griffin Hunter. She didn't need to go through the pain of losing him again. She'd spent six years blocking it out. She wasn't sure she had the emotional resources to do it twice.

Closing her eyes, she reached into the neck of her blouse and pulled out the long silver chain she always wore, fingering the oversized locket at the end. No one else knew that inside the locket lay the tiny silver heart Griffin had given her on their last night together. In all the time since then, despite her unbearable pain, despite the bitter memories, she had never, ever been without it.

She wanted to put her head down on the steering wheel and

weep.

Chapter Eight

The afternoon was as unproductive as the morning had been. When Cassie called Neil, he told her the insurance company wouldn't be faxing him anything until Monday.

"Sorry. The weekend, you know. But I'll call you Monday when they come in." The sound of papers rustled over the phone. "I did call Jesse Markham, and he said one of his daughters would drop by and see you. Do you need some help going through the house? I'd be happy to offer my services."

No, thanks. She didn't need him pawing through her mother's things or anything else that might turn up. "Thanks anyway, Neil, but I can manage. As a matter of fact, I think it's something I need to do by myself."

"Well, I know you want to get back to Tampa as soon as you can, Cassie, and I'd say that's a good idea. I'll do whatever I can to expedite things."

She had just started the massive job of cleaning when Carol Markham dropped by. "Nice to see you, Cassie. I'm sorry about your mother. My condolences."

"Thank you."

Carol was the youngest of Jesse's daughters and four years older than Cassie. Some said she'd been on the fringes of Diane's crowd, but she looked very prim and proper now.

"We're all on our way to the lake for the weekend," she said with a breezy air. "How about if I come by late Monday morning? We can do a walk-through and fill out the listing agreement. Sound okay?"

And if it isn't? It seemed Stoneham closed up for the weekend, just like it always had.

"That will be fine." Did she have a choice?

Carol's next words made her tense. "Oh, and do something about the yard. Your mother really let it go. Call Griffin Hunter, or I can do it for you. He'll fix it up in a jiffy. Bye." She handed Cassie a business card and breezed out the door.

Call Griff? Over my dead body. There had to be someone else she could call. She was still more shaken by their encounter than she could admit to herself.

She was interrupted again when Donald Brandon called to tell her he'd confirmed the memorial service for Tuesday, if that was all right with her.

Why did everyone ask her that when she had no real choice?

"Fine, Donald. Thanks." She rubbed her forehead, where a headache was beginning to build.

"I spoke to the minister, and he's agreed to perform the service. He's also notified the cemetery, and they'll prepare the grave site, right next to your father."

"Thank you," she repeated. "I appreciate you handling all of this."

"I hope everything meets with your approval." His slippery voice slid over the wires.

"I'm sure it's fine, Donald," she told him again. Did he want her to express undying gratitude? "Whatever you arrange will be all right with me."

"I've run off some funeral notices," he continued. "We'll get them around this weekend."

Stoneham's newspaper published once a week, on Wednesdays. The usual method of notification of events between times was flyers in all the local stores. No high-tech age in this town.

"Fine, fine. I'll touch base with you on Monday morning."

"I know this must be a trying time for you," he went on. "Perhaps you'd like to have dinner with me tomorrow night? A little companionship is always nice."

Another dinner invitation. What was it with all these men and meals? She'd never had so much as a hamburger with them when she'd lived here before.

"I don't think so, Donald." She bit down on her impatience. "I have a lot of work to get done in the house."

"Well, all right. But if you change your mind, just give me a call."

Her original plan was to finish most of the downstairs by the end of the afternoon, but all the interruptions had given her a headache that had set up shop behind her right eye.

Tomorrow. As long as I'm stuck here for a few days, I might as well not kill myself. She pulled her pad of paper across the counter toward her and listed things to check—utilities, mail, the newspapers. Whatever she couldn't sell, she'd have to arrange for shipping to Tampa. Or give it away, which might be the best solution. There wasn't anything she wanted, truth be told.

Then there was the yardwork. Carol Markham was right—the grounds were a mess. The signs of neglect were everywhere. A buyer would be put off by that and the fading trim. She'd ask Neil to recommend someone. Landscaper as well as painter. There had to be someone she could hire besides Griffin Hunter. Having him around would just open the can of worms she was trying to close.

Monday she'd get copies of the will, the death certificate, and probate papers from Neil and take them to the bank so she could transact her business there.

She sighed. Why had she ever been so foolish as to think she could accomplish this over the weekend with no problems? Everything, it seemed, conspired to keep her here long past the limit of her endurance.

The ringing of the phone again startled her.

Now what?

"Just checking to make sure you're doing okay."

Harley sounded so steady and soothing, Cassie almost cried at the warm familiarity. "Not great, but okay," she told him.

"I spoke to Neil, and he said he'll do what he can to help you wrap things up here as fast as possible. Time to bury the past, right, Cassie?"

She sighed. "I thought I'd already done that, but it seems fate dug it up again. Thanks for checking on things. The sooner done the better."

"I agree. Let me know if there's anything I can do."

Life had indeed conspired to tear open the scars of the old wounds, and she wondered now if they'd ever heal.

On impulse, she picked up the phone and dialed Claire.

"Oh, Cassie, I'm so glad you called. I just this minute got home and was checking for messages. How's it going, gal?"

"It looks as if life has connived to keep me chained to this stupid town," she complained. "Nothing's changed here, that's for sure."

"Is there a lot you have to do? Do you want me to come out there and give you a hand?"

"Claire, you don't know how wonderful it would be to have you here, but no, thanks just the same. You have obligations, and the stuff isn't that complicated, just tedious. Everything gets done on Stoneham time."

"How's Mister Silver Heart?"

Claire was the only one Cassie had ever confided in about Griff. She'd fled to her that terrible summer and cried off and on for days, overwhelmed by the awful sense of betrayal. After that, unable to return to Stoneham and see Griff and Diane in the bloom of wedded bliss, unable to cope with her parents' blindness where Diane was concerned, she'd spent every school break and summer at Claire's. The warmth Claire's family surrounded Cassie with almost—*almost*—killed the pain that still lived in a tiny corner of her heart.

"I'm sure he's just fine," she answered. "I'm avoiding him at all costs." Telling Claire she'd already run into him would open a dialogue she wasn't ready to have.

"You know, I guess it's none of my business, but this might be a good time to take care of your unfinished business with him, too."

"Griffin and I are more than finished," Cassie said, her tone heavy. "It's over and done. Period. You know that."

"Sure, sure," Claire soothed. "That's why you wear that locket with the tiny heart inside, right?"

"Claire...."

"All right, all right. But call me if you need to gab. I'll be in and out all weekend, but I'll keep my cell phone with me. Take care, sweetie."

After ending the call, Cassie realized she'd had nothing since coffee that morning, which might account for part of the headache. She was too tired from dealing with the hassle of the day for anything elaborate, and she felt the grime of the house covering her. Okay, a shower, cool clothes, and a sandwich and milk. Just what she needed.

Passing Diane's room on the way to her own, she again stopped in the doorway. She could almost smell the scent of her sister's rich perfume, hear her throaty voice as she hummed to herself. Had someone flown to close to her flame, burned themselves, and retaliated? She turned away to escape the sense of choking when something nudged at her consciousness.

Forcing herself to wipe everything out of her mind, she put on her reporter's brain. What had she noticed that didn't register? What was wrong or out of place? Her eyes lit first on the dresser. That was it. Every drawer was open, just a fraction, as if it had been closed in haste. Her mother would never do that. She was known for her prim neatness.

Cassie opened each drawer, looking through the contents. Again, everything was almost neat, but if you knew the history, you could see things had been marginally displaced.

Next, she turned to the closet. The folding doors were open a fraction, again as if someone had been in a hurry. The inside of the closet was messier than the drawers. It was apparent someone had been looking for something and might have been running out of time, not able to be so careful here.

The fine hairs on the back of her neck stood up, and a shiver ran down her spine. Tomorrow, she would do a more thorough search of this room. It was obvious, though, someone had been in here searching. When? And for what? Most important of all, who had a key and could come here whenever they pleased?

The thought was more than unsettling. Tomorrow, first thing, she would call a locksmith and have all the locks changed. She knew it was the weekend, but she'd pay double-time for this. She'd never sleep, knowing there was a stranger out there who could enter the house at will.

She stood under the shower a long time, letting the water wash away the day and its troubles. Then, dressed in shorts and a T-shirt, she headed downstairs. Too edgy to sit, she stood at the counter, eating a sandwich with ice cold milk to wash it down.

The laptop she'd brought with her stared back at her from the kitchen table, and she thought about plugging it in, but the effort of booting it up seemed more than she could handle. She could go through her mother's room, but she needed a good night's sleep to tackle that. At last, with nothing else to do and not feeling in the mood for television, she decided to sit out on the back patio for a while.

"I figured you'd be out here sooner or later." Griff's voice was like warm velvet in the darkness. As dark as it was, she hadn't noticed the figure in the big lounge chair until she was almost next to it. "Sit down, Cassie. You can't run away from me in your own house. We have things to talk about, and, by God, we're going to do it now."

Chapter Nine

Cassie's throat tightened, and her stomach recoiled. Too many emotions battled inside her—anger, apprehension, desire, and the one she'd buried so deep she didn't think it would ever surface again. Love. She couldn't make words come out of her mouth. She turned to run back to the house, but he was out of the chair like lightening, gripping her arms with incredible force.

"Oh, no you don't," Griff said, his tone harsh, "Not this time. You're going to sit in that chair and listen to me if I have to tie you down."

He forced her onto the lounger he'd just vacated and sat down on the edge beside her. One arm stretched across her body, pinning her in place, with no wiggle room.

"I'd appreciate it if you'd let me get up this instant." She put every bit of the cold fury she felt into those words. "And get away from my house."

"Not until you hear what I have to say. You can scream if you want, but think of the explaining you'll have to do when someone shows up to rescue you."

He was so close≈ she could smell the mixed scents of soap and aftershave on his skin, clean and earthy and male. There was just enough light from the moon to give her a good view of his features. His face still had that wicked, sexy look, and his eyes, no longer hidden behind sunglasses, burned into her. But the laughter that always danced in them was gone. Instead, they looked like two dead pools of navy, reflecting no light at all. Still, his gaze could make hot-

and-cold flashes chase themselves over her body.

Her heart squeezed at the painful thought of all they'd lost. She clenched her fists, digging her nails into her palms.

"If I agree you can have your say, will you let go of me? And then will you go away?"

"Yes." He nodded. "But you have to listen to everything."

"I cannot imagine what you think I want to hear."

She held herself rigid, trying not to touch any part of him. If she did, all the stored desire, the remembered passion, would come flooding back, and she'd be powerless to refuse him anything.

"I have plenty to say, whether you want to hear it or not. Are we clear on this?"

She nodded, but when she looked into his eyes, she was shocked by the incredible pain she saw.

"How can I make you understand it all," he asked her, "when I still have trouble with it myself ?"

"What can there even be to understand?"

"God, I don't even know where to begin here." He looked away for a moment, his eyes distant. "If I tell you that no matter what you saw or heard, you were the one I wanted since high school, I know you won't believe me. Why should you? But it's the truth. That night on the porch, when I told you I was waiting for you? You thought it was a line, but that's just what I was doing. Just as I'd done a lot of other nights. Waiting for you to walk by."

"Bull," she said. "Diane was always the one you wanted. Not me. I wasn't loose enough for you and your friends."

And Diane was the one he'd married.

"You're right about that. Even in high school, you were the ice queen. You could destroy guys with just that cold, frosty look of yours.

Did you know that? Everyone was afraid to approach you." His voice dropped a little. "Me more than anyone. It took a lot of guts to do what I did that night."

"I don't believe you." Was that why she had so few dates in high school? She'd deliberately kept everyone at bay, unwilling to be painted with the same brush as her sister. Still, there hadn't been anyone who'd interested her enough to make her drop her guard.

"Shut up and let me finish" His words were sharp and clipped. "I meant every word I said to you those two nights. Everything. I was more than ready to stop running with that crowd. I thought, when you came back from your trip, maybe we'd see what kind of relationship we could build."

Cassie could still remember the shock when her mother broke the news of Griffin and Diane's marriage. Afraid she'd fall apart on the spot, she'd greeted the news with a stiff smile, then locked herself in her room. Unwilling to face anyone and listen to the painful details, she'd endured hammer blows to her heart and shut out the world.

"You must have run out of patience because, when I came back, there you and Diane were, the happy couple. No doubt having a good laugh at my expense."

Griffin grabbed her so hard, his fingers bit into her flesh so hard they hurt. He shook her until her head snapped back and forth. "Did you think I wanted you to walk out of my life?" Deep grooves etched his face. "Do you think I wanted to marry Diane? Is that what you thought I had in mind? We might have had our fling, but Diane had a fling with just about everyone. You didn't marry girls like her. You only took them to bed."

"I didn't know what to think," she whispered, shaken by his fury. "I-I thought you'd just amused yourself with me, for some reason."

And burned me in the process.

His eyes blazed into hers, like twin lasers. His fingers pressed her flesh even harder. "She was pregnant." He spit the words out as if they tasted bad. "Diane was pregnant."

"What?" Cassie felt as if someone had punched her in the stomach. "She was what?"

"You heard me. She was pregnant. She swore it was mine." He raked his hand through his hair. "I'm a lot of things, Cassie. I know what my reputation is, and I've sure done everything to deserve it. But this was my responsibility, and I wasn't going to opt out of it."

"You didn't have to marry her." But she knew those were empty words. Griff was right. He'd accepted responsibility for his father, and he would have done no less for the supposed mother of his child.

"Is that how little you think of me?" He shook his head. "I know you always looked at me as just another piece of trash, like everyone else in this town did. But believe it or not, I have some sense of accountability for what I do. Especially when it involves another person. A child." He continued gripping her arms, holding her in place. "Besides, I didn't think a child should have to suffer for an irresponsible act."

"My folks must have had a fit."

"They didn't know. No one did but me. I thought they'd have a hemorrhage over the runaway marriage, but Diane was twenty-two, so there wasn't much they could do about it. Besides, no matter what she did, they were always accepting of it. I never could figure that out."

"Diane drew people like moths to a flame," Cassie said, her voice bitter. "She had our folks wrapped around her little finger. And everyone else, too, it seems."

"I tried to see you when you got back," he went on, "but you were here one day and gone the next. I didn't know how to find you, and I couldn't very well ask your parents."

"I got out of town as fast as I could." She tried to shift to get more comfortable, but Griff's position made it next to impossible. "I spent the summer with my roommate. Did you think I wanted to stay around and watch you and Diane play house?"

"I was desperate to explain it all to you." He looked away from her. "I didn't know what the hell to do. My dad was drinking himself to death, and I had a wife who only wanted a name for her child and someone to pay the freight."

"I'd have thought she would get an abortion," Cassie said, hating her bitchy tone. "A baby would have cut into her playtime."

"I asked her about it, you know. God knows I wanted her to, whatever that makes me. Having a child with Diane was never in my plans. She said she was afraid of them. That something might go wrong. So there we were, pregnant Diane, drunken Dad, and me, all in the house down the street." His words held the sound of bricks hitting concrete. "Can you think of a more fun scenario?"

"What did you think I would do?" she asked. "Play the doting aunt? Or didn't that even cross your mind?"

"I didn't think at all, Cassie, and that's the God's honest truth. Fuck. I was just trying to take it one day at a time."

"And then Diane was killed."

"Yes." He exhaled heavily. "Then Diane was killed. But I can tell you, the ink wasn't even dry on the marriage license before she was out running around again. I wanted her to settle down because of the baby, stop drinking, take care of herself, but you know Diane."

"Better than I ever wanted."

"I knew she was still sleeping around." Hostility edged every word. "Hell, Diane could never be faithful to anyone. It wasn't as if I cared one hell of a lot, except I didn't want her to hurt the baby." He drew in a shuddering breath. "I'd already planned to divorce her as soon as she gave birth and file for sole custody. The Barbours' dog was a more fit parent than she was."

"I understand you were the one suspect they had," Cassie murmured.

"You got it." He shoved his fingers through his hair again, a gesture of pure frustration. "I know I haven't always been a nice person, Cassie, but murder is a little out of my league. No matter what the circumstances."

"They never found out who did." She spoke so low, she didn't know if he could hear her.

"No. No, they didn't. I'm sure half the town still thinks it was me."

"But you have a business," she protested. "And it seems everyone hires you."

"As long as I stay in the yard and don't come in the front door, they're very happy to pay me for my work." His lips twisted in an ironic imitation of a smile. "I guess it's okay to hire a murderer if he hasn't killed someone close to you."

There was such pain in those words her heart ached for him. Don't do this, Cassie. Don't play with that fire again. Let him talk and then tell him to go.

"Okay." She forced the words out. "I've heard what you have to say. Now you can go."

"Do *you* think I killed her? How about it, Cassie? Do you see me as a killer?" His tone was flat, his eyes hooded as he waited for her answer.

"No." She whispered the word. "No, I don't."

He leaned closer, his face so near she could feel his breath on her skin.

"Griffin...." She tried to push her head back into the chair, away from him.

"I never got to tell you that night that I love you, Dewdrop," he said, his voice quiet. "Even though I gave you my heart. I figured we'd have plenty of time for that later. I wanted you to get to know me as a person, not just by my reputation."

Cassie's heart almost stopped. Whatever else she might have said caught in her throat. Of all the things he could have told her, this was the last thing she'd expected. And the name. His nickname for her. The sound of it made her heart crack open.

Damn him!

"Say something," he prodded. "Tell me to leave right now, or I'm going to kiss you."

Cassie couldn't move, couldn't speak. She couldn't do this, couldn't let him touch her. Part of the reason for her return to Stoneham was to get him out of her system once and for all. She wanted to make him pay for the hell he'd put her through. If she let him touch her now, she'd be his again.

She willed herself to jerk away, to get up, but her muscles wouldn't obey her command. Then his mouth was on hers, parting her lips, probing gently with his tongue.

The kiss started out easy, tentative, but then Griff's hand tangled through her hair, pulling her head to him, holding her in place. The kiss deepened, and she couldn't fight it. without even thinking she reached her arms around him , holding him to her. The kiss went on and on, his tongue making an erotic sweep through her mouth, teasing and tasting everywhere it touched. She didn't have the strength to break the contact.

When Griffin lifted his lips, he looked at her, hard. "It's still there, isn't it, Cassie? This thing between us. You can lie to yourself, but you can't lie to me."

"Griff, I—"

Then he was kissing her again, feeding from her mouth, ravaging it with his tongue. He held her to him so tight she almost couldn't breathe.

"This won't go away, you know. I still love you." His words were thick with emotion. "God, how I love you. And admit it or not, you feel the same way." He sat back, releasing her, and brushed one cheek with his fingertips in a single gentle stroke. "You haven't married, have you? Or found anyone to get serious with? I thought not."

"I had my reasons," she whispered.

"You don't have to tell me what they are. The kiss says it all. You gave me a precious gift, Cassie. I didn't take it lightly, whatever you think. I didn't have a real choice in what happened before. I won't let you run away from me this time. You can take that to the bank." He touched the locket around her neck. "What's in there, Dewdrop? A picture of me?"

She shook her head. "No, it's not."

"You still own my heart, Dewdrop. Nothing ever changed."

And just like that, like fingers brushing away a magic curtain, six years disappeared as if they'd happened yesterday. The memory of his sleek, muscled body, the golden curls on his chest, the feel of his fingers on her, in her, was like a drug in her system.

He stood up, towering over her.

"This yard hasn't been touched in forever. I think your mother just kind of gave up on everything. I don't have anything scheduled for tomorrow. I'll be back in the morning and get to work on it."

She couldn't believe the switch in conversation. Had she just imagined him saying those three words that were turning her upside down? Her body ached for his hands, his tongue, his hardened erection, and he was talking about landscaping?

"I don't think—"

"That's right. Don't think. Just let this take us wherever it goes." He bent and brushed his lips over hers. "Good night, Dewdrop. See you tomorrow."

Then he was gone.

Cassie sat on the patio for a long time, playing with the locket and where his lips had made contact with hers. She called herself all kinds of a fool, knowing she stared danger in the face. She had to find a way to protect herself from this fire threatening to consume her again. Once burned was more than enough for her.

Griffin Hunter could whisper all the sweet words in her ear he wanted. She knew the truth. In the vernacular, he wanted to fuck her, and just like before, he'd do whatever it took to accomplish it. She just wished she didn't feel this awful, aching need.

Chapter Ten

Sleep eluded Cassie. She tossed, restless, dozing off and on to be awakened by the memory of Griff's mouth on hers, his maleness so close to her. Images of the past kept floating in her head. No matter how she tried, she couldn't chase them away.

When the numbers on her watch read at six o'clock and the sun was already trying to slip in around the edges of the window shade, she got up to work on the house. She stepped into the shorts and T-shirt she'd thrown over a chair, pulled her hair back in a ponytail, and hurried to the kitchen. In seconds, she had the coffee pot going. Too bad she couldn't wave a magic wand and make her wonderful single-serving pot appear. Today she reminded herself to eat, popping bread in the toaster while she filled a mug.

She was munching on the last bite when she heard a truck pull into the driveway. A glance at the clock told her it was almost six thirty. Nobody started life that early in Stoneham. Peeking through the curtains, she saw Griff lifting equipment out of a pickup labeled *Hunter Landscape Services*. Ignoring the flutter in her stomach, she opened the door and stepped out on the porch.

"I think this is a very bad idea." She tried to sound as firm as possible. If she let him into one corner of her life, he'd take the rest. She couldn't do it again. Sure, he'd said he loved her, but could she believe him? Trust him, after everything?

He looked up. "Planning on doing the yard work yourself?"

"No, but—"

"Okay, then. I try to get as much done as I can before the worst heat of the day. I thought I'd get all the hand work done before starting the mower. Don't want your neighbors throwing rocks at me."

She started to tell him again to go away, but her mouth had its own idea of what to say. "Would you like a cup of coffee?"

He stopped arranging his tools and looked at her for a moment then nodded. When he spoke, his tone was as reserved as hers. "Yes. That would be nice. Black, no sugar."

"Easy enough." *Cassie girl, you are playing with fire again. How many times will you hold yourself in the flame?*

She ignored the alarms going off in her head and poured coffee into a mug for Griff, refilled her own, and took them both out to the porch. She sat down on the top step and motioned for him to join her.

"I appreciate the hospitality." He sipped his coffee. "Not what I expected after last night."

Last night. She was still trying to decide if she had imagined it or not. Had he said he loved her or had she imagined it? Was the unbelievable story he told true? From beneath her lashes, she stole an all-encompassing look at him. His jeans and T-shirt hugged his body like a second skin. As he sat down, muscles flexed smooth and effortless beneath the fabric. When she got to the bulge in his crotch, her gaze slithered away.

Don't go there.

The aviator shades were in place again, making his eyes unreadable. Cassie wished hers were, too. When he turned her face toward him, she was afraid of what he would see there.

"We still have a long way to go, sugar," he said, in his deep, liquid voice, "and I'm not rushing things. But I'm taking advantage of every minute you're here. Be warned."

She didn't know what to say to that. She was torn between wanting to run and wanting to throw her arms around him and bury herself against him.

"So," he said, changing the subject. "How's it been going? Anyone giving you a hard time?"

She shook her head. "Not unless you count the fact that you can't get anything done until next year around here. I forgot this place operates on Stoneham time."

He threw back his head and laughed. "Oh, yes. Nobody hurries for anything around here. What's on your plate that you're so anxious to get finished with?"

She ticked off her items for him. "Cleaning out the house, listing the house, probating the will, having the funeral service, all that stuff. Neil McLeod's handling the legal work, but he doesn't seem in any bigger hurry to get stuff done than anyone else."

"Get used to it, Cassie. You've been away too long. Nothing's changed."

Except my life. "By the way. Who would I call as a locksmith to bribe for some Saturday work?"

"You have to be kidding." He cocked an eyebrow. "What's so urgent it can't wait until Monday?"

She told him about Diane's room. "I'm sure it's nothing more than my imagination, but it makes me nervous thinking someone I don't know about has a key to this house." A thought struck her. "You didn't happen to come over and go through that room, did you?"

"I haven't set foot in this house since Diane died," he said, obviously angry at her implication. "And if I did, I wouldn't be sneaky about it." He drained his coffee. "I don't like the sound of this, though. Especially with you staying here all alone. Let me make a couple of calls."

He pulled his cell phone off the belt clip and scrolled through to find the number he wanted. Cassie listened while he cajoled someone into coming over, in the end almost threatening. "Just do it," he said. "You owe me enough favors, it won't kill you to pay one back."

"I don't want you to impose on anyone for me." Cassie folded her hands on her knees in a prim gesture.

Griffin disconnected the call. "Phil Morgan does most of the locksmith work in town. He hates to work on Saturday, but I rattled his cage a little. And I'm not imposing. He wouldn't mind calling me if he needed some work in a hurry."

"Thank you." She didn't know what else to say. "I appreciate it."

"Is the room still the way you found it?"

She nodded. "I checked everything then put it back the way it was. I thought of calling the police, but I changed my mind."

"When I take a break, I want you to show it to me." He handed her back the mug. "Thanks for the coffee. I need to get to work."

Cassie dragged out the cleaning supplies she'd bought, found her mother's broom and vacuum cleaner, and began methodically divesting the house of its accumulation of dust and neglect. She didn't know how long it had been since someone had cleaned the rooms, or what her mother had been able to do.

She made a mental note to call Harley in the afternoon and ask him more about her mother's condition. She felt bad about not getting back to him yesterday, but her mind had been on other things.

A lot of other things. And with all the answers she'd been looking for, she seemed to have come up with more questions than ever.

Chapter Eleven

Cassie had just finished with the living room when the doorbell rang. When she opened the door, Griffin stood there with Phil Morgan.

"How you doin', Cassie?" Phil had been a big player in Diane's group, but now he seemed intimidated by her little sister's presence.

Cassie smothered a laugh. "Fine, Phil. Just fine."

"Sorry about your mother. She was a nice lady."

"Thank you very much."

Griffin stepped into the house and took charge. "Cassie, why don't you let Phil know what all he needs to do. Then you can show me that thing you were talking about before."

"Oh! Of course. And thanks for coming out on a Saturday, Phil." She made herself smile at the man. "I know I cut into your time off, and I'm more than willing to pay for it."

He just nodded then followed her as she showed him all the doors, even the one from the garage into the house. He made notes on a little pad of paper as they walked, nodding to himself.

"Okay," he said when they were finished. "Let me get my stuff, and I'll have it done in no time. I've got a portable key machine, so you'll have a whole new set before I leave."

She was more grateful to him than she could have said.

"I want to see Diane's room," Griffin murmured, coming up behind her. "Let's do it while Phil does his thing."

She felt strange standing with him in this room, a painful picture of him and Diane together on this bed slamming into her brain. Could

66

she ever ask him all the questions tumbling in her mind? She tamped down her thoughts to focus on what they were doing.

"You're right," Griff said. "Your mother invented neatness. Her housekeeping may have suffered the last few months, but she never would have left stuff this way. And, of course, it's been six years since Diane set foot in here."

He frowned as he looked around, standing still for a long time as if memorizing details. He walked around the room once more, taking his time now, studying in the disarray in the closet, searching for some kind of indication of why someone had been there.

"What I can't figure," he said at last, "is what they'd be looking for. Diane didn't have anything of real value. Not even our wedding ring. I got what I could afford. And why now?"

"I asked myself the same thing. I can tell you my parents didn't change a thing in this room after Diane died. Did she spend much time over here?"

"As much time as she did anywhere, I guess, including our home." The venom in his voice was obvious. "But she didn't have anything worth taking. Something else is going on here, and it bothers me that I can't figure it out."

Phil was just finishing up when they walked out onto the porch. He closed the workbox on his truck and brought a set of keys to her.

"The same key will open all the doors," he told Cassie. "I didn't know how many you'd need, so I made four. I guessed you were looking for extra security, so I also put deadbolts on the three outer doors."

"Thank you very much," Cassie told him. "This has been a big help. Let me get my checkbook, and I'll pay you. Oh." She stopped. "It's an out-of-state check. Is that okay? I promise you it's good."

"No problem." His smile was just a tad uneasy. "Uh, just pay me for the materials, and we'll call it square."

"But that's ridiculous." She raised an eyebrow. "What's going on? You came out here on a Saturday, which is at least double time. I insist."

"Uh...Griffin?" He shifted from one foot to another.

"Pay him what he says, Cassie. He owes me too many favors to charge for his time."

She saw it was useless to argue with them, so she wrote out a check for the locks and Phil all but ran to his truck.

"I think that man's afraid of you," she said, a smile twitching the corners of her mouth. "Do you beat him on a regular basis?"

"At least once a week," he said, a solemn expression on his face. Then he then winked at her.

Her heart stuttered, and she had to turn away. This was absurd and ridiculous, and she had to stop it.

He went back to the yard work, and she tackled another room in the house. When her stomach grumbled, she knew it was time for lunch. She debated about offering Griffin something, knowing she was wading into deeper and deeper waters, but finally went to the door and hollered to him.

"If you like tuna fish, lunch will be ready in ten minutes."

He looked up from the side yard, startled. He wiped at the sweat on his forehead with his arm. "Okay. But I need to find a place to wash up."

"You can use the bathroom downstairs. Come on in." She went back to the kitchen to fix their lunch. *What are you doing, Cassie?*

In a minute, the front door opened and closed, and footsteps moved down the hall. She was just setting their plates on the table when he came into the kitchen. His presence filled the room. His hair was still damp from running wet hands through it, and he had put on a clean T-shirt. Muscles rippled beneath the tanned skin, and he smelled of maleness and the outdoors. Her unruly hormones did a happy dance.

Damn!

Despite the past, despite the pain she still carried with her every day, she wanted nothing more than to throw herself against his body and hold on for dear life. And that was a sure recipe for disaster.

Chapter Twelve

"I think you'll need to soak the towel I used, for about a week," Griff told her with a tiny grin. "Sorry about that."

"No problem." She fussed at the table settings. "I hope this is okay."

She had prepared tuna sandwiches with chips and pickles and large glasses of iced tea.

"This is fine. You didn't have to fix anything for me. Most days I just take a break and run down to the sandwich shop."

"I didn't mind. I was making something for myself anyway." Could she just stop being so fidgety? She felt like a fly that couldn't find a place to light.

It's just lunch. What's the big deal?

"Thank you for getting Phil out here and helping with the locks."

He shrugged. "No big deal. He does owe me, and it was important to get it done. I'm not saying someone has a key to this place, but no sense taking chances."

"I can't imagine why anyone would want to go through Diane's room." She brushed a stray hair off her face. "It just seems so strange. What on earth could they be looking for?"

"Do you know what kind of visitors your mother had in the last few months?".

Cassie shifted in her chair. "I know this sounds awful to say, but I haven't spoken to my mother in the past six months."

Griff gave her a strange look. "Did you two have a fight? I know you haven't been back here since...well, for several years, but I guess I assumed you all were still talking."

Cassie set her sandwich down, wiped the corner of her mouth, and tried to think how to answer the question without putting herself in a difficult position. "You have to understand," she began. "It all had to do with Diane. She and I were total opposites. She was bright, vivacious, a charmer from the day she was born. I was kind of the afterthought. Dull gray. Nobody asked or expected very much of me."

"You sell yourself short."

Cassie took a swallow of her iced tea then went on. "No matter what Diane did, my folks were one hundred percent absorbed with her. They chalked up her wildness, her reputation, to 'youthful hijinks,' as my dad used to say. She was the bright light in their lives."

She paused, gathering her thoughts.

"When Diane died, I was still so...well, I was still dealing with what happened when you two got married, and I couldn't make myself come home for the funeral. They never forgave me. When Dad died, my mother all but told me to stay away. That was fine with me. We've only had limited contact since then."

"I messed up your life a lot, didn't I." It was a statement more than a question.

"Truth be told, I think I guess did that all by myself." Her voice was low, quiet. "Anyway, I don't want to talk about it right now, if that's all right. Would you like some more iced tea? Or another sandwich?"

Griffin reached out and caught her hands in his. "I don't want iced tea, and I don't want anything else to eat. I want you to look at me."

She stared at her lap.

He tugged on her hands. "Cassie? Lift your head and look at me."

With great reluctance, she raised her eyes to meet his, thinking what a bad idea this had been. She should have just let him get his own lunch.

"We either keep picking at this thing until it starts to bleed," he said, "or we open it all at once and hope it will heal."

"I keep telling you," she said in a sad tone, "there just isn't anything to say. This was a mistake, Griffin. I'm sorry. I appreciate your help with the locks and the yard, but when you're finished, I think you should just go." *Before I make a fool of myself again.*

"Not a chance." He shook his head. "For one thing, I discovered something last night, and you should have, too. Whatever was there between us six years ago is still there. It's always been there for me. Diane got in the way, and there's just no polite way to say it any different."

So, he did remember what he'd said. But did he mean it?

He paused, watching her, then went on. "I know she was your sister, but she just wasn't the nice person your parents thought she was. Diane was selfish, self-centered, and she used people. She always hovered at the edge of a precipice, daring everyone to fall over it with her. When we were all running around like idiots, it was okay, because she could drink and fuck with the best of us."

Cassie jerked.

Griff tightened his grip on her hands. "Does that word offend you? I'm sorry, but there's just no other word for it. None of us in that crowd bothered much with morals at that time. We were wild then. All of us. Some nights I even slept in the drunk tank with my father. That's just the way it was."

"Is that the way it was with us?" she demanded. "Just...an exercise?"

"No," he said, emphatic. "But that's another topic for discussion. I'm just trying to make you see something here. Diane was just a good time, a hard ride, as they say. One more place I could run away from the disaster my family had become. But I never loved her. She knew it, I knew it. I guess I hoped, when I married her for the baby, we could start something new."

"Did you?"

"Not even for a minute." A shadow of sadness swept over his face. "Diane didn't want to be married, but your folks would have had a fit if she was single and pregnant. The money wasn't so great then, either, which bothered her a lot. I don't know what she expected, but it sure wasn't what she got. And, of course, there was my dad."

"I heard he passed away about year after Diane," Cassie interjected.

"All I can tell you is it was a blessing for both of us."

"I'm sorry." She didn't know what else to say.

"Yeah, well, aren't we all. Thank you."

He still held her hands in his, preventing her from leaving the table. "When she told me about the baby, I took it as some kind of sign to clean up my act. But Diane wasn't about to let a baby cramp her style. She bragged that she didn't even look pregnant. Most nights all we did was fight, and she'd slam out of the house. It was a freaking disaster."

"Is that what happened the night she died?" Cassie asked in a soft voice.

"You mean the night she was murdered? The night the whole town thought I killed her?" His tone was venomous. "Let's call it what it is, Cassie. You can't dress it up with nice words."

"I just...I don't...."

73

"The night Diane was murdered, we had a big fight. That's what you wanted to know. Right?"

She nodded, looking at her lap again. He sounded so angry.

"I guess I'm just damned lucky I went to Phil's house instead of staying home and getting smashed. Two other people dropped by, and we drank beer and watched a game on television. Otherwise, I'm sure I'd be on the inside looking out through bars right now."

Without raising her eyes, she said, "I never believed you killed her, Griff. I didn't think you could do something like that."

"You're a majority of one, I'll tell you that. People still look at me cross-eyed."

"But you do everyone's landscaping and everything," she pointed out again, and frowned. "They still hire you."

"Because they don't have a choice. It's me or no one." He dropped her hands, stood up, and took his dishes to the sink. "We still have a lot of unsettled issues between us, Cassie. And we're going to settle them before you leave here. Make no mistake about that. If I have my way, Tampa has seen the last of you." He headed toward the front door. "I'll let you know when I'm finished, so you can take a look."

She sat in her chair a long time after that, trying to straighten out her brain and her emotions. Griffin Hunter, Stoneham's worst bad boy, had grown up. As a man who'd walked through hell, he was even more dangerous. Before, he had been a forbidden pleasure she hungered for, beckoning her.

Now, he was older, his wildness under control but still there below the surface. Letting him into her life again was a big mistake, but she seemed powerless to stop it. If she kept opening the door for him, he'd walk right in and consume her. And that scared her.

Still, if she was honest with herself, this was the reason she

74

hadn't wanted to come back to Stoneham. Here she'd have to face the fact she'd never stopped loving him all these years. No matter how much she kept denying it to herself, there it was. That's why she still wore the locket.

Those kisses last night. Powerful kisses that she had willingly accepted, that stirred something inside her. The imminence of more was just hanging out there, tempting her, keeping her on edge.

And his words. "I love you."

Could she trust what he said? What could she do with it? Could she admit that she'd loved him all her life?

Those two nights with him so long ago still haunted her memory. She had indeed saved her virginity for him, hoping shamefully that one night she would be the one in the bad boy's arms. Even after the disaster of his marriage, the months and years of crying and anguish, nothing could erase that exhilaration. Seeing him now brought it all back.

Walk away. But she knew she wouldn't. She had built a fantasy on secret dreams and two stolen nights. Could she let down the bars long enough to find out if that fantasy was real?

Chapter Thirteen

Cleaning the kitchen took the longest of all the rooms, and by the time she finished, Cassie needed a break. She decided to take the opportunity to call Harley Graham.

"Good to hear from you, Cassie." His words boomed across the connection, somehow so comforting. "Everything going okay there?"

"Yes, Harley. Just fine. Thanks."

"Ran into Neil," he commented. "He told me you and he had met, gotten things started."

"Yes, we did." She sighed. "I didn't think everything would take so long. I guess I was dreaming if I thought I could do it in three days."

"Not around here, girl." He chuckled. "By the way, I'm passing the word about the funeral service on Tuesday. Hope you don't mind."

"No, that's all right. I don't expect a big crowd, and that's just as well."

"You may be surprised, honey. Your folks lived here a long time."

Cassie thought a moment about how to frame her question. "Harley, did my mother have a lot of visitors during her last few months?"

He paused, and she could imagine the faint lines of a frown forming on his forehead. "I don't know what you mean. She had two or three friends who looked in on her. Neil came by every so often to check on her and get her to sign some papers or other. Thad Williams, the senior partner in that firm, used to do all the legal work for your folks. When he retired, Neil took over, but Thad still came around to see her now and then. What's this all about? You looking for someone specific?"

"No, no," she said, quick to answer him. "I guess I was just trying to get a picture in my mind of what was going on here."

"Well, if there was anyone else who came to see her, they'll for sure be at the funeral. You can check everyone out for yourself."

"Thanks, Harley. And thanks for setting everything up here for me."

"No problem." He paused. "I happened to drive by your house a while ago and saw Griffin Hunter working in the yard. You hire him to do some work?"

"Uh, yes, well, that is, Carol Markham suggested I get him out here to neaten things up. I'm listing the house with her."

"Be careful, Cassie. Griffin may be a lot older and run a good business, but I still don't think I'd trust my daughter with him, if I had one."

A knot formed in her stomach. "Thanks for the advice, Harley, but I can handle Griffin. I'm older, too. Remember?"

"Just call me if you need me. You know I'm always here for you."

That went well. Cassie leaned back against the counter. *No one to suspect of breaking and entering except solid citizens, and a blatant warning about Griff.* Her headache was returning, too. She tore off a paper towel, wet it with cold water, and put it on the back of her neck.

"Are you all right?"

She hadn't even heard the object of her thoughts come in. He stood inches away from her, crowding her again, towering over her.

"I'm fine," she said, again giving a fast response. "A little overwhelmed by everything, I guess. I just got off the phone with Harley."

"You're not sick, are you?" Concern flashed in his eyes.

"No, thank goodness. That's all I'd need right now." She moved the towel around to cool her cheeks. "I'd told him I'd check in with him today. I also wanted to see if he knew who was visiting my mother these past few months. I'm trying to figure out who'd be searching for something here."

Griff cocked an eyebrow. "Did you get anything from him?"

She snorted. "A list of respectable citizens and a warning not to succumb to your charms."

Griff smiled at that. "Looking out for his surrogate daughter, was he? It's nice to know my reputation is still intact. You'd do well to listen to him. I have plans."

She started to say something, but he took her hand and pulled her toward the front door.

"Right now, I want you to come outside and see what I've done. The place sure was a mess."

Cassie couldn't believe how he'd transformed it. The grass was neatly mowed, the shrubs trimmed perfectly, all the beds weeded. Even the shriveled rose bushes had perked up. He walked her around the side yard and into the back. The flower beds had sparkled back to life, and all the edges of the lawn, including around the patio, were trimmed with great precision. He had put fresh mulch around the crepe myrtle and sycamore trees.

"Griff!" She couldn't hide her amazement. "I can't believe it's the same place. This is fantastic. You do incredible work." She couldn't stop staring, overwhelmed by what she saw. "Did you learn all this from your father?"

"Yeah, right," he snorted. "Some from working with him, some on my own by trial and error." He glanced away. "Two years ago, I started taking landscaping classes at the junior college in San Antonio. I learned a lot there."

She looked at him, her mouth gaping. *Griffin Hunter going to college?* She felt like she'd stumbled into a different dimension.

"Close your mouth, Cassie, you'll catch flies. Did I shock you? They say education is for everyone, you know."

"It's just that...."

"That you never expected it of me, right?" His moved closer to her, his presence crowding her. "What *did* you expect of me, anyway? Did you just want to give up your cherry to the town bad boy so you could have your own naughty memories? Was that it?"

The day had been too long, the tension too much, the frustration too great. She sank onto a lawn chair and burst into tears. She swiped at her face with the wet towel, knowing she looked as undone as she felt.

"Cassie?"

In an instant, he knelt beside her, brushing away the hair escaping from her ponytail, wiping away the tears running down her cheeks. "Honey, I'm so sorry. That was a rotten thing to say. And I didn't even mean it. Look at me, sugar. Come on."

Sugar. She could still hear him, his seductive voice whispering in her ear while he did unbelievable things to her body. While his fingers probed inside her, slick with her liquid, and his thumb did things to her clitoris that six years hadn't erased.

The tears she had saved up all this time came tumbling out. She rocked back and forth, crying in huge gulping sobs, not even caring what she looked like. She just needed to cleanse her body of the pent-up suffering.

She hadn't noticed Griffin leaving her until suddenly he was back. "Here." He handed her a glass of water and two aspirin. "Take these and drink all the water."

She obeyed his gentle instruction. Her body slowed its paroxysms and returned to normal. "Thank you."

"I think you've done quite enough work for today. The house looks great, but you look a mess, and you're exhausted." He took the glass from her and pulled her out of the chair. For a space of a heartbeat, he held her against him, their bodies touching, his rigid cock pressing against the softness of her stomach, her hardened nipples pushing into his chest. Then he released her and took her hand. "Come on. What you need is a hot bath and a nap."

"A bath?"

"Works wonders, they tell me." He led her into the house and helped her put away the cleaning supplies. "I'd take you out to dinner tonight, but I'm not in the mood to drive fifty miles to a restaurant. If we parade around in Stoneham, your reputation will be shot by tomorrow. Take your bath, take a nap, and I'll be back about seven thirty. We'll order some pizza, okay?"

"Pizza?" Didn't she just sound like an idiot, parroting his words.

"Yeah. You know, the flat dough with all the stuff on it. And I'll hide behind the door when the delivery boy gets here." He grinned.

She gave him a shaky smile in return.

"That's better," he said. "So. Seven thirty, okay?"

"Do you think this is such a good idea?" She knew she sounded shaky.

"I think it's a fine idea. And you will, too, once I get back here." He pulled her to him again, cradling her against his chest, stroking

80

her hair, soothing her. "I'll see you in a while, okay?"

She nodded. "Okay."

He started toward the front door then stopped. "We're going to face this, Cassie. You may not want to, but you've got so much bottled up inside you, and I have so much to say. There's no running away this time. I'll see you later."

Chapter Fourteen

Cassie had to admit Griff was right; the bath was great medicine. She'd stuck some bubble bath in her suitcase for whatever reason, and she dumped most of it into the tub. Leaning her head back, she sank into the welcoming warmth and let the softly lapping water and heady aroma do its work.

She'd gone and made an ass of herself with her meltdown, that was for sure. She cringed just thinking of it. What a fool he must think her, but it was an emotional catharsis long overdue. Maybe now she could take care of business in Stoneham, shake the dust from her shoes, and get on with her life.

But the question she kept trying to ignore just wouldn't go away. What was she going to do about Griff? When she thought of him it was with a mixture of dread and anticipation, her dilemma continuing to swirl around her. The imprint of his lips still lingered, and the memory of his touch wouldn't go away. She'd come back to Stoneham still so full of anger, determined to close that chapter of her life. Since then, all she'd done was let herself be drawn tighter and tighter into his web. He had asked the right question of her, though— what did she want from him? Too bad she didn't have a pat answer. Did she want to push him out of her life forever, or was she willing to risk her heart one more time?

This was a different Griffin Hunter than the untamed, careless boy who had taken her to his bed. That's what he had been then, a boy, even at twenty-four. This was an older Griffin, matured by the challenges life had thrown at him. A man, and a greater threat than the boy had ever been.

On a sigh, she let her hands drift to the nest of curls between her legs, recalling how Griff's hands had felt so long ago, teasing at those same curls, invading her body with a magic touch. This was a fantasy of long familiarity, played out whenever the memories of him became too hot to turn off. She spread her knees wide, letting the hot water lap against her skin and rubbing her fingers against her labia. She tingled just from thinking of those two nights with him, and she squeezed her puffy skin between thumb and forefinger.

She regretted not bringing her vibrator with her, the poor substitute for Griff that had eased her frustration on many nights. Instead, she let one finger slide over her clitoris, between the lips of her sex, past the throbbing flesh that begged for stimulation. When she slipped a finger into her pussy and slid it back and forth, she closed her eyes and imagined it was Griffin's hands, Griffin's fingers. Her vaginal muscles clenched around the intrusion, and she moved her hand in and out, faster and faster.

When she placed her thumb on her clit, she imagined it was Griff's thumb, circling and teasing. Her hips jerked as the heat built inside her. Bracing her feet on the bottom of the tub, her head barely above water, she increased the tempo, bucking against her hand until she could feel the tremors start. Then she was there, her whole body clenching as the spasms rippled through her.

But her fingers were not Griff's, her hands were not his. Nothing she could provide on her own was a substitute for the thick hardness of his cock as it probed at her entrance and pushed up inside her.

She lay in the tub, weak and just mildly satisfied. Why had she done this? Instead of bringing herself relief, she'd stimulated herself to an edge she might just fall over.

Better make up your mind, girl. The evening is approaching. Open that door, and there's no going back.

She dried her hair and brushed it until it shone. Tonight, she let it fall loose to her shoulders, unrestrained by a clip or ponytail holder. She pulled on fresh jeans and a summer sweater in deep rose, fastened little gold hoops in her ears, and swiped pink lipstick across her mouth. Putting on the war paint, she told herself. Did she even have a clue as to what she was doing?

At seven-thirty, waiting for the doorbell to ring, she was startled by a tap on the back door. She pulled aside the curtain on the little window. Griffin stood there, grinning at her.

"I didn't even hear you drive up," she said, opening the back door. "Why didn't you come to the front? Don't tell me you're worried about the neighbors."

"Yes and no." He stepped into the utility room and threw a small canvas bag on the counter.

"What's that?"

"My stuff. I'm spending the night."

Just like that. For a long moment she felt suffocated. Her chest hurt, and she couldn't breathe.

"You can wipe that look off your face. I have other reasons, which I'll tell you about over pizza." He grinned again. "Although, I can't say I haven't entertained naughty thoughts about you."

"What reasons?" Her voice strangled in her throat.

"The kind that explain why you didn't hear me." He gave her a stern look. "I walked and came in the back way. No one sees me arrive here or leave." He propelled her into the kitchen. "First, let's order the pizza. I'm starved."

Insisting she answer the door to the delivery boy herself, Griffin shoved money into her hand to pay for it. He avoided her probing questions while they ate, and Cassie tried to sit as relaxed as she could. But the sexual stimulation she'd given herself in her bath had left her whole body one big throbbing pulse.

If I could go ahead and attack him, then send him on his way. I don't know if I even want to know the real reason he's here. Or care.

After they'd finished the last crumbs and cleaned everything up, he took her hand and pulled her into the living room. Sitting on the couch, he tugged her down beside him.

"First of all, I don't want you to freak out about what I'm going to tell you. I have to let you know, though, because it's why I made up my mind to spend the night."

A tiny thread of fear wriggled through her.

"The whole business with Diane's bedroom bothered me," he began. "What could someone possibly want that an airhead like Diane would have? Then, when I was working in the yard, I saw where someone had been digging around some of the shrubbery, close to the house."

"What?" *What the hell?*

"It wasn't landscaping work, I can tell you that." He rubbed his jaw. "They were digging for something and then trying to cover it up. Then I remembered Diane had planted some of those bushes with me, when she was doing her 'let's do some yard work together' thing. It dawned on me someone might have thought she'd buried something there."

"I can't imagine what it would be." Cassie was astounded. Diane wasn't a complicated person. What would she have that would cause this stir of activity?

"Something's going on," he continued, "and I don't feel easy about it. With your mother gone and you here by yourself, whoever it is might decide to get bolder. I don't like the idea of you being all alone here."

"But where will you sleep?"

"You could always invite me into your bed, sugar," he drawled, but when her entire body tensed, he became serious. "I'm sorry, Cassie, That wasn't funny. And I owe you a big explanation about this afternoon."

He stood up, stuck his hands in his jeans pockets, and stared out the window at the fading light.

"I don't even know where to begin here. I can't apologize for my life, and I won't. I was what I was, and I did what I did. Nobody held a gun to my head. Even before my mother died, I lived for the excitement. I liked my bad boy reputation. After that, it was easy to use her death as an excuse."

He paused, still looking out into the dark.

"The disaster with Diane never should have happened. Oh, I liked her all right, and she was great in bed. But nobody in that crowd ever expected anything lasting of anyone else. That's why we could be so free with each other. The pregnancy shocked me. There was just one time I didn't use a condom, but I guess that was enough.

"I told you being married was the last thing she wanted," he went on, "but she wanted money. Her mistake was in thinking I had any. She was bored when I told her I thought we should clean up our act." He kept his back to her as if afraid to face her while he talked.

Cassie sat immobilized, barely breathing, just listening. "What about us?"

She had to know the truth, whatever it was.

"I wanted you the first time I saw you in your little cheerleading

86

outfit." The words exploded in a whooshing breath, as if the confession had been hidden too long. "But I knew you'd never go out with me. You were just the stuff of my dreams. Then you went away to college, and time went by. The first summer you went off somewhere to work, but the next year, when you came back, I took a look at you and realized I was in love."

"In love." She echoed his words, tasting them, testing them.

He turned to face her, a rueful look on his face. "Beats all, doesn't it? You were *my* guilty little secret because I don't think I even believed in love. Shocked the shit out of me. And that was a problem, you see. Because, how would I ever get you to think that way about me? I wasn't just out there by accident that night, Cassie. I sat on my front porch for three nights running, hoping you would walk by and I could get you to come up and talk to me. I never expected what happened to happen."

"Didn't you?" The words seemed stuck in her throat.

"No. But I sure as hell hoped. Please don't think I took it lightly, because I didn't. Those two nights we had together kept me going for the past six years. I gave you my heart, Cassie, and then you ran away with it. I've never gotten it back." He stood in silence for a long moment. "When I tell you now that I love you, I'm not just saying what I think you want to hear. I've never said that to anyone else. Not even Diane. Or, maybe, especially her. Because you're the only one I've ever loved."

Cassie didn't move, not knowing what to do next.

"I don't expect you to say anything," he told her. "I just wanted you to know. I don't have any illusions about the future, but it was important to tell you how I feel." He turned and moved next to the couch. "I also wanted to apologize for this afternoon. That was a rotten thing to say. I've just been storing up so much anger all these years, it jumped out without my thinking."

"Why didn't you ever call me?" she asked. "You could have found me if you really wanted to."

He shrugged. "Too ashamed. Too proud. Besides, what did I have to offer? What could I say? 'Hi, Cassie. Your sister's dead. The town thinks I killed her. I didn't, and now I want us to be together?' Do you know how that would have sounded?"

"You could have told me how you felt," she insisted, her heart fracturing more and more as she listened to him.

"Would you have listened then? Ask yourself that. Now," he said, pulling himself together with visible effort, "if you could direct me to some sheets and blankets, I'll fix myself up on the couch. I'd feel weird sleeping in your parents' room, and I sure as hell won't sleep in Diane's."

They stared at each other through the gloom, the gathering dark underlining the silence. She knew she should run upstairs, lock herself in her bedroom, and, in the morning, run back to Florida as fast as she could. Instead, she just kept looking at Griffin, searching for some kind of answer.

Finally, she broke the spell. "You could sleep in mine. With me." She said it so softly she wasn't sure he heard her.

He gave her a hard look, his eyes like cold steel. "Don't say that unless you mean it, sugar. I haven't got that much control left in me. When I bury myself deep inside you, I won't let you walk away again."

She could no more have stopped what she did next than halt a runaway train. She had lived with her memories for six years. She'd sworn she'd never come within ten feet of him again, but now, here, she knew what a false promise that was. As badly as she'd been burned, the flame still beckoned. Not knowing what would happen afterward, if he even meant half of what he said, she still obeyed the insistent call of her body. Standing up, she took his hand and led him to the stairs.

With her back to him, she said, "It's been a long time since I've done this, so I'm a little out of practice. Of course, they say it's like riding a bicycle; the body never forgets."

Chapter Fifteen

She faced him in her room, more nervous and afraid than she'd ever been in her life. Even more than their first time together in his spartan bedroom. Griffin's memories of her, just like hers of him, were light years past. Would he still find her as desirable? Would the passion still be there?

She lifted her hands, palms outward. "Help me."

He captured her hands in his. "Cassie, I have to tell you this before we go any further. I have nothing to offer you. And you have to know, if you hook up with me, this town will be pointing its collective fingers at you. It won't be pretty."

"Do you think I care one bit what this jerk town thinks?" She twisted her lips in a bitter parody of a smile. "What has it ever done for me?"

He rubbed his fingers in a sensuous glide against hers. "Last chance to back out, sugar. You're up here in your bedroom with the town bad boy. My reputation hasn't changed." His face was dead serious. "But neither have my feelings for you."

"Maybe this is what I always wanted, even before our first night together." She couldn't believe she was saying this. She gripped his fingers hard. "Maybe you were *my* secret fantasy, and I've still been wanting you all these years. You didn't warn me the last time, or didn't it mean anything to you?"

"You can't imagine how much it meant." His voice was tight. "What about you? Did it mean as much to you? Have other men been able to set you on fire like I did?"

"No one," she whispered. "Not ever."

How could she even begin to tell him the way the touch of other men had turned her off, how no one else could awaken that hot flame of desire in her, make her body shiver and tremble in anticipation.

In the next moment, he cupped her face in his hands, leaned down, and kissed her. If she thought his kisses the other night had been exciting, tonight, they made her blood race. Threading one hand through her hair, he pulled her lips tighter against his. She opened her mouth to him, and he explored it with slow sweeps of his tongue, making her respond with hers. This kiss was like a feeding frenzy that went on and on. Weak, she leaned against him, unable to stand on her own.

Lifting his mouth from hers, Griff backed up to sit on the edge of the bed, guiding her toward him with gentle hands, and undressed her. He took his time, not hurrying anything, each piece like wrapping paper exposing another piece of the gift. He held her steady as he dragged her sweater over her head and tossed it aside. Then, with teasing slowness, he traced the tips of his fingers over the swell of her breasts above her bra. He palmed them, the touch of his skin searing hers.

She held her breath as he stared at her, his gaze drinking in every inch of her.

"Damn," he breathed. "Perfection. Just fucking perfection."

He grazed her nipples with his thumbs, touching the pebbled surface as if it were crystal. She felt them contact into hard points. She let out a long. choppy breath as he kissed each of them in turn, sucking them until they enlarged in his mouth, swirling his tongue around their tips, then closing his lips over larger portions of the creamy flesh.

She swayed, weakened by the assault of sensations, he held her in place with his hands firm on her hips.

"God, you are so beautiful." His tone was reverent, almost awestruck. "Cassie, Cassie. You are still the light in my heart."

He unsnapped her jeans and slid the zipper down, the rasp of it sounding so loud in the room. Pushing the jeans down, he nudged her to step out of them, leaving just the tiny scrap of silk that passed for her panties. Then that was gone, and she was naked before him.

His eyes raked over her as if relearning every inch of her body. He touched the tip of one finger where her thighs met, slid it up into the curls on her mound then down through their silkiness.

Cassie gasped at his touch, almost falling forward. With his knees, he nudged her thighs farther apart and moved his finger lightly between them, seeking the warmth of her folds. He stroked one finger along the length of her labia, probing the outer edges, his touch eliciting a delicious shiver from her. He tightened his grip on her, holding her in place, and held up his finger, wet with her moisture.

"Fucking damn, Cassie. You have no idea how hard it makes me to know you're slick for me already. Remember that? Remember my fingers touching your sweet little cunt lips? Does it still feel good, sugar? You know it does. And I'm about to make you feel a whole lot better. Sweet, sweet Cassie," he said in a husky voice. "How could I ever have been so stupid as to lose you?"

Somehow, then, he was out of his clothes, and she was in the bed next to him, cradled against his body. His free hand drifted to the apex of her thighs again, and she opened her legs for him without prompting, urging him to delve even deeper. He pressed his palm against her damp mound while he kissed her eyelids, the tender spot behind her ear, the hollow at the base of her throat where her pulse beat a rapid rhythm.

He touched every outside inch of her sex, teasing the curls, stroking the softness of the slick skin, taking his time with his exploration. When he found her already swelling clit and moved his thumb over it, she jerked as if arrows of lightening had shot through her. She lifted her hips toward him in a pleading gesture, and a soft moan escaped her lips.

"Easy, sugar," he told her, almost whispering. "We've got all night, and I'm in no hurry. Open your legs wider for me. Come on."

When she did, she was rewarded by the thrust of his fingers into her hot, hungry sex. She couldn't stop the little cries of passion erupting from her mouth.

He moved his fingers in and out of her in an easy glide, stroking the nub of her clit with his thumb. He seemed to know when to slow down, when to speed up. He brought her to the edge again and again before backing up then driving her to the point where every inch of her body quivered with hot need.

He kissed her abdomen, his lips open and hot against her skin. Reaching far inside for her most sensitive spot, he curled his fingers to rasp against it then drew back. With his touch and the sound of his voice, everything came flooding back to her, every touch, every caress, all the secret yearnings in her dreams all these years.

"Do you remember this, Cassie?" His words rumbled low and deep in this throat. "Do you remember how it felt? Talk to me, sugar. Tell me what you like. How it feels. Tell me what you like me to do."

Cassie gasped in remembered pleasure. The pain she'd worn like a hair shirt was gone, dissipated in this one moment. Just like that, the past six years disappeared, and she was back in his bed with him, consumed by an uncontrolled passion. This was where she should be, no matter what.

She moved against him, hungry, needy, wanting him closer. Her hands roamed over his chest, pulling at the crisp chest hair. He groaned with pleasure as she found his flat nipples and teased them with her fingernails. Heat spiraled through her, pooling between her legs, and an insistent throbbing pulsed through the wet muscles of her heated channel.

"It's all right, Cassie. I can wait to hear you say what you want. Right now, your body's doing all the talking I need. God, how it's talking," he whispered. "I love you, Cassie. God help me, I love you more than my life."

Her eyes glazed, and her movements quickened. His fingers danced over her, slid into her, teased at every sensitive spot.

"Griffin." She could barely get the word out.

"Yes, darlin'? Tell me. Come on, tell me that you want this. And this. And this. Come on, Cassie."

She pulled at him, sliding her hands over his hot skin. She couldn't stand it. Her mind whirled.

"Tell me. Did anyone else make you feel like this?"

"No, no, no." She thrashed about, tossing her head back and forth, rocking against him. "Nobody. Just you."

"You know it, sugar. Just me." He put his lips to her ear, stroking the inside with the tip of his tongue. "You're mine, Cassie. No one else's. Say it," he commanded her. "Say it now."

"Yes. All right. I'm yours. Please, please, please." She begged him, almost sobbing with need. Her body shook with frustration, reaching for that elusive peak of fulfillment, the moment when her womb would contract, her vaginal walls would clench, and spasm after spasm would roll through her body.

He laughed, a low, throaty sound. "All right, then. Here we go. Come for me, Cassie. Just like before. Let me feel you come. Now." When she pushed against him, her body arching toward him, he leaned close to her ear and whispered, "I love you, Cassie."

That was all it took. Rockets went off in her head, and she thought for sure she would fly apart. The tremors deep within her went on and on and on, convulsing around his fingers, her body straining against his touch. Wave after wave of ecstasy washed over her. Small tremors like aftershocks fluttered inside her. Her release consumed her, as if it would never reach conclusion. Then, at last, he brought her down and the tremors slowed.

She lay back against the pillows at last, panting, her heart racing so loud she thought he would hear it. Pleasure still pulsed through her. She looked up at Griffin, and his face held a satisfied look. But, with his next words, she could feel herself responding again.

"I want to be inside you," he whispered in her ear. "I want to feel you around me, feel your hot wetness on my dick. God, Cassie, I want to bury myself in your soul."

"God, Griff."

"I want to taste you, feel my tongue stroking those hot, wet walls of yours. I've never forgotten how sweet you tasted."

She tried to mold her body to his, her legs clasping around him as she urged him to enter her. Panting, vibrating from the intensity of her orgasm, still she was ready for him again. She wanted him at the very center of her body, penetrating her vagina, the tip of his penis touching her womb. She wanted to feel him convulse inside her like that night so long ago.

"Hold on a minute, darlin. Don't move." He slid back from her and fished a condom from his pocket.

She tugged him back to her. "No," she said, defiant. "Just like before. Nothing between us." She was possessed with the need to feel the nakedness of his cock against her drenched inner skin. And, even more, to bind them together, skin to skin. How could she possibly have denied to herself what she felt for this man?

He spoke through gritted teeth. "Cassie, I'm in no position to start an argument with you now."

"Then don't," she told him. "Please. Just do it."

He leaned over her. "When you're in this all the way, sugar, then we'll talk. Right now, I'm about to forget my own name, so just let me do this before I lose any shred of control."

"No. No. No." She tried to wrap her legs around him again and pull him back into position, hardly able to believe what she was saying. Somehow it was important to her that there be nothing separating the contact. The specter of pregnancy didn't frighten her. "This is what I want," she cried. "Please."

"Ssh, darlin'. We'll have plenty of time to think about that. But not now."

He unwrapped the condom and sheathed himself, teeth still gritted. Then, with a groan, he pushed her hands aside and mounted her again, positioning himself between her legs.

Cassie reached down to take him in her hand, guide him into her

"Okay, Cassie," he told her, his voice unrecognizable. "Now."

With a slow movement he slid into her hot, wet sheath. Beads of sweat popped out on his forehead, and she wiped them with her fingertips. Needing more, she rocked back and forth, urging him on.

"That's it, sugar," he rasped. "Yes. Oh, God, Cassie."

He thrust hard against her, grinding his pelvic bone against her sensitive nub, pulling her hips tight to him. Their sweat-slickened bodies moved together, faster and faster. She tensed, clutching at him, clenching around him. Cassie felt his hot, thick shaft filling every inch of her channel, stretching her tight vaginal walls, damp flesh clutching steel-hard flesh.

And just like that, the explosion caught them again, whirling them into a space filled with fireworks. Their climax was so intense it shook both of them. Cassie convulsed violently, arching wildly, pulling him deep into her body. Slick skin slapped against slicker skin, sliding against the cool, cotton sheets as his shaft pulsed again and again inside her.

At last, they collapsed together, Griff's head on Cassie's chest, both of them gasping for breath, their rapid heartbeats thudding in union. She tangled her fingers in his hair and whispered his name over and over.

"I love you," he said again, feathering light kisses on her cheeks, her forehead, her eyelids.

The words were so soft, for a moment she wondered if she had imagined them.

"I love you, too, Griff." How good it felt to say it. After all the years she had denied it to herself, now she could tell him without reservation.

Time seemed to expand as they lay there, twined together, his hand stroking her with infinite tenderness. When he tried to move, she held him in a tight embrace, her grasping muscles refusing to let him pull out of her body.

"Condom," he whispered, and pulled out to dispose of it before trouble came calling.

Then he was back beside her, pressing his mouth close to her ear.

"I'm back in your life now, Dewdrop. And I plan to stay."

As she drifted off to sleep, she managed to smile and say, "Good."

Chapter Sixteen

Cassie opened her eyes and stretched like a cat then felt the warm body next to her and smiled. She hadn't been this happy in a long time. She turned on her side to run her fingertips over the man who owned her heart. It was still dark outside, the moonlight shining in through the window.

"Can we do it again?" She kissed his shoulder, wondering where her boldness was coming from.

"Cassie." With obvious effort he turned and faced her. "Look at me, sugar."

"What is it? I'm not sure I can think right now." She gave him a sleepy smile. "Someone wore me out."

"We have to talk about this." The expression on his face was serious.

"About what? Why are you always wanting to talk?" She tensed, not sure she wanted to hear what he had to say even as she stroked a finger along his arm. "I can think of better things to do."

"Because we have things to discuss." He shook his head. "You almost convinced me to do something crazy, and I have a feeling that subject isn't closed with you. How could you be willing to take such a chance? What if you got pregnant?"

"I want to." The words just popped out of her mouth like jumping beans.

Whoa, Cassie. Take a step back.

But she wasn't sure she wanted to. They had so much lost time to make up for.

"Cassie, honey, you don't know what you're saying."

"Oh, yes I do," she insisted, pushing herself upright." I've waited a long time for this. I didn't think I'd ever have it again. I hated you for so long despite the fact I never got over loving you. And now?" She gave him a slow smile. "Having your baby would be the frosting on the cake."

She heard herself talking and wondered if she'd hit her head, but she couldn't seem to shut her mouth. And she *did* want Griff's baby. Last night had ignited that need stronger than ever, and she didn't want to wait.

"And then what would you do?" he asked.

"What do you mean?" A tiny chill crept into her with a sudden blast. What did he mean? "Are you saying you wouldn't want to marry me?" She stared up at him. "You were willing to marry Diane. Was this just sweet talk to scratch a six-year-old itch?" The words were out before she had time to think.

He tried to roll away from her, but she refused to let him.

"Don't pull away," she demanded. "You pushed this thing. Now you have to tell me where we're going with it."

Again, she couldn't believe the words coming out of her mouth. Just because he said he loved her didn't mean he was planning a long future with her. Did it? Everything was moving so fast. Still, being together with Griff again let her know she either needed it all or she had to push him out of her life. A life he could easily turn upside down.

Silence hung between them.

"Do you know what you're saying?" he said at last, shaking his head. "I was selfish tonight. I saw you, I wanted you. I wanted to make you mine. But like I told you, I'm a pariah in this town, a marked man. People would talk about you all the time if we were together."

"So, this was just about getting me into bed for one night?" She shook with anger. "That's your unfinished business?"

"No, sugar, it's way more than that." His voice was low. "I never thought you'd come back. When I saw you, I.... God, Cassie. You think letting you go again would be easy? I said I love you, and that isn't a lie. But if I love you, I have to think about what's good for you. How would you live here, anyway? You have a job, a life to go back to. And I'm stuck here, in small town hell."

She chose her words with care. "A job is a job. I can get one anywhere. Since the night I left here, there hasn't been anyone else for me, Griffin. As angry and bitter as I was, when I looked at any other man, I saw your face. I was sure I'd never see you again. Then my mother died, and here I am. We just did things and said things to each other.... Do you think it would be easy for me to walk away from that, regardless of what the town busybodies do or say?"

"Let me sit up." This time, he forced her to let him roll away and sat with his back to her. "I'm trying to do what's right for you, Cassie. I love you, but life isn't even the same for us."

She moved closer, reaching for him, bereft at the loss of contact. "No, it isn't. But that doesn't mean it's bad. We could make it good together. You keep saying you love me. Do you mean it?"

He looked down at her, caution in his gaze.

"Do you really love me?" she prodded.

He was mute for so long, she panicked. What was she doing, anyway? Yesterday, she'd wanted to erase him from her life. Today, she wanted his child. First, he said he loved her then he said it was a mistake. She was crazy. He was *making* her crazy. She held her breath, waiting for his answer.

It seemed forever until he spoke. "I have loved you for as long as I can remember," he told her, his words slow and deliberate. "If I'd been someone other than who I was, I would have told you a long time ago. But what could I offer you then? What can I offer you now? Not respectability. You have to realize that."

Now, she was the one who pushed away. Hard. "I guess I forgot to ask that question. Is that what I'm supposed to do? Ask what you can offer me?"

She raged, all the lovely indolence of sex gone in an instant.

"Just what is it you think I want, Griffin Hunter?" She clamped down on the surge of anger. "Answer me that."

"I told you." He uttered his words in a flat monotone. The moonlight glancing in through the window outlined the sharp angles of his face, giving it a harsh look. "I'm an outcast in this town. People tolerate me, but the men lock up the women, and the women harbor secret thoughts of shameful sex with the town exile. Not to mention the fact that Diane's death will always hang over my head. I had no right to do this tonight. You have to want more out of life than what a relationship with me will do to you."

"Tell me that you love me again," she insisted.

"God, Cassie." He drew a ragged breath. "You just don't give up. All right, I love you."

"You know, I was the one holding back, afraid to give myself to you again, and you came on here like gangbusters. Now, I'm ready to jump off a cliff with you, and you want to pull away. How stupid is that?"

"Cassie," he groaned.

"I want to show you something."

With fingers that trembled she opened the locket still hanging on the slender chain. When Griffin saw what was inside, he clenched his jaw. Emotion flashed deep and dark in his eyes.

"A long time ago, you gave me your heart and told me to take care of it for you. I've been doing that ever since." She pulled him down beside her and curled up close to him. "You keep saying we have a lot to talk about. Well, we've talked. And I'll bet we've got a lot more talking yet to do. Maybe I've got more to lose than you do, although I doubt it. But if I'm willing to chance it, why aren't you? Or were you lying to me just now."

With a moan, he pulled her into his arms and slanted his mouth hard against hers. This wasn't just a passionate kiss, it was a searching kiss, a probing kiss, claiming her, his tongue seeking answers.

"All right, Cassie." He lifted his lips and stared straight into her eyes. "You want the truth? Fine. I want you more than my next breath. I feel as if I've loved you all my life." He raked his hand through his hair, desperation lining his face.

"Then...."

His words fell like block of concrete. "Then you'd better be prepared for a hard ride. If you've got the guts to do it, though, who am I to argue?"

In answer, she shoved him back on the bed, leaned over him, and took his shaft in her hand and stroked it with slow sweeps of her fingers, feeling the ridges that pebbled the velvety skin. "You're right, we have a lot to do, so we'd better get started."

She knelt beside him and leaned forward. When the heat of her mouth enclosed his hardening cock, he almost came off the bed. Her tongue swirled and dipped and licked, covering his hardening erection with the warm moisture of her mouth.

"Jesus, Cassie." His hands gripped her head, his fingers weaving through her hair.

She lifted her mouth from its journey. "Am I doing it wrong?" This was something she'd read about in great detail but never had the desire to do with anyone else. "Help me, Griff. Teach me how to pleasure you." She bent to her task again, loving the sweet, salty taste of him, the feeling of his penis growing and expanding in her mouth.

"Gently." His hoarse words sounded like rusty steel. "Touch my balls, Cassie. Tease them with your fingers. Yesss," he hissed, as she cupped the heavy sac and stroked it from back to front. "That's it. Oh, God, you're killing me."

She swirled her tongue at the tip of his cock, stroking the drop of liquid she found there over the rest of the head, then sucking the entire erection into her mouth. She moved her hand on his balls in cadence with the rhythm of her mouth, sucking and caressing and licking, until time lost all meaning for her.

She heard Griffin's harsh cries, felt his body thrusting against her, as she lost herself in the erotic joy of pleasuring him.

"Cassie, I'm gonna come," he groaned, trying to lift her head away.

She responded by clamping one hand around his cock, pushing him harder into her mouth, and stroking the shaft with her tongue. The hand at his testicles felt the pre-orgasmic tightening, and then, with a harsh cry, he exploded into her mouth.

Liquid jetted down her throat, and she swallowed reflexively, still sucking and stroking until the last convulsion of his climax had left him. When she lifted her head, her mouth was wet with his semen, and she licked every drop of it from her lips.

"Cassie," he moaned, pulling her toward him. "Oh, God, Cassie."

He kissed her, and, against his mouth, she whispered, "Now, you belong to me, too."

Chapter Seventeen

Whenever Griffin looked back on this night he thought of it as a reawakening. The first frenzy of stored passion abated, followed by long, slow exploration. *Do you like this? How does that make you feel?* Griff was experienced while it was evident Cassie was not, a fact that thrilled him. He was delighted to use his expertise to bring her to one shattering orgasm after another.

They had always made love in the dark, but now it was important they see every inch of each other. Her body was lush and ripe, her nipples still taut and darkened with passion, the inside of her thighs still slick with her juices.

In the brightness of the lamplight, he watched as she took his shaft in her hand, staring at it in wonder, caressing it, exploring the tip with her finger, the touch so gent that, even as spent as he was, he almost came in her hand.

Swearing at his near loss of control, he covered her hand with his and moved it to the side, maneuvering her to lie flat on her back. With hungry eyes, he examined every inch of her body, touching it in all the secret places, memorizing her. He ran his fingers over the hollows at her hip bones, teased at her navel, brushed his hands against her breasts now swollen and heavy with passion. With delicate strokes he laved the hard, rosy nipples, grazing them with his teeth then soothing them with his tongue.

With a gentle touch he bit the tender spot between her shoulder and her neck, nipped at the pulse pounding at the base of her throat. Not even her arms were left untouched.

Kneeling before her, he pulled her legs over his shoulders, leaving her entire vaginal area open to his assault. With gentle fingers, he parted the lips and just stared his fill at the slick, pink flesh and soft, pouty lips exposed there. He separated them more, a fraction at a time, until her entire channel was exposed to his heated gaze. He brushed back the curls clinging there, damp with the fluids of her sexual release, so no inch of her luscious skin was hidden from his sight.

"Do you like this, darlin'? Can you tell me yet what you want? Can you say the words?"

Cassie lay there moaning.

"It's all right, sugar. I can read you, even if you don't say the words. But, one of these nights, you will, Cassie. You'll feel free enough to talk to me like I talk to you."

Then, lifting her hips, he carried her to his mouth, and, in one swift stroke plundered her with his tongue. In a frenzy of feasting, he lapped every internal inch of her, scraping his tongue against the sensitive flesh, flicking the tip against her clitoris now so sensitive just the merest touch made her jerk in response. Her skin was so tender, so delicious, he thought he would never get enough of her.

The more he stroked her with his tongue, the louder the mewling sounds emanated from her throat. Only his strength kept her anchored in place as he took her higher and higher, using his tongue and his teeth to touch every nerve in her hot, secret places. He was like a man possessed, so famished for every inch of her that he couldn't find enough ways to take her.

When a low, moaning sound escaped her, and body began the clutch of orgasm, he pressed her thighs apart with his forearms and opened her vaginal entrance with his fingers as wide as he could.

While his penis twitched to slide into her, he was obsessed with watching her body convulse in passionate response to him.

His breath jerked as he watched her sweet pink flesh clench and unclench and heard her screaming his name as her climax rolled through her. His hungry gaze reveled in the sight of her hot fluid pouring from her opening and into the cleft of her buttocks.

His cock was so swollen, his body so aroused, he needed every bit of control to contain himself. He wanted to plunge himself inside her and never pull out, but he wanted more of her body first, more possession to slake his need. Griffin had been with a lot of women in his life, but compared to Cassie, everything else had been calisthenics. Cassie touched his heart, his soul, making him want to brand every inch of her as his.

Her fists were still grabbing the sheet and her body still shaking when he flipped her over and kissed the length of her spine, wet, moist kisses, punctuated with swift stabs of his tongue. He was like an addict, unable to get enough of her. No matter how much he drank of her essence, he couldn't slake his thirst.

He nipped at her ankles and slid his mouth up the insides of her legs, delivering little feathery touches that had her squirming with desire. Every spot was an erogenous zone—her calves, the backs of her knees, the juncture of her thighs at the crease of her buttocks. She moaned as he pressed each moist imprint on her tender skin.

When he reached the base of her spine, he kneed her legs farther apart, separated the luscious globes of her buttocks, dipped his head low, and lapped the juice that, only seconds before, had seeped from her body. His hands cradled her as he pulled her up to him and his tongue sought the rosy inner flesh that had given up its secrets to him.

She bucked under his ministrations, calling his name over and over, begging, pleading, demanding his entry into her body. As his tongue licked away the last of the liquid, he stroked the cleft with his thumbs, pausing at the tight opening he had yet to penetrate just long enough to hear her cries intensify.

Barely remembering in time, he reached for another condom and rolled it on with shaking fingers. Then he pulled her to her knees, separated her folds and, with one swift stroke, thrust himself into her from behind.

The moment his cock was buried in her to the balls he stopped, unwilling to have the feeling of ecstasy end too fast. This was where he belonged, he'd always known it. He'd cherished the little spark of hope that this would happen for so long he had trouble believing this was real. Cassie. The woman who'd stolen his heart. The woman willing to step into the mess that was his life, without regrets.

Gritting his teeth to restrain himself, he began a slow, steady, thrusting movement, his hot hands holding her hips, as he described to her in erotic detail everything he was doing to her and everything he wanted to do.

Then the delicious feel of her snapped his control. One final stroke, and he emptied his seed into her, his hands at her abdomen pulling her tight against him.

Exhausted at last, she curled into his body, spooning him. He threw his arm around her and pulled her tight, holding her as they fell asleep. They didn't wake up until the sun shone full in the window, the bright rays disturbing their slumber.

Cassie lay there, savoring the feel of Griffin against her, every muscle relaxed in the greatest sense of peace and security she'd had in a long time. Every muscle in her body was sore, every bone ached, but it was a satisfying feeling rather than an unpleasant one.

He'd been relentless, taking her every way possible, teaching her how to pleasure his body as he'd pleasured hers. Each time he'd carried her to new heights of passion, her brain told her she couldn't take any more. But he'd soothed her, petted her, taken her back down, then started in all over again.

They'd done things together she'd only read about, yet none of it made her self-conscious or uncomfortable. With Griffin, exploring new boundaries was exciting to the senses. Because she loved him. There it was. The thing she'd been running away from since she'd left Stoneham. Without Griffin, her life had been a succession of colorless days. Now, here they were, together, and she wasn't about to let it fall apart again, no matter what she had to do.

And no matter what anyone else said. Gossip couldn't hurt unless you let it.

Relaxed and in blissful lassitude, she was startled to feel the tip of Griffin's erection pressing against her, and without even thinking she shifted her legs to open for him.

"A great way to start the day, sugar, don't you think?" he breathed into her ear, lifting one of her legs and draping it over his hip. His hand stole toward her clitoris, searching it out in the still damp curls and pinching it between two fingers. She jerked in response to the stimulation.

"Will we ever get enough of each other?" Even as her body protested another assault, heat still stirred in her loins.

"I hope not." Adjusting her to accommodate him, he entered her from behind then put his hand on her stomach to hold her tight against him. He rocked against her, his fingers reaching into her lips, still swollen from the night before, testing her for readiness. She relaxed to take him, and he thrust deeper into her. In the slowest, gentlest coupling yet, they climaxed just like that, holding each other and molded together.

"I love you, Cassie Fitzgerald" he said, and today his tone was more certain. "You know you're mine now, with all that goes along with that."

She nodded. "I love you, too, Griffin Hunter."

He leaned his head next to hers and spoke into her ear. "Nobody ever knew about us, Cassie. Not a soul."

She stilled in his arms. Why was he telling her this? Was she going to get yet one more argument?

"I know you've had to wonder, all this time," he went on. "Those two nights we had together were private between you and me, and too important for me to trash with loose talk."

"I was never quite sure." She turned her face, wanting him to see her as she spoke. "When the wedding and everything happened, I didn't know what to think. All I can tell you is the last six years have been hell for me."

"Me, too, Dewdrop. Me, too." He stroked her arm, her cheek, and kissed her temple, his heart thumping against her back. "For the first time in years, I feel peace stealing over me. Soothing me. I don't know if I can find the words to tell you what you mean to my life, but I'll spend forever doing what it takes to make you happy."

At last they managed to push themselves out of bed. After they showered together, Cassie went downstairs to make coffee while Griffin shaved. He came into the kitchen as she was pouring liquid into two mugs, and she stood on tiptoe to give him a light kiss. His hair was still damp from the shower, and he carried the tantalizing scent of soap, aftershave, and his own maleness.

"I need to go home and change," he told her. He wore the chinos and sport shirt he'd had on last night. "What are your plans for today?"

"I've got to finish cleaning the upstairs," she said. "It's driving me nuts. I don't know how my mother stood it. I also want to go through her room and see if she has any papers I might have missed. Harley said Neil took care of everything, but I want to find her checkbook, things like that."

"Want to take a little drive?" he asked.

"Where to?"

"Just some place I'd like to show you. Not far."

She raised an eyebrow, staring at him, but his face gave nothing away. "Can you give me a couple of hours? Then I'll be ready."

"Sure. We'll stop somewhere for lunch." He sat in silence for a few minutes. It was apparent he was running through some things in his head.

Cassie knew they had a lot of ground to cover, and, for the moment, she was content to let him take the lead. But when he didn't say anything, she broke the silence. "I've made up my mind about something."

He looked at her, his expression wary. "And that is?"

"Neither of us will have any peace in our lives until there's some resolution to Diane's murder. I get the feeling the police didn't look any further than you, and when that didn't pan out, they just stopped looking. Maybe they hoped you'd do something to kill your alibi."

"And how do you figure we can to change that?" he asked, his voice laced with bitterness.

"First of all," she told him, "Dangler said he'd get me a copy of the police report and the autopsy. I've worked on newspapers long enough to know how to read police documents. Then I want to go to *The Stoneham Recorder* and have them pull their back issues for me. I read what I could online, but *The Recorder* didn't have a website then. I'm thinking maybe there might be something in one of the articles that will point us in a new direction."

"Cassie." He raked his fingers through his hair. "You aren't a trained investigator. You can't just go charging into something you know nothing about."

She wasn't charging, just investigating. If they could come up with a new lead or fresh piece of evidence, if Dangler wouldn't follow it up, she'd hire a private detective.

She stared into her coffee cup. "I discovered my mother had quite a little nest egg," she said in a matter-of-fact tone. "She left it to me. Maybe I can use some of it to make up for all the tragedy."

Griffin just looked hard at her for a long moment before he spoke again. "The money is immaterial. You can't stay here alone at night as it is. The risk is too great, with someone running around out there trying to find something. I'd worry too much about you. If you start digging into this, it ups the risk factor. We need to move you to the motel where you'll have people around you."

"Stoneham Tourist Cottages? Puhleeze." She shook her head. "Anyway, I've already come up with a solution." She swallowed her smile. "You'll just have to move in with me."

"Cassie." He slammed his mug on the table, sloshing the coffee over the rim. "Damn it. That is the stupidest thing I've heard. Do you have any idea how tongues will wag? The vestal virgin and her sister's killer?"

Cassie burst out laughing. "If that weren't so funny, I'd be insulted. Give me a break here. Anyway, it's my home, and I can invite anyone in that I want. Besides, do you have a better solution?"

He opened his mouth to protest further, but the phone rang.

"Hello? Oh, hi, Neil. How are you?" *Neil McLeod*, she mouthed.

"Fine, Cassie." McLeod sounded so pompous today. "And you? Everything okay?"

"Yes, thanks, I'm doing fine. You saved me a phone call, as a matter of fact. I was wondering what time I can come by the office tomorrow to sign whatever documents you have. I want to start completing the process so I can wrap things up."

"One o'clock if that works for you. But I feel I must bring up something that disturbs me."

She frowned. "I can't imagine what that could be."

Griffin was busy wiping up the spilled coffee, but she knew he was listening, watching her face as she spoke.

"Was that Griffin Hunter I saw when I dove past your house yesterday?"

"Yes, that was him." She bit back the swear word she wanted to use. "Tell me, Neil, did everyone in Stoneham just happen to drive by my house?"

"Now, no need to get huffy. I just want to make sure you know having him there is dangerous."

God, could he sound any more condescending?

"Dangerous," she repeated slowly. "Well, I appreciate your concern, but I'll be just fine. And before you ask, yes, he will be coming back. As a matter of fact, he's staying with me while I'm here."

Griffin paled, but Cassie grinned at him, convulsing with laughter.

"What?" The word was so loud it all but jumped out of the phone. "Do you understand the situation?"

"Yes, Neil, of course I understand. But I assure you, I'm quite safe with him." She didn't seem to be able to stop herself from baiting him. "He hasn't killed anyone recently, has he?"

"No," he blustered, "but—"

"Well, there, you see? Thanks for calling. I'll see you tomorrow about one." She disconnected the call, still tamping down the laugh that wanted to erupt.

Griffin looked at her with anger and hysteria battling in his eyes. "You know I want to shake you, you idiot? That was a stupid thing you just did."

But then, without warning, a great laugh welled up and burst from him.

Cassie stopped holding herself in, and, in a moment, they were both screaming with laughter, releasing the remaining emotion they'd both stored up for so long.

"You know Neil was on the phone to his wife as soon as you hung up," he told her, when he at last he could catch his breath. "By noon, the whole town will be in an uproar."

"So what? They need something new to talk about, anyway. I just hope it doesn't affect your business."

"I'll worry about that if I need to. Who knows, I might have plans nobody knows about." He sighed. "I guess I'm ready for it if you are. But darlin', I hope you do understand what's going to come down on us."

She put her arms around him. "As long as we're together, Griff, that's all that matters."

He sighed against her hair. "I don't know what I ever did to deserve you, but I plan to do my damndest to make sure you don't get away."

"We'll make it. I'm tougher than you think." She grinned. "Tougher than this town thinks. Just watch my style."

Chapter Eighteen

Cassie swiped at her forehead with the back of her hand, pushing some errant strands out of the way. At last, she'd finished the upstairs, everything but Diane's room.

Griffin returned, changed into jeans and a T-shirt, and scuffed boots of soft leather. She'd just put the spread back on her mother's bed when he walked into the room, startling her.

"Your front door was unlocked." His tone was accusing.

"I'm sorry. I can't believe I didn't pay more attention, especially after changing all the locks."

He frowned at her, worry creasing his forehead. "Well, you need to start doing that when you're here alone. Anyone with a mind to can just walk right in."

"I promise I'll remember from now on. What's that?" She pointed at the box he was carrying.

"Just what's left of Diane's things." He lifted it and looked at it as if it was a strange animal. "Your father came and collected all her clothes and stuff. These are just odds and ends I never had the stomach to go through."

Cassie placed her hand on his arm. "Why don't you put it in my room, and we'll go through it tonight."

He didn't move, just stood watching her.

"What? Do I have a smudge on my face?" She wiped at it with the cloth in her hand and grinned up at him. "I promise I'll shower again."

He shook his head, watching her closely. "So, you've made up your mind about this? Just plant me on your front porch for everyone to see?"

"When you told me we were far from done, that we had unfinished business, did you think I was going to sneak you into the house like a thief in the night?"

He shrugged. "I didn't think that far. When I saw you, all I could think of was wiping away the past six years and getting you in my arms."

"We have nothing to hide, Griff. If we're going to have a relationship, I won't do it hiding behind bushes." Defiance surged through her. "You have a problem with that?"

He held up his hands in mock surrender. "No, Dewdrop, I sure don't, but I'll ask you again. Are you sure you want to take on this town?"

She looked into his eyes. "You said you've never told anyone else you love them. Am I right?"

He put his hands on her shoulders and pulled her next to him, tilting her face up. "No, Cassie, I've never said that to anyone before. If I had, it'd have been a lie. Because ever and always, there was never anyone but you."

"Are you healthy?" she asked, wondering why she hadn't thought to ask before.

The muscle twitched again. "Yes. I get tested on a regular basis. I'd be a fool not to."

She didn't want to know what prompted his religious attention to that. She just hugged him again then stepped back. "Well, then. We're all set. And the town can just go to hell. What's in that other hand you've got behind your back?"

She tried to peer around each side of him, but he sidestepped her. "Close your eyes."

"What?"

"Come on, Cassie. Close your eyes."

She squeezed her eyelids shut, wondering what was coming next.

"Okay. Now, open them."

Her eyes widened when she saw what he was holding.

"One perfect rose," he told her, holding it out to her. "I planned to get you a dozen, but I saw this one in a bud vase by itself. It's perfect with the petals just about to open." He leaned down and placed a soft kiss on her lips. "That's what you are for me, Dewdrop. A perfect rose about to flower in our love."

Tears pricked her eyelids. The last thing she'd expected from Griff was romantic language and gestures. She took the box from him, setting it on the bed, and threw her arms around him, almost knocking the rose from his hand. "Oh, Griff. I truly, truly love you."

"Go get cleaned up." He kissed her forehead. " I want to fix this so it blooms for a long time."

She was showered and dressed and they were outside ready to leave, when a car pulled into the driveway behind Griffin's truck. Cyrus McLeod, Neil's father, got out and came to her.

"Nice to see you, Cassie." He kissed her on the cheek.

"What can I do for you, Cyrus?" She was sure he was the advance guard, and she wasn't in the mood for him. "I thought you'd be in church."

"I was hoping we could visit a minute, honey. Got a cup of coffee for an old family friend?"

"As a matter of fact, we were just leaving." She noticed he'd ignored Griffin altogether.

Cyrus looked over at the man standing so protectively with her.

119

"Griffin, you think you could give us just a minute here?"

"Stay where you are, Griff." Cassie's tone was firm, but polite. "Cyrus, if you have anything to say to me, you can say it in front of Griffin. And if it's anything negative about him, you can save your breath."

Griffin moved to stand behind her, his hands resting on her shoulders in a definite signal of possession. And maybe, she thought, protection. She leaned back into him, drinking in his strength.

"See, now, that's the thing," Cyrus told her. "There's a lot of things you just don't know, honey. You need to listen to me before you make a big mistake here."

"Neil called you, didn't he?" She spoke through gritted teeth. "He needs to mind his own damn business."

"Now, Cassie," he soothed. "He's just concerned about you, like the rest of us. We all saw Griffin here yesterday and figured he was after you. No other decent woman will have anything to do with him."

Cassie was so angry she found it hard to speak. She clenched her fists at her sides, trying for some control. "You listen to me. Seems the whole town decided to drive by my house yesterday and spy on me. I'm sorry that's all you people have to waste your time on. I know everything I need, and, if you're interested, Griffin wasn't after me, I was after him. Now, if you could move your car, we have someplace to go."

She brushed past the man and climbed into the passenger seat of the truck.

"Nice to see you, too, Cyrus." Griffin inclined his head then went around to the driver's side, fighting a smile.

McLeod stood at the edge of the driveway, face grim, watching the two of them. At last, he got into his car and backed out into the street.

Griffin burst out laughing, a good warm sound that rumbled up from deep inside him. "I'd give a month's income to have a picture of the look on that man's face when you blew up at him. But I'll tell you, he won't forget that for a long time. And the whole town will know about it before the day is out."

"Forget the town." Cassie pounded her fist on her knee. "I hate this town. Maybe I always have. My sister may have been the town tramp, but when she was murdered and they couldn't pin it on you, they just brushed it off. When my father died, nobody seemed to care, and I'd guess my mother was just left to wither away in this house. Now, everyone's on their high horse because you and I are playing house? Give me a break."

Griff reached over and placed a warm hand on her thigh. Just the touch of his fingers on her skin sent shivers up her spine. "I don't think I ever realized what a little spitfire you are." He chuckled. "It'll give me a whole new perspective tonight when we're in bed."

"It will for sure make it interesting when we're married," she teased.

"Cassie." His tone turned serious. "I'm asking you again because this is important. It's about a lot more than sex. Are you very sure this is what you want?"

"And I'll ask *you* again." She played with his fingers in her lap. "Aren't you?"

"More than you can ever know. This isn't something I take lightly. That farce with Diane notwithstanding, and my reputation aside, this is what I've always wanted. If you can believe that."

"I believe it." Lifting his fingers to her lips, she kissed each one in turn then turned his hand over and licked his palm with a delicate stroke of her tongue. "So stop asking me the same question over and over, or I might change my mind."

He shifted in his seat. "Cassie, if you keep doing that, we'll have a wreck for sure."

She grinned at him then dropped his hand back in her lap. "I'm saying this for the last time, Griffin Hunter. This was the last thing I expected when I came back here. I came prepared to hate you for the rest of my life. But I love you, I want to marry you, I want to have your children. If I have to live in this cesspool of a town to do it, so be it, but it would be nice if we could both get out of here."

"Then maybe you'll be interested in what I have to show you. If you're determined to do this, our little trip becomes even more important."

"So mysterious," she teased. "How about a hint?"

But, try as she might, she couldn't pry any more information out of him. The more she asked, the less he told her, fending her off in a joking manner.

"Just wait," he said. "I want you to see this without any preconceived notions."

Their closeness in the truck filled the air with snapping sexual tension, and they forced themselves to use restraint. They stopped for lunch at a roadside diner that served the best hamburgers she had ever eaten and dawdled over chocolate shakes. But, even there, they took every opportunity to touch hands or brush against each other. Even just sitting across from one another, heat smoldered in their eyes, and they shared unspoken promises of the night to come.

The dashboard clock read three thirty when they pulled into a town about twice the size of Stoneham.

"Where are we?" Cassie peered through the side window, trying to catch a familiar sight.

"Marble Hill."

"But I mean, where *exactly* are we?"

"About an hour from Austin. Just keep your eyes open."

As Griff eased through town, she took in the limestone buildings lining the main street, an eclectic mix of businesses and offices. On the side streets, he pointed out where the schools were, the clinics, all the things that make up a town.

As they headed out the far side of town, Cassie noticed a large nursery on the left, just out on the highway. "Do you buy any of your stuff there? It looks like a pretty big place."

"Sometimes." A tiny smile tipped up the corners of his mouth. "I'll show it to you on the way back."

They had driven another ten minutes when he turned off on a narrow road. On both sides, pasture land stretched to the horizon, dotted with oaks and sycamore and the mountain cedar so prevalent in the Hill Country. On one side of the road, cattle grazed, on the other, horses gamboled in the sunshine. The scene was a picture suitable for painting.

Griff pulled up and stopped next to a *For Sale* sign set at one corner of the fence. "Come on." He took her hand and led her along the fence line. "So? What do you think?"

Cassie was bewildered. "I think it's beautiful. There's a big hill back there that would be perfect for a house, and all this land for livestock. Why? Who owns it? Is someone building a house here? Do they want you to do the landscaping? Is that how you know about it?"

He turned her to face him. "I hope I am," he told her. "No, that *we* are. Dewdrop, I've been wanting this for a long time. The old home town is nothing but a dead end for me, and I'm ready to kiss it good-bye. Besides everything else, no matter what anyone ever finds out, I'll always be linked to Diane's death."

"You'd really move?" She wished he'd take off the damn sunglasses hiding his eyes.

"In a heartbeat. That nursery you saw at the edge of town is also for sale, and I've been talking to them, trying to see what kind of capital it would take to buy it. I've been wavering on this for months, waiting to see if either the land or the nursery sold. If they did, that could be my convenient excuse for failure."

She tilted her head, one eyebrow cocked. "Did you want to fail?"

He wiggled a hand back and forth. "Maybe before, but not now."

"Why not now? And why didn't you tell me about this earlier?"

He wrapped his arms around her and pulled her close. "I had to make sure you meant what you said. You don't know how afraid I was you were just getting me out of your system. Or maybe getting back at me."

"Oh, Griff." She swallowed the tears clogging her throat.

"If there's going to be any you and me, it isn't going to be in Stoneham. We'd be two outcasts, and that's not what I want for you."

"How would you manage this? It's a big financial commitment."

"I could get a decent price for my house if I put it up for sale. The business, too. And I've got enough saved for escrow to hold everything until I have the rest of the money." He tipped her face up to him. "I love this kind of area, but what about you? Think you'd like living out here in the hills?"

"Are you kidding? It's beautiful. The town looks great, and the schools are probably terrific." She threw her arms around him and hugged him tight then stepped back, looking up at him again. "But do you know enough about running a nursery?"

He laughed. "All the upright souls in Stoneham would be shocked to hear this, but remember me saying I took a couple of courses at the junior college in San Antonio?"

She nodded.

"Well, as a matter of fact, I got a degree in landscaping with a minor in business management." He blushed. "Pretty surprising for the town hellion, right?"

"Griffin! My God!" Cassie was astounded. If someone had told her she would go back to her old hometown, fall into bed with the man who broke her heart, and promise to make a new life with him, she'd have sent them for therapy. Yet here she was, doing just that.

"I know. I have trouble believing it myself."

She was speechless.

"Well, say something," he said, his tense posture signaling his nerves. "You love it? You hate it? What?"

For an answer, she pulled his face down to hers and kissed him, mouth open, tongue searching. She thought she'd never get enough of the taste of him. "I love it. And I've got some ideas, too."

"Then let's do this right." He pulled off his sunglasses, a serious look on his face. "Will you marry me, Cassie? Will you risk the rest of your life with me?"

"Yes. Yes, yes, yes." She planted another kiss, this one quick. "Now, let's go home and talk."

The euphoria of the afternoon lasted until they reached her house and walked up on the porch. Griffin had taken her key and was about to open the door when he stopped, hand frozen.

"What is it? What's wrong?"

"Cassie, it looks like our housebreaker has been at work again."

Chapter Nineteen

"What do you mean?" Cassie shook.

"There are scratches around the lock." Griff squinted at it. "Like someone tried a key that didn't work and played around with it. Stay here while I check the other doors."

She waited on the porch in a fit of nervous impatience, twisting her hands in agitation. Why was this happening? What was going on?

He was back in five minutes. "Whoever it was tried every door. I guess we're lucky they didn't break a window or anything. Cassie, I think you should call the police."

"No." She was emphatic. "I can just see Dangler looking at us suspiciously and forming his own ideas. We'll take care of things ourselves."

"Darlin', whoever it is could be dangerous."

"Then you'll just have to protect me." She gave him a shaky smile. "Let's go on in."

Griff unlocked the door then went back to his truck, opened the lid on the bed, and took out two suitcases.

"Griff?"

"Yeah?" He carried the luggage up to the porch.

"I want you to know how glad I am you'll be staying here with me."

"*Living* with you, sugar. And not a moment too soon. Someone wants inside this place in a bad way, and I'm not leaving you unprotected." He set his suitcases down and framed her face with his hands. "I can't let anything happen to you. Not now when we've finally gotten this thing right." He placed a soft kiss on her lips. "Okay, let's get a move on here."

She helped him put his things away in her room. Then she brought her laptop to the kitchen and made him sit at the table with her. Booting it up and opening a blank page, she slipped into reporter mode with ease, firing questions at him as she would interview someone for a story.

"We have to figure this out," she insisted. "Nobody else is going to do it, so I guess it's up to us."

"I'm just not sure we can find out anything." He rubbed his jaw. "God knows, no one would like it better than me, but after six years, the trail has to be ice cold."

She cocked an eyebrow at him and jutted out her chin. "I'm a reporter. I may write sports stories now, but I cut my teeth on everything under the sun. It doesn't matter what you're looking for, the questions are still the same: who, what, where, when, and why."

"All the same, Miz Reporter," he warned her, "you need to be careful. People don't like anyone digging into things around here."

"I guess not," she told him, "since they didn't do much digging into Diane's murder."

"And someone is after something in this house," he went on. "Something that might have to do with Diane's death."

"Okay, I'm not arguing with you about that. I was the one who thought something was out of sync to begin with, remember?" She nibbled at her lower lip. "Besides, what else here could be of possible interest to anyone? So come on. Let's get started."

In full reporter mode, Cassie took him through every detail of the night Diane was killed, pulling things from his brain he didn't even know were there. Under her experienced prodding, a picture emerged for her.

In three months of marriage, Diane had done little to alter her pattern of living. She still worked during the day, a make-work job at their father's office he'd created for her. Anything for Diane, Cassie thought, tamping down the shreds of resentment. And, each night, when Griffin got home, she was already dressed, primped, and perfumed, eyes flashing, urging him out to enjoy the night life. She blew off his argument that all her running around wasn't good for the baby. If he wasn't willing to show her a good time, there were plenty of people who would.

"Money was tight then," he told Cassie, "and I was taking jobs more than an hour away just to bring in the extra cash. I tried to explain to her I was tired, that we didn't have extra money to blow now that I was supporting both of us as well as my good-for-nothing father."

"What did she say?" But Cassie could imagine Diane's reaction.

"She'd just get that sneer on her face and head out of the house, slamming the door as she left without me." A bitter look twisted his features. "My father was a continuing problem, too. The only good thing was he was seldom home when we were. He slept all day and drank all night."

"I'm sorry. I really am." She chewed on the end of her pen. "Was there anything different about Diane right around that time?"

He frowned. "Yeah, I guess. She was edgy in the weeks right before she...died." A muscle ticked in his cheek. "Something was on her mind, but I thought it was the pregnancy. She was dreading the arrival of the baby, and I already figured out if anyone was going to care for that child, it would be me."

"Just how were you going to do that, working all day?" Cassie was losing a battle with the anger welling in her.

He shrugged. "I hadn't figured it out yet. I couldn't even get her to stop drinking."

"Didn't she know about fetal alcohol syndrome?" The anger turned into a cold rage. Cassie's entire life had been derailed for a child her sister didn't even want.

"Oh, yeah." He couldn't hide his bitterness. "But she was determined to enjoy the high life as long as she could."

"I'm surprised she didn't get an abortion. It would have solved a lot of problems."

"Before she told me, maybe she'd considered it. I don't know. But when the subject came up, she told me the idea terrified her, although we'd all have been better off. Except, by that time, I was already emotionally invested in the baby, and I'd never have let her do it."

Cassie got up and snagged two cold beers from the fridge, opened them, and passed one to him. She took her time drinking from her bottle, trying to cool the fury burning inside her.

Damn Diane anyway.

"Most of the time she made it a point to ask me to go with her," Griff went on, "but not that night. We'd started fighting as soon as I got home. Money and her drinking were the big topics. One thing led to another, and we started screaming some pretty ugly things at each other. Then she just stormed out and screeched off in her car."

"Did you get the idea she had some place specific to go?"

"Maybe. I don't know. I keep trying to remember. If I hadn't been so pissed off, I'd have called around to see where everyone was and find out who she was with. But I was getting to the point where I almost didn't care."

"What did she do when she went out by herself?"

He shrugged. "Hang out with the same people I used to run with. Only by then I was looking at things from a different point of view. And like I said, I couldn't afford it." He made a face. "Somehow, after finding out about the baby and getting married, it all didn't seem quite right any more. Or as exciting."

"Impending fatherhood will do that to you," Cassie said with a tinge of resentment.

He picked up the hand closest to him, separating her fingers and lacing his own through them. "The whole thing wasn't anywhere near what I had planned. There I was, in a huge hole I'd dug for myself and missing you more every day. I was sure you hated me."

Her pulse accelerated at the touch of his hand. She'd tried to hate him all this time, but that had lasted until his kiss. Well, love and hate were two sides of the same coin, weren't they?

She turned to the laptop again. "She didn't give you any hint about what was bothering her?"

"None. I knew marriage and the baby were cramping her style, though. Diane was never one to be monogamous."

Cassie gripped the laptop until her knuckles were white. She'd known exactly what Diane was like—needy and greedy, unconcerned about the lives she ruined.

She wet her lips. "Let's go back to that night again. Do you think she was meeting someone? Is that possible?"

"I guess anything is possible." Griff leaned back in his chair, eyes closed. All of a sudden, he leaned forward and opened them. "I almost forgot. She had this little purse, more like something you keep your makeup in, I think. The last couple of weeks, she carried it with her everywhere. When we went to bed at night, she took great care to stash it somewhere. At first, it bugged the shit out of me, and I tried looking for it when she was asleep. Then I just gave up, figuring what the hell."

"Obviously she had something she didn't want anyone else to see. Too bad we don't know what."

With Cassie's prodding he filled in the details of the rest of the evening. He'd changed clothes, called Phil, and invited himself over. Two other guys were there, and they all watched a game on television, drinking beer and talking about nothing. He'd gotten home around one, but Diane was still out. Angry and depressed, he'd gone to bed and was immediately asleep. At three o'clock in the morning Barry Dangler and one of his deputies banged on the door and woke him up.

"A patrol car, checking Stoneham Park for late night couples, spotted something in one of the bushes by the ravine." Griff's hands gripped the beer bottle. "It was one of Diane's shoes. They discovered her body in the ravine. Her dress was torn, and she'd been beaten to death."

"Was she raped?" Cassie made her tone of voice as uninflected as she could.

He shook his head. "No. They found no evidence of it."

"So tell me how they decided you were the prime suspect? You were in bed when they came to tell you."

"It wasn't rocket science. The whole town knew why we got married and what a disaster it was. I guess Dangler just figured I'd had enough and killing her was the best solution." He pushed back from the table. "Enough. Let's leave it until tomorrow. I'm sure whoever's trying to get into this house has something to do with everything, but I'm done talking about it for today."

"You're right. Anyway, Dangler said he'd have the incident and autopsy reports for me tomorrow. Maybe I can find something in them. Then we'll decide where to go next."

He rubbed his forehead.

"Headache?" she asked.

"Just a little one. A couple of aspirin and I'll be fine."

Cassie shut the computer down, got up, and went to stand behind him, rubbing his temples. "I give good head rubs."

He caught her hands and pulled her around to face him. "Let's go upstairs," he said hoarsely. "I've got something else that needs rubbing more."

Chapter Twenty

This time it was different, the first frenzied hunger somewhat abated. They took their time with each other, exploring, experimenting, learning all the little signals that lovers in tune with each other use.

Griffin paid careful attention to every part of her body, touching her, tasting her, kissing her until she was almost mindless. Her breath caught; his tongue stroked deep inside her mouth.

"This is not sex, Cassie." His voice was hoarse and strained. "You can bet on that. I love you so damn much. Making love with you comes straight from my heart, sugar. "

"I couldn't be like this with anyone else," she whispered, and knew the truth of it.

She met him, just as eager as he was, her tongue as heated an instrument as his. Their kisses were almost like the act of sex itself, and heated their blood until they were filled with rivers of fire.

Cassie grew more bold, more sure of herself with him. Before, he had taken the lead, and she'd been the recipient. But her one act of daring the night before had given her a taste of something she wanted more of.

She took his swollen, throbbing cock in her hands, tracing the veins on the sides, sliding over the soft skin that hid the ridged flesh beneath it. Her fingertip slid over the smooth, velvety head in wonderment. With great care she probed at the tiny slit at the top, licking the salty fluid that seeped from it with tiny, delicate laps of her tongue. When she leaned forward and ran her tongue the length of him, he groaned, burying his fingers in her hair, holding her head in place.

"More, sugar." His voice was thick with desire. "God, your mouth is like warm honey. Do it, darlin. That's it. Yes, let me feel that tongue. Cassie, Cassie, Cassie. You take me to heaven, did you know that?"

When she took his balls in her hand and did the same thing with the heavy, weighted sac, he almost came off the bed. His muscles clenched with the effort to maintain control, but she was having none of it. The taste of him the night before had just whetted her appetite.

She took a page from his book, running her tongue over the seam at his hips, flitting over his abdomen, down the insides of his thighs. With her fingertips, she sought and found his flat, male nipples, pulling and teasing at the tips as he did to hers, excitement rushing through her as she felt them swell and harden.

She was wild with wanting him, with welding him to her. When he tried to pull her up to lie on top of him, she shook her head, taking him in her mouth again. Then, taking him deep, she tickled and squeezed his balls, feeling them tighten in response. With her hands and her tongue, in the rhythm she'd learned so easily and quickly, she coaxed his orgasm from him with relentless determination. When the hot liquid splashed on her tongue, she swallowed in triumph, sucking deep and hard to get the last salty drop.

"Damn, sugar." He groaned. "You're sure a quick learner. I'm a wreck. But I think you did yourself in, darlin'. As tired as I am, as active as we were last night, you didn't leave anything for yourself."

She moved up to lay her head on his shoulder, inhaling the musky scent of him. "That's all right," she assured him, a tiny grin on her face. "We've got plenty of nights ahead of us. I love you, Griff.

With all my heart."

She reached up to kiss him and discovered he wasn't kidding about being tired. He was already asleep. Smiling, she nestled her body close to his. Even the aching, unfulfilled need was worth it, when she knew she had the ability to give him so much pleasure.

It amazed her she could be so uninhibited with him, so unselfconscious. But she was learning when the love between two people was as real as this, every physical act was an expression of that love.

She was right in what she told him. They had a lot of time to make up for it.

Although she was up not long after sunrise the next morning, Griff was already gone for the day. A note sat propped against the full pot of coffee.

"A full day's schedule. See you at six. I love you." He had drawn the outline of a rose on the paper, with one drop of moisture clinging to a petal...a drop of dew.

She knew what it meant for him to have written that. She was sure that, in his whole life, she was the only one he'd ever been this open with, this trusting. This was his way of telling her she could trust him, too. She smiled, pressing the note to her heart.

She called Neil and reminded him to expect her at one and to please have all the papers ready for her to sign. Then she called Donald to check on the funeral arrangements and the cemetery. Next, she called the police station to remind Barry Dangler she'd be by in the early afternoon for the reports on Diane's death. The bank she'd worry about after she had the probate papers in hand.

The two calls she dreaded making, she put off until last.

When she reached Mike Rivard, he was so silent at the news she was resigning and wouldn't be coming back, for a minute she thought he'd hung up. "Mike? Are you there?"

"Yes." He sighed. "I guess you know what you're doing, Cassie. But you're leaving me in a real bind here."

"I know, and I'm truly sorry. It's just that things here are, well, different than I thought. I have more loose ends to take care of than I expected."

"What's his name?" he barked.

"What? What do you mean?" She was startled.

"Any time a reporter as good as you are walks out on what could turn into a plum job, it's over a girl. Or, in your case, a guy." More silence. "I hope he's worth it, sweetheart. I guess I should wish you good luck."

"Thanks, Mike. You can't know how much I appreciate the way you're taking this."

"Who knows? Maybe one day you'll decide you like the Florida life again, and we'll find a spot for you."

She thanked him a second time. "I'll have to make a trip back to get my car and close things up. I'll stop by and see you when I pick up my check."

"You'd better," he growled.

She felt a little sad after she hung up. Mike had been good to her, but she had no regrets. She'd given him value for every dollar he'd paid her.

Her call to Claire was both harder and easier. Harder because they'd been so close for so many years and, for the first time, would be going their own ways. Easier because Claire made it so.

"The bad boy must be really good," she joked. "Six years and the past disappears just like that."

"I know, I know."

"Just remember, girlfriend. I was the one who listened to you cry all those months and patched up the cracks in your heart."

Claire had been her lifesaver. Not just for giving her a place to call home until graduation. She'd introduced her to the right people in Tampa, which made getting her first job a lot easier.

"When this is all over, I'll tell you the whole story," she promised, "and you'll understand."

"What about your car and your apartment? You can't just dump them."

"I have a new lease on my desk I'd need to sign if I were staying. Otherwise, I'm up the end of next month. I think I'll take next weekend, fly back, and take care of stuff then drive my car back. And the rest of my clothes."

"Bring that hunk with you." Claire laughed. "I'm dying to get a gander at him."

Cassie spent the rest of the morning tearing Diane's room apart, looking for something, anything, that someone would be searching for. She emptied drawers and checked under and behind them, pulled everything out of the closet, looked under furniture. She even crawled beneath the bed to see if anything was hidden inside the box springs. Nothing.

As she walked out of the room, her cell phone rang, and she fished it from her pocket.

"Glad I caught you, Cassie." Harley Graham's voice held that paternal tone to it. "I think we need to discuss something, honey."

Her stomach clenched. "Are you all ganging up on me?" she demanded.

He was silent for a moment. "I'm not trying to lecture you, but you've been away from this town for a long time. There are things you don't know, things best left alone. Griffin Hunter isn't someone you should be letting into your house and your life."

"Is that right?" She gripped the phone so hard her hand hurt. "Well, thanks for your concern, Harley, but Griffin and I are doing just fine."

"Let me give you a piece of advice, then. If you're so dead set on hooking up with him, I suggest you leave your sister's death alone. Stir things up too much, and Hunter could end up in jail."

She seethed, hanging onto her temper with a frayed rope. "I'm going to pretend we didn't have this conversation, Harley. I have to go now. Bye."

She had to restrain herself from throwing the phone across the room. After checking the time, she showered, ate a quick sandwich, and left for her appointment with Neil, girding herself for yet another attack. She'd dressed in cool navy cotton slacks and a sleeveless navy and pink top, pulling her hair up in a ponytail and tying pink and blue ribbons around it. Silver hoops at her ears completed her outfit. Texas had turned up its thermostat, and she needed comfort, not style.

She checked herself in the mirror. Not bad. Casual without being too informal. Just the right note.

Neil and Cyrus were both in Neil's office when she got there. Her stomach knotted at the sight of them. This would not be fun. She was not in the mood for a lecture and all she could see in this meeting was disaster.

"You're looking lovely, as always." Cyrus rose to take her hand. "You look well."

Okay, we're going for charm today. "I'm fine, Cyrus. Thank you. I didn't expect to see you here today. I didn't think things were so complicated it would take both of you to handle it."

"Just making sure we cross all the T's and dot all the I's," Neil told her. "Sit down, Cassie. Would you like some coffee? Iced tea?"

"Iced tea would be nice, thank you."

Neil buzzed his secretary with the request then leaned back in his chair.

Cassie looked at both men for a long minute. "All right, let's have it. Is this more of what you came to visit me about yesterday, Cyrus?"

"I want you to understand we have your best interest at heart," he began.

"I'm sure you huddled together after your stop at my house, so why don't we just cut to the chase? If you want to talk to me about Griffin Hunter, forget it. End of discussion."

"Cassie." Neil's voice was firm. "You've been away from Stoneham for years. College, then work. I'm sure you don't even remember the reputation he had when you lived here. And let's not forget Diane's death. As far as the town is concerned, he's still the top suspect. He's not someone you want to spend time with."

She mentally counted to ten. "I know a lot more about Griffin than you think." She sounded much calmer than she felt. "And I'll bet more than you or anyone else in this town does. Besides, he was cleared in Diane's death, remember? I appreciate your concern, but please stay out of my personal business."

"You know, your mother's estate could be considered sizable by some," Cyrus persisted.

Cassie gaped at him. "You think Griffin's after my money? How absurd. And even if he were, that's also my business. So. Did you file the papers this morning? The courthouse can't have so much business that you didn't get it done. And the insurance forms."

The two McLeods looked at each other.

"What? You think you'll hold me hostage with paperwork?" She leaned forward and stared each of them in the eye in turn. "Guess again. I thought we could do this in a friendly manner, but I'd be just as happy to get a lawyer from San Antonio to straighten this out."

Cyrus stood and looked at Neil. "I'm done here. Maybe you can talk some sense into her, but I doubt it." His posture was rigid, his gait stiff as he walked from the office.

"You're making a big mistake," Neil told her.

"Then it's my mistake. I appreciate your concern, but everything's fine. Show me what I have to sign."

At the end of a half hour, they were done. Neil used every opportunity to interject comments, but she ignored him. She sat while he faxed the claim forms back to the insurance company, making sure she got a name and phone number so she could follow up herself. Then she put all the copies of the paperwork in her purse and stood to leave.

Neil walked her to the office door. "Are you planning to stay in the house or sell it? Just curious, you know."

"I'm listing it with Carol Markham. She came by and dropped off her card the other day. Thank you for arranging that."

He put his hand on her arm, a gesture that made her skin crawl.

"You'll need some help going through everything," he said. "I'd be more than happy to do that. Your mother had great confidence in me these past years."

She shook her head. "Thanks anyway, but I think Griffin and I can manage."

"Cassie, you're taking a viper into your nest. You don't know what you're letting yourself in for."

"On the contrary. I know exactly who I'm taking into my house."

"Then at least rethink this nonsense about reopening Diane's case. Let her rest in peace."

Cassie's jaw dropped. "In peace? With her killer still running around loose? You see, I'll never believe Griff did it, so the real killer is still out there somewhere."

"Honey, do yourself a favor. Clean everything up and go back to Tampa. You have a nice life there."

"Thanks for everything, Neil. I think I can tackle it from here." She left him standing with a polite smile pasted on his face.

She didn't fare much better with the chief.

"It's all over town," he told her.

"Oh? And what is it you're talking about here? The funeral? Does that mean I should expect a big crowd?"

"Cassie, you know what I mean. I shouldn't have to spell it out for you." His words were heavy with censure. "There isn't a person in Stoneham who doesn't know you're playing house with Griffin Hunter." He fixed her with a grim stare.

"Well, Chief," she snapped, "I'm so sorry everyone here hasn't anything better to do than discuss my private life."

"I think you're deliberately missing the point. Forgetting about your sister for a minute, you come from a fine family. I knew your folks real well. Griffin Hunter is pure trash. He'll be nothing but trouble for you."

She gritted her teeth to keep her temper in check. "I'll keep that in mind. Do you have those reports for me?"

He picked up a large envelope from his desk, tapped it against his fingers before handing it over. "I don't know what you expect to find here. There isn't much. If you don't know how to read them, you might misunderstand a lot of stuff."

She didn't want to tell him that for a solid year in Tampa all she did was read police dailies, looking for any kind of story to follow up. He might change his mind about giving the envelope to her.

"You might also want to remember there's still a chance to discredit Griffin's alibi," he added.

"After six years?" She shook her head, incredulous.

"Fine, Cassie. Whatever. I'll see you at the funeral tomorrow." As she stood to leave, he rose, too. "You let me know if you need anything, okay?"

She wanted to tell him it would be a cold day in hell before she asked anyone in this town for anything, but she kept her mouth shut. This week, she still needed people to talk to her. She didn't want to burn her bridges just yet.

Her final stop was the bank. Howard Cook had been their banker for as long as she could remember. She knew from her sparse contact with her mother he'd been a big help selling her father's accounting practice when he died, and investing the money for her.

He came out of his office to get her as soon as she walked into the lobby. "Neil called and said you'd be down," he said. "Nice to see you, Cassie. Come on into my office, and we'll take care of stuff."

"Thank you." She swallowed a sigh, wondering what *this* encounter would be like.

He fussed with getting her in a comfortable chair, asked his secretary to bring them coffee, then opened a folder he had on top of his desk, and looked at the top sheet. "Neil told me you had all the right papers, honey. This should be real simple. All we need to do is add your signature to the account, take your mama's off, and we'll be set. Or you can open a new one and transfer it, if you want."

"I want to draw it all out."

Howard's eyes snapped wide open. "Cassie, there's a tidy sum of money here. All the direct deposits from the annuity go in here. That'd be a mess for you to change."

She almost laughed at his expression. "I'd like a cashier's check, please, and I'm taking care of the arrangements for the annuities."

Howard sat back in his chair, hands folded in front of him, his gaze firm on her. "Forgive me for intruding where I'm not wanted, but I understand you've been, uh...seeing Griffin Hunter since you got to town."

"Yes." *Here we go again.* She took care to keep her face blank. "In fact, I'm thinking of taking out an ad in the paper, just in case there's someone who might have missed the news bulletin."

Howard leaned forward in his chair. "Now, honey, this is just a small town where everyone takes care of everyone else. That's all."

"Like you took care of my sister?" she snapped.

His face turned an ugly shade of red. "Your sister brought her troubles on herself. You've always been the nice girl in the family. I guess folks just want to keep it that way. You'd do well to remember that, despite his alibi, Griffin was the one person with a real motive."

"Well, you can tell *folks* I appreciate their concern, but I'm doing just fine. I don't believe Griffin killed my sister. Not for a minute. He's not after my money, but, if he were, it's my money to give. Now, may I have a cashier's check? I'll sign the form to close the account."

At last, Howard gave in with poor grace, and, in fifteen minutes, she was done.

"I hear you're selling the house."

"My, my, the town has been busy. Yes. I'm listing it with Carol Markham."

"Well, if you need any help going through all that stuff, sorting through things, you just let me know."

She escaped with her temper still intact.

Before heading home, she drove to the other side of town, to the tiny Bank of America branch. They'd opened just before she left, serving everyone who didn't want Howard Cook sticking his nose in their business. That's where her account was in Florida, and, in just a few minutes, they'd taken care of her deposit. She felt somewhat better getting her financial affairs out of the gossip sheet.

Tired and sweaty, she headed home. But rattling around in her mind was the question of why people were so eager to help her sort through the things in her mother's house. What was it these men thought she'd find? And were hoping she wouldn't find.

She got that itch on the back of her neck that plagued her whenever she was on the trail of a dicey story. Someone was up to no good.

Chapter Twenty-One

She lay on the living room couch, a cold rag draped across her forehead and a glass of wine at her fingertips, when Griffin got home.

He leaned over and kissed the tip of her nose. "Hard day, sugar?"

"You don't know the half of it." She pulled off the washcloth and sat up, fire in her eyes. "I swear to God, Griff, I don't know how you live in this place."

He chuckled. "Get the third degree today, did you? And warnings about bad boy Griffin Hunter?"

"You don't know the half of it. Everyone wants to mind my business for me. I don't think they'll be quite as friendly after everything I said, though."

"Did you give 'em hell, sugar?" He grinned.

"You bet." She went to him and tried to put her arms around him, but he held her away.

"I need a shower before you touch me. I have every kind of dirt and fertilizer stuck to me."

"I'll come shower with you." Her boldness continued to grow.

The blue in Griffin's eyes turned a shade darker. "Come on, then," he told her, in his low husky voice.

Under the hot, steady stream, they took great care soaping each other's bodies. Not an inch of skin on either one was left untouched, but, when Cassie stroked Griffin's hardened cock, he pushed her hand away.

"Uh-uh, sugar. I'm not wasting it tonight. I have plans for later." He nuzzled her ear, licking the rim with the tip of his tongue. "I want to do things with you that haven't even been invented yet. I wish I could suck you into my body and keep you there forever." Then, in direct contradiction, he leaned her against the shower wall, spread her legs with his feet and used his fingers to bring her to orgasm.

"No fair," she gasped.

He laughed, a warm sound rumbling up from his chest. "You recover faster than I do."

Cassie was in no mood to cook, so Griffin went to pick up Chinese takeout. She refilled her wine glass and sat down to read what she'd gotten from Barry Dangler.

The incident report didn't offer much. The patrol officers first on the scene had given their story of finding the body. The crime scene people hadn't been able to do much with the site. None of the ground around the area had yielded any good prints to analyze, and scour as they might, they could find nothing to indicate who might have been with her.

She turned to the autopsy report, which was a pretty straightforward document. Diane had been choked—although that wasn't the cause of death—struck several times on the head with something hard, and her body tossed down into the ravine. Any of the blows to the head could have killed her. And, just for good measure, the fall also broke her neck.

Cassie was halfway through the rest of the details when something stopped her cold. She read it three times to make sure she was not mistaken. She was shocked, enraged, furious—every kind of angry she could think of. If Diane had been standing in front of her, Cassie would have killed her herself. She pounded her fist on the table until it ached then threw the folder across the room. She needed to tell Griff about this.

Taking deep, gulping breaths, she paced the room, somehow pulling herself together. She'd wait until after dinner to tell him. Let him eat first. Give him some time to settle down after a workday. She hoped she could manage it.

By the time Griff returned, she had arranged her face into a pleasant mask.

Somehow, she pushed everything to the back of her mind while they ate, although the food tasted like sawdust. She talked about her meetings that day, even laughing about all the warnings people had given her. *What an actress I am.*

When she told him about closing the account with Howard Cook and moving it to Bank of America, he laughed.

"I'd give a week's pay to have seen the look on his face when you asked for the check. Serves the old bastard right. I always thought he blabbed too much about the business of the people who banked with him."

"Moving the money just made sense, anyway, since I already have an account with B of A. It just gave me a lot of satisfaction to do it."

While they cleared away the debris, she mentioned the other thing that stood out in all her conversations. "Everyone wants to help me clean out the house. Including the chief. And Carol Markham, who stopped by with the listing agreement."

"It sure makes you think there's something here someone wants," he commented.

"Yes, but what?" She was as puzzled as she'd been before.

"We can talk about it later. It's still light, and it's cooled off. Let's go sit on the patio."

"Good. There's some stuff I need to go over with you." Stuff she was sure would send him through the roof.

They settled into the lounge chairs, Cassie clutching the folder she'd gotten from Dangler. The line from the report slammed back into her consciousness, if indeed it had ever left. One sentence, so damning, so destructive to so many lives. She swallowed against the nausea, determined to calm herself.

She glanced sideways at Griffin. "I quit my job today."

He turned to look at her. "How'd your boss take it?"

She shrugged. "After the whining and bitching, he was great. He wished us well."

"You told him about me?"

"Didn't have to. He guessed, and I didn't deny it." She cleared her throat, choosing her next words with care. "I thought I'd go back this weekend. I still have my return ticket. I need to close up my apartment, make plans to get rid of everything. Pick up my car."

"Can you do it all in two days?"

"Probably not, but Claire can handle the cleanup details for me." She waited to see what he'd say next.

"You'd better give me the flight info so I can make my reservation," he said at last.

"I was hoping you'd say that." She reached out and took his hand. "Besides, I want to show you off to Claire." She also wanted a chance for him to see the person she was while she'd been doing what she now saw as marking time. "I'll get my ticket. It's in my purse on the counter. I changed the reservations to Thursday."

"I'll do it. You sit there. Tomorrow, I'll take a minute to reschedule my Friday jobs. No problem." He went into the house to make his arrangements.

She tried to settle the butterflies tap dancing in her stomach.

She'd procrastinated long enough. When Griff came back out, she'd have to tell him what she'd discovered. Rage surged through her again, and she forced it back.

The screen door slammed. "All set," he told her.

She waited until he'd dropped into the lounge chair again. "I pried the information about Diane's murder loose from Chief Dangler today. The description of the crime scene was pretty graphic. Lots of blood."

He grimaced. "I wouldn't know. They gave me very little information. They were interested in seeing what I could tell them."

"I know they did a DNA swab to see if any of the blood on her body was yours."

He nodded. "Yes, they did."

"Griff, there's no easy way to say this, so I'll just say it straight out." Her hands curled into fists. "The baby wasn't yours."

Chapter Twenty-Two

Griffin didn't say a word. The silence grew between them until it was almost palpable. Cassie sat very still, trying to relax the knot in her stomach and keep her hands from shaking. Reading it hadn't been half as bad as saying it out loud.

"Are you sure?" His voice sounded hollow, as if he were at the bottom of a well.

She bit her lip. "Yes. It's all right here in the lab reports and the autopsy. There was no DNA match whatsoever."

"God damn it," he exploded, and launched himself out of the chair. He paced the patio, running his hands through his hair, jaw clenched, tension radiating from his body.

She waited in nervous silence. It was obvious no one had told Griffin the results of the tests at the time. Were they waiting for him to slip up, admit to something? How many people had Dangler shared this information with?

"I should have demanded a test from the beginning." He bit the words off. "Your sister was a tramp, Cassie. I'm sorry to say it, but it's the truth. She slept with anyone who appealed to her." He dry-washed his face. "Of course, I wasn't any better."

"Griff—"

"Let me finish." It was evident he was so angry he could barely get the words out. "They knew. All this time, they knew. No one told me. I grieved more for the baby than I ever did for Diane. Shit."

Cassie willed herself to sit still, let him work out the battle within himself.

"Diane knew, I promise you." His words were rough, vicious. "And I was the poor sucker she reeled in to take on her responsibility. I have not one doubt that when that baby came, she'd have been gone, and I'd have been left to handle things. We both know Diane was not the maternal type."

He paced some more, cursing a steady stream, fists clenched. At last, he drew a deep breath, seemed to gather himself, and sat down again. "That opens up a whole new can of worms, doesn't it?"

"Yes," Cassie agreed. "It does. I hate to ask, but do you have any idea who the father could be?"

"Not a clue." He shook his head. "But I think she took care choosing who she went to with her news, picking the one of us that would be the easiest mark. Also, I was the only one running any kind of business. Everyone else was sort of drifting through life and holding down a succession of odd jobs. If she was going to dump the baby afterward, she at least had enough conscience to want it to have some kind of security."

Her chest tightened. "Griff, I wish I knew what to say."

He pounded his fist on his thigh. "I think she wanted to make sure she cut you out, too, Cassie. Diane was always jealous of you, and, somehow, she knew how I felt about you."

"Jealous of me?" She was astounded. She tried to read his face, but darkness had descended like a black drape and there was no light coming from the house. "In God's name, why?"

"You were the smart one, the bright one, the one with all the awards. Diane played your parents for all they were worth because her charm was all she had going for her."

She couldn't assimilate the information. She'd had no idea how Griffin Hunter felt about her until those fateful two nights. How had

Diane known? Could it be true her sister had done this on purpose?

"You always overlooked Diane's shortcomings," he went on. "Two such very different sisters. Diane, the wild child, grabbing at life with both hands, and you, the object of every respectable man's dream. You had no idea how all those proper young men felt about you, did you? You didn't even know how great sex could be until that night, did you, sugar?"

She shook her head.

"Damn," he growled. "All this time, just wasted."

Without warning, he was on her, pulling at her, lifting her from the chair in both arms. Then they were on the grass, his body pinning hers beneath him. He slammed his mouth against hers, tearing at her clothes with his free hand until she was completely naked. His tongue stabbed into her, bruising the inside of her mouth, reaching deep into the dark hollow.

She heard the clink of his belt buckle, the rasp of his zipper, felt his movement as he jerked his pants down.

"This is what I always wanted," he breathed into her ear. "This. Not Diane. Not anyone else. Just you, and me inside you."

In one swift movement, he thrust her legs wide apart, bracing his arms under them so she was wide open and exposed to him. He didn't seem to care if she was wet or ready because this wasn't about her. With a brutal thrust he was inside her, buried in her, her pussy tight around him.

"Mine, Cassie. All this time, you should have been mine." His voice was hoarse, guttural. "Well, you're mine now." He plunged into her, going deeper each time. "Take me, Cassie." He all but sobbed as he drove into her. "It should have been you. Always, always, always."

She didn't flinch at the pain of the intrusion, didn't try to push him away, even as his engorged penis stretched her, scraping her inner walls. She could feel his rage, his pain, his despair at the destruction of his life all pouring into her. In just seconds, he came with shuddering force, hips jerking, harsh, guttural sounds emanating from his throat. She clung to him with her legs around his hips and rode out the storm with him.

Then it was over, as fast as it had started. He lay panting on her chest for a moment, then heaved himself off and stood, pulling up his pants and zipping them. She whispered a silent thank you that the houses on either side were only one story. No prying eyes to look down on them.

"Well, that showed a lot of class," he said, not looking at her. "Now you know what kind of bastard I am. You should pay attention to all those warnings you heard today."

She forced herself to her feet. She didn't even bother with her clothes, just stood naked on the lawn, his semen drying on her thighs. The first thing that hit her was how much he'd needed this. The second, like a blast of cold water, was the absence of a condom. Should she mention it now? Later? Would he blame her and shove her out of his life?

She went to him and slid her arms around him, pressing her face against his back. He was taut as a drum, every muscle in his body rigid.

"I guess they'll have a lot more to say tomorrow," she said, her voice gentle.

"I should tell you to run, Cassie, just as far and as fast as you can. Go back to Tampa. Get your job back. Get the hell away from me if you want to save yourself." He wouldn't turn around.

She stepped in front of him. "You don't mean that. That's just rage, Griffin. And pain. You have a right to be angry and hurt and all of those things. You've had your life almost destroyed. But if you want me to leave, if your mind is made up, you have to tell me you don't love me. Can you say that?"

"I just about raped you, for God's sake. The woman who means more to me than my own life." He shook his head in disgust. "That would be enough to chase away anyone with brains."

"Tell me you don't love me," she insisted, "and I'll throw you out of the house right now." She shivered in the night air, wrapping her arms around herself to ward off the chill. "Well? Can you say it?"

Griffin looked at her as if seeing her for the first time. "My God, you're freezing. Here." He picked up his shirt and made her put it on, pulling it together in front. He looked at her for a long time. "If I wanted to do the best thing for you, I'd say whatever it took to get you to run me off. But I can't. Because I do love you, Cassie. God save us both."

"Well, then." The knot inside her eased. "Let's go inside and figure out what to do. I think we've given the neighbors enough of a show for tonight."

She picked up her clothes and her papers and walked inside the house, displaying more dignity than she felt. It was important for Griffin to know she understood what had just happened and why, and that it made no difference at all between them.

In a moment, he followed her.

Chapter Twenty-Three

They faced each other in the kitchen. So much pain still lined Griffin's face, Cassie wasn't sure she could stand it. She wanted to reach out and touch his cheek, but she needed first to make him understand she was okay with everything, that she understood his wrath, and it hadn't changed her feelings for him.

"I don't even begin to know how to apologize to you." Desperation filled his words. "I can't explain what I did. Even at my very worst, I never treated a woman like that. I just needed to be inside you, to feel us connected, to bind us together. I needed something clean, something real. And I needed to get rid of all that anger."

She took one of his hands in both of hers and leaned forward, rubbing her face against his chest, hearing his heart thudding beneath her ear. "It's all right. I know. I understand. You can't chase me away. What kind of love would we have if I couldn't understand what drove you to this, what was behind it? It will take a lot more than that to get me to walk out of your life."

"God, you're amazing." He pulled her tight against him.

Cassie looked up at him, trying to send him messages with her eyes. "Diane did a lot of damage to both of us. I don't even know yet how to deal with my own feelings, so I can hardly imagine yours. But we have to get past all of this."

"I think...I think just now, I wanted to erase every trace of her from my body, to make sure there was no one but you. I wanted to take back all the wasted years. I just...."

"It's okay. I understand. I do. We have to go forward, Griffin. And we have to do it together."

"I don't deserve you." He kissed the top of her head. "God knows I love you more than anything. If you'd run, I don't know what I would have done."

"Okay, then." She swallowed hard. Just spit it out, she told herself. "Griff, uh, we didn't use a condom."

He stared at her, opened his mouth, closed it again. "Fuck."

She forced a grin. "But it's okay. It is. I promise." *Please let it be okay.*

At last, he managed a lopsided smile. "Then I guess it's a good thing we're getting married."

She relaxed against him. "It is indeed. And now I think we need another shower and some coffee. Then we can take a better look at this situation." She tugged his hand. "We can shower together and save water."

The shower did more than wash off the grass and dirt from their bodies. It washed away the fury, the feeling of helplessness, the desperation that bubbled up after six years of hell. Griffin stood in the shower stall under the spray, just holding Cassie against him, letting her strength flow into him until they both began to feel waterlogged. When they stepped out, he kissed her for a long time, a very gentle kiss, but one that said more than any words. And when they were dried and dressed again, it was better between them. Something unspoken had wrapped around them and taken them to a new place of trust and commitment.

Cassie made coffee then filled a mug for each of them. They sat at the kitchen table, where so much of their life seemed to be playing out for the past couple of days.

"Now," she told him, "we have to figure out why nobody ever told you about the DNA and who the real father of that baby is."

"Easy." There was no concealing the bitterness and underlying rage in his words. "In a town this size, it wouldn't be difficult to match DNA. Someone's gone to a lot of trouble to cover this up and make sure the focus remained on me."

"I hate to do this to you right now," she told him, "but you've got to try and come up with some alternate names. Someone else who could have been the person who killed her."

"I know, I know." He pinched the bridge of his nose. "I've just blocked so much of it out of my mind that it's hard to bring it all back. Besides, Diane used her charm on everything in pants. It didn't matter if it was me, the dentist, or the bag boy at the grocery store."

When they had listed everyone they could think of in the document she opened, Cassie leaned back in her chair. "This isn't getting us anywhere. We'll end up listing every man in town."

"No kidding."

"There has to be a better way of doing this."

They sat in silence for a long moment.

Cassie snapped her fingers. "Did they give you Diane's things after the...afterward?"

Griff frowned. "What things?"

"You know, her clothes, any personal items. Stuff like that."

"No. I didn't even ask. Why?"

She stared unseeing at the computer screen in front of her, lower lip caught between her teeth. "Didn't you say Diane always had that little purse thing with her?"

He shrugged. "I guess. What about it?"

"I'll call Dangler in the morning and ask about it. I'll bet it's still being held as evidence, even though the case is cold. If it's not there, it could be what our mysterious stranger is looking for."

"He'll be angry again because you're still digging this up, you know. Dangler, I mean. He still thinks I did it."

She thinned her lips. "Too bad for him."

Griff narrowed his eyes. "There's one other thing we haven't considered."

"What's that?"

"Dangler could be covering up for someone," he pointed out. "The people who hold power in Stoneham take care of each other. If he knew, or even suspected who Diane's lover was, he might just be doing a favor for an old friend." He felt sick. The possibility was very real, and if that was so, their job would be a lot harder and a lot more dangerous.

They were both so emotionally drained, and even the coffee couldn't keep them awake. Climbing into bed, they fell asleep holding each other like lost children.

***

When Griff got up at his usual early hour the next morning, Cassie rose with him. The day would be a busy one for her, no doubt unpleasant, and she wanted time to prepare herself.

"Come to the funeral," she urged him.

"Better for you if I don't," he argued.

"Do you think I care what any person in this town thinks? This is my choice, not theirs."

He pulled her to him and held her close, his lips brushing her hair. "Listen to me this once, Cassie. This will be a difficult day for you as it is. Don't make it worse for yourself. And it will be if I show up at the church."

She hated to admit it, but he made sense. Whoever chose to attend would make their disapproval evident. Worse yet, they would make Griffin feel uncomfortable, and she didn't want that. "All right. But be here when I get back, okay?"

"You bet." He hugged her, gave her a light kiss then was gone.

Carol Markham had left the listing agreement, and Cassie signed it, tucking her copy in the folder with the other papers she was accumulating. Then she called the agency.

"You can come by before noon to pick it up," she told Carol when the woman came to the phone.

"Oh, honey, I don't want to make you do business on the day of your mama's funeral," Carol protested.

"My mother won't be any less dead," she said, her tone pragmatic. "I'm sorry if that sounds cold, but I need to get this taken care of."

Next, she called the insurance company and asked for the claims processor whose name she had pried loose from Neil. He came on the phone in seconds.

"Yes, Miss Fitzgerald, we have all the paperwork and everything's in order." He paused. "On the life insurance, we'll send you a check, but on the annuities…."

"Yes?" she prompted.

"I'm not sure cashing them out would be a wise move. We could just transfer your name as the beneficiary, and you'll receive checks every month."

"I understood I could opt for the lump sum cash-out." She'd been very specific when she asked Neil about that. "Can you tell me how much that would be?"

The claims agent cleared his throat. "A little over two hundred thousand dollars."

Cassie dropped into a chair, stunned. *So much money!* Despite what Neil had told her, she was unprepared for the reality. When he said he'd been prudent investing the money for her, he hadn't been kidding. "You're right. That's a significant sum, but my mind's made up. Let me give you my bank account number, and you can do a wire transfer."

She couldn't wait to tell Griffin. What a shock!

Her next call was to the management agency for her apartment in Tampa to tell them of her plans. She wasn't signing the new lease agreement but would drop off a check to them on Friday for one more month's rent, to give her time to do whatever was needed. No problem, they said.

Her final call was to Barry Dangler.

"Yes, we still have all your sister's things." He sounded abrupt. "But since it's an unsolved case, they can't be released."

"Okay. Can I just come by and look through them?"

"What is it you're searching for, Cassie?" It was hard to miss the fact he was hostile and resentful. "Is there something you think we missed?"

"No. I just wanted to see the stuff. Is that all right? Is there some problem I'm not aware of?"

Silence drifted over the connection for a long moment.

"No problem," he said at last, "except her killer is still loose. Bury your mother today, Cassie. Call me tomorrow, and I'll make the arrangements. But I'm telling you, get off whatever crusade you're on and close the door on this."

Her head ached again. She dug aspirin out of her purse and swallowed two with the rest of her coffee. She dreaded the afternoon more than she wanted to admit to herself. If she was lucky, only a few people would show up and the service would be short.

Just before noon, Carol came by to pick up the listing papers. "I just want to say again how sorry we are about your mother." She wore her sympathetic face. *Did she practice in front of a mirror?* "It was too bad you weren't able to come home for your sister's funeral, or your father's."

Cassie refused to rise to the subtle dig. "Thank you for taking care of this." She handed the signed contract to Carol with exaggerated politeness. *Just sell the house and get out of my life,* she wanted to tell her.

"What are you planning to do with the furniture and things?" Carol asked.

"If whoever buys the house wants it, they can have it. I won't be needing it."

"I imagine you'll be going back to Tampa?" She studied Cassie's face with avid curiosity.

"My plans are somewhat up in the air at the moment." *Get out of here!*

"I hear those plans might include Griffin Hunter." The woman's eyes held an avaricious glitter.

Cassie sighed. She wished all these people a short trip to Hell. "If you don't mind, I need to get dressed for this afternoon. When you need to show the house, just let me know. I put my cell phone number on the contract, so you can get hold of me wherever I am."

She managed to push the woman out the door and close it behind her. The headache blasted back with the intensity of a rocket-propelled grenade. The sooner she and Griffin got out of this town the better.

At last, she put on the one dark dress she'd brought with her and her low matching heels. A deep breath and she was ready.

Chapter Twenty-Four

All Cassie could think of was the opening line from *A Tale of Two Cities:* "It was the best of times; it was the worst of times." More people came to the service than she'd expected, filling the small chapel at the mortuary. People she didn't even recognize crowded every corner. Curiosity-seekers, she decided.

The room was hot and stuffy, the air cloying with the scent of the flowers banked tastefully around the platform the casket rested on. She couldn't begin to imagine who sent them, unless people were salving their consciences. The babble of voices, hushed though it was, didn't do her headache any good.

Donald Brandon greeted her with his practiced unctuous attitude, patting her hand and mouthing condolences. "I've made all the arrangements for the cemetery following this. They'll be expecting us."

"Thank you."

She recaptured her hand and turned to the coffin. She and her mother had never been close, even on the best of days. But her death marked the closing of a chapter in Cassie's life, and she felt a strange sadness. Here was a woman who never knew how to enjoy life, except through a daughter who brought violence and evil into it.

Donald positioned himself next to her, acting as the official greeter. Every time he spoke, his words grated on her nerves, the oily syllables sliding like water on glass from one sentence to the next. She longed for a Star Trek transporter.

Beam me up, Scotty.

Neil was there with his wife. At best a nodding acquaintance of Cassie's, Leslie McLeod mouthed platitudes of comfort then moved away.

"I'm happy to see you haven't dragged Hunter along with you today," Neil said with approval.

"More for his sake than mine." Cassie curled her lips in a nasty expression. "I didn't want to subject him to the brand of etiquette this town practices."

"You know, you need to take time to think about what you're doing," he admonished her. "I hate to sound like a broken record, but—"

"Then don't," she snapped. "I've had about all the advice I can take. By the way, I took care of everything with the insurance company this morning, so that's one more chore you can cross off your list."

Neil shrugged and moved off to join his wife.

Next in line was Cyrus, with his obvious disapproval in contrast to his sympathetic words. "Your mother was a wonderful woman.

"Yes. She was." What else could she say?

He scowled. "I don't think she'd be happy at the path you're taking."

"Cyrus." She was beyond exasperation. "Could I please just bury my mother without another lecture?"

He looked as if she'd slapped him. "Of course, Cassie. I'm sorry to intrude on your grief."

Last came Thad Lewis, Cyrus's former partner and Leslie's father. He bit back whatever he'd been planning to say. "I understand you're listing the house," he said instead. "Carol will get an appraiser out, but I've been doing a bit of that since I'm not practicing much anymore. I'm sure you'd want someone to evaluate the things inside the house so you get fair market value."

"Are you offering to go through the house with me, Thad?"

Another one?

He missed the dangerous edge to her tone. "Why, yes, as a matter of fact. At your convenience, of course."

"Thanks anyway, but I've got it covered." She studied his face, looking for some kind of clue behind his words. "You know, it seems like a lot of people are anxious to go through what's in the house. You wouldn't have any idea why, would you, Thad?"

He backed away. "I'm sorry if I offended you in any way. I was just trying to be helpful."

The pastor, Andrew Howell, provided the sole soothing note in the room. He drew her to one side, away from the sideways glances, and spoke with her about her mother and what he planned to say.

"I know this sounds terrible," she told him, "but my mother and I hadn't been close in years. If ever. I'm sure whatever you've prepared will be just fine."

"You're fortunate to have so many friends to help you through this." He glanced around the room.

"Forgive me, Pastor, but these are not my friends. They're gossips, sniffing around my private life." She knew she sounded like a bitch, but she didn't care. "My sister was murdered, my father drank himself to death over it, and my mother died well out of touch with reality. And of course, in case you haven't heard, the icing on the cake for them is the fact that I'm playing house with the town pariah. So, if you mean it when you say you want to do something for me, get this over with so I can get away from everyone here as soon as possible."

If he was shocked by her words, Andrew Howell was too trained a professional to show it.

"Of course. Yes. I am here to serve your needs." He led her to a chair in the front row.

Cassie was sure the service was nice, but it washed over her like a passing cloud. Only the fact that the pastor's lips stopped moving and Donald touched her arm signaled her it was over. Then she got trapped in an argument about transportation to the cemetery.

"I think I should drive you," Donald told her, trying to guide her to the door.

"No, thank you." She jerked her arm away. "That's very nice of you, but I'd prefer to drive myself."

"Leslie and I will be happy to take you." Neil materialized beside her, his wife next to him, her face remaining blank.

"Please." Cassie moved to the side. "Thank you, but I need this time to myself." She all but ran to her car, leaving everyone staring after her, their unasked questions hanging in the air.

The graveside ceremony was blessedly brief. She dropped the traditional white rose on the casket, turned, and walked away. It saddened her she felt nothing, not even regret.

"Cassie." Barry Dangler hurried to catch her. Had he been at the service? She didn't recall seeing him. He huffed as he jogged to where she stood. "Here." He handed her an envelope. "The list of items we catalogued the night Diane was killed. You sounded like you wanted this right away, so I thought I'd bring them with me."

"Thank you." She almost choked on the words.

"If you want to come by and see them for yourself, just call me." He stopped to catch his breath. "Here's the last piece of advice I'll try to offer you. Leave it alone. Go back to Tampa. You won't be doing yourself or anyone else any favors by pushing this thing."

She gave him a hard look. "Doesn't it bother you that it's been six years and you've never found even one lead to who killed her?"

"No." His face was set in a hard look. "I know who killed her. One of these days, I'll break his alibi, and we'll have him."

"After all this time?" She was flabbergasted.

"I'm a patient man."

"Why didn't you tell Griffin the baby wasn't his?" She threw the words at him like darts.

Dangler showed no reaction. "I was sure he knew. That's why he killed her."

"Well, he didn't," she spat at him, climbing into her car. "Maybe it's time for you to start looking somewhere else."

Her tires squealed as she pulled away from the curb. Her head was pounding again, and her rage was so fierce she could almost touch it. Hot tears spilled down her cheeks, blurring her vision, until she pulled off onto a side street and gave vent to all the stored-up anguish. She cried until her eyes ached and her chest hurt, beating the steering wheel with clenched fists. A long time passed before she was calm enough to start the car again.

She lay soaking in the bathtub, every bit of strength gone, when Griff called her name.

"Up here," she yelled.

He took one look at her and kneeled beside the tub. "Not the best of days, was it?" He smoothed stray curls away from her forehead.

"That's no lie. I have stuff to tell you, but not now. I'm too exhausted to think."

He cared for her as he would a sick child, with a tenderness she would never have thought him capable of. He let the water out of the tub, lifted her out and dried her with a gentle touch, then found one of his large T-shirts and slipped it over her head. She stood, unresisting, while he ministered to her.

When he was through, he carried her to her bed, slid her under the covers, and lay down beside her. Cradling her in his arms, he crooned soft words to her until she dozed off.

Chapter Twenty-Five

The room was dark when Cassie woke up. She was aware Griffin's body was still spooned against hers, his arm thrown over her hip. She moved slightly, and in an instant he was alert.

"Better?" He brushed her hair back from her face.

"Much." She laced her fingers through his, so grateful for the feeling of his warm skin, his hands so tender and magical.

"Lousy day, right?"

"Worse than most." She turned over and sat up. "What a bunch of sanctimonious hypocrites. If I'd had a gun, I think I'd have shot everybody there."

He chuckled. "Such bloodthirsty words from such innocent lips."

"These people are amazing," she told him. "I feel like I'm living someone else's nightmare."

He insisted she eat something, even if it was just soup. "Just eat as much as you can. If you don't put something in your system, you'll get sick."

She obediently spooned the soup into her mouth and munched on a cracker.

He watched her finish it while he ate the sandwich he'd made for himself.

When the bowl was empty, she sat back and recapped the day for him. She told him about the funeral service, about Neil and Cyrus and even Donald. And about Chief Dangler and what he'd said.

Griffin's eyes darkened as he listened, his jaw tightening when she got to the part about the chief, but he sat in silence until she finished.

"Someone killed her, and it wasn't you." This had become Cassie's mantra. "And no one in this town is going to look any further to find out who it was. It's going to be up to us."

"We're hardly detectives," Griffin pointed out.

"We couldn't do a worse job than the police have already done, which is nothing," she replied. "Griffin, if we don't find answers to this, it will dog us forever, and we'll never have any peace."

He picked her up and sat down again, cradling her in his lap. His lips touched her hair, her forehead, her eyelids, her cheeks. His heart thudded against her, and she spread her palm over his chest, letting the beat travel into her body.

"I'm tainted, Cassie," he reminded her once more. "You should keep that in mind."

"You know what?" She sat up with such suddenness she almost knocked both of them over. "That's getting old real fast. Do you think I didn't know who or what you were that first night I let you take me up to your bedroom? Do you think I don't know who you are now? I'm an adult, Griffin. I make my own choices. This is one of them. How many times do I need to tell you that?"

In answer he kissed her, a gentle brush of lips at first, then harder with his tongue probing and insistent. His hands roamed over her body, touching her everywhere, branding her as his. At last, he lifted his head and looked at her. "All right, then. We go on from here. But it won't be an easy ride, sugar."

"If I wanted easy, I never would have walked up onto your porch that night."

They knew one of the first things they had to do was make some sense out of the signals Cassie was getting from everyone. She thought again of all the offers to help her go through the house. Which of them had an ulterior motive? Was it more than one? Was the little clutch bag what they were looking for, or was there something else out there even more damning? If the baby hadn't been Griffin's, then there was a man out there with a dreadful secret to hide. A good enough excuse for killing.

They looked over the list of items the chief had given Cassie, studying it, but nothing in the catalogue of Diane's belongings gave them any kind of hint.

"What did you do with the rest of her things after...afterward?" she asked.

"Boxed them up and gave them to your folks. I missed a few of her things, which I brought to you the other night. That's it.

She tilted her head, forcing him to look at her. "So, good chance they're still in this house somewhere."

"I guess. Your mother looked like she wasn't ever going to let go of them."

"We have to find them. There may be something there." She stood and carried their plates to the sink. "I can't think any more today. Tomorrow, while you're working, I'm going to go through this house room by room. I need to make lists anyway, what I want to keep, what I want to get rid of, stuff like that. It will give me a good chance to dig through this house again."

He lifted an eyebrow. "Don't you want to wait until I get home tomorrow night?"

"No. I need to get into this. Besides, it will keep me busy during the day."

"We should leave here after lunch on Thursday to get to the airport in San Antonio on time," he reminded her. "When I go by my house to check on it tomorrow, I'll pick up some clothes for the weekend. I don't want your friends to think you found me in a homeless shelter."

Cassie burst out laughing. "Claire could care less what you look like. She'd probably like it if you didn't wear any clothes at all."

"What kind of friends do you have?" He grinned.

"You'll like Claire, and she'll like you, and she's the only one whose opinion I care about."

He gathered her in his arms. "Don't you think it's time to go to bed?"

"Make me forget," she whispered. "Make it all go away."

In the bedroom, he stripped her clothes off, glad for a lack of buttons, and was out of his own in seconds and lying next to her. His hands sought the familiar shape of her breasts, his tongue probed her ear, and his hot breath whispered over her skin.

"Cassie," he crooned. "God, touching you is like touching a flame. You make my blood boil and my skin catch fire."

Cassie ran her hands over his lean, muscled body pressed against her side, the mat of hair on his chest teasing at the side of her arm. The rough stubble of his beard abraded her cheeks, making them instant erogenous zones. No matter where he touched her, or how, she was so aroused her body begged for satisfaction.

Needing to connect with him, she turned and reached for his cock, already hard and throbbing, the soft tip probing against the flesh of her thigh. When she wrapped her hand lightly around it, he groaned and his body tightened in response.

"Your touch is like a feather. So light but so hot. God, Cassie, I can't get enough of you." He laved her ear again. "Come on, sugar, talk to me. Tell me how I make you feel. It's okay," he murmured. "I want to hear you say it. Tell me from your heart."

She had never dreamed of doing what he asked, of verbalizing. But then, she'd never dreamed she'd be fulfilling all her erotic fantasies with him, either. Somehow saying the things he wanted to hear cemented the connection between them even more.

"Say it, Cassie," he urged.

"You make me feel...good." She gasped.

"Hot?"

She nodded, her brain so scrambled she couldn't think.

"Tell me, then." His mouth closed over one breast, his teeth rasping the nipple, biting it, tugging on it. His hand slid down her abdomen, trailed through the silken curls, and his fingers slipped beneath her labia.

Without any urging, she opened her legs, thrusting her hips at him. "Yes, hot. Empty without you inside me."

"Do you like my fingers inside you, sugar? Talk to me. Tell me what to do."

"Put...put your fingers inside me. Oh, God. Yes! Like that!" She felt him slide two long, lean fingers inside her, and then she couldn't stop talking. "Fill me with your fingers, Griff. More. More. That's not enough." She shoved her hips at him. "Give me more. I want you way inside me. Do it. Do it."

She couldn't believe she was saying these things, but Griffin stripped away all her inhibitions, all her reserves. She did want more, that soul-shattering feeling no one but him could give her.

"Inside me, Griff. Feel inside me. I'm already wet for you."

He nudged her legs until her knees were bent and her feet were flat on the mattress. "God, you're dripping." He slipped another finger inside with the other two, stretching her, the muscles loose and pliable. Curling the fingers, he lightly scraped her inner walls with his nails, smiling in satisfactions when she jerked in response. "I could leave my fingers inside you forever," he whispered, "feeling your muscles clamp around them. Your hot, slick moisture is like warm cream. Oh, sugar, you are so sweet you take my breath away."

Cassie was wild, her senses on overload. Every coupling with Griffin seemed more intense than the last. She craved his fingers, his tongue, his thick, hard cock. There wasn't a nerve in her body that wasn't inflamed. The more he touched her, the more she wanted.

"Fuck me with your hand, Griff." In her life, she had never whispered graphic, erotic words to anyone, but with Griff, she couldn't seem to stop herself. Everything he did and said excited her. "Do it. Hurry." She pressed herself upward against his touch. "Yes. More. Oh, God, I can't stand it anymore. Put your mouth on me. Please."

"All right, darlin'. Let's see if the little nub likes my tongue as much as your mouth does." His lips closed over her clitoris, sucking it into his mouth as if he'd never let it go. When he caught it between his teeth, the bite as gentle as a fairy kiss, her hips thrust at him so hard she almost knocked him away from her.

"Don't stop," she gasped. Her entire body seemed focused on the one little spot, jolts of electricity spiking through her, every nerve screaming at the intense stimulation.

He sucked hard, his tongue relentless as his fingers stretched her vaginal walls. When he lifted his head, his lips were slick with her moisture. Her face flushed with desire.

"You taste like fine wine, sugar. Better than anything that comes in a bottle. I could get drunk on you, Cassie, you know that?"

"Yes, yes. Drink me, Griffin. Use your mouth. Oh, God, please,

please." She was desperate in her need, her body begging for release, for satisfaction.

His fingers kept working their magic, moving her closer and closer to her peak, and all the while he crooned to her in his low rich voice.

"Sometimes, when I'm working, I think about how you taste. How you feel, like velvet and satin. I don't know which turns me on more, darlin'—making you come wide open, so I can watch those pretty pink muscles clench, feeling you with my hand, or having you clamp tight around my dick while I spurt into you. When I think how it feels to have my dick inside you, my zipper just about pops open."

She moved harder against his hand, moaning soft little sounds, her body arching in her frantic search for fulfillment. "Make me come, Griff. Please. Now. Now. Now."

Her skin was slick with the sheen of perspiration, and her breasts swayed with each toss and turn. The walls of her sex fluttered against his fingers

"Come for me, Cassie." His mouth was against her ear again, his tongue dipping and swirling. "Let me feel all that good hot liquid pour into my hand."

His words pushed her over the edge, and she climaxed, bucking wildly, grabbing his hair, screaming his name over and over. His fingers stroked and probed and teased inside her as she came in what seemed an endless orgasm.

When the fierce movements of her body slowed, he eased his hand from her and brought his fingers to his mouth. He licked the tips.

Through slitted eyes, Cassie watched him licking her dew from his skin, and the beat of her pulse deep in her channel began all over again. She'd barely finished with one orgasm and another was already building.

With her body still throbbing with aftershocks, Griff moved over her and sheathed himself with a condom from the nightstand.

"We don't need one anymore," she protested.

He paused and looked hard into her eyes, his face serious. "If we made a baby that tine, Cassie, it was meant to be. But if we didn't, let's get this mess straightened out before we try again. Okay?"

She sighed. "O-okay. But hurry."

His fingers opened her as if he was peeling back the petals of a flower, and he entered her with one hard, swift thrust. She was so damp with her own moisture he slid in with ease, seating himself to the hilt.

"Like that better, sugar?" His words were thick with desire. "Like my cock inside you? Oh, Cassie, you don't know how good you feel. Or what heaven it is being inside you."

Her tender flesh surrounded him like a velvet glove, the little spasms still gripping her walls like so many tiny flames against his cock. The hard points of her nipples stabbed into his chest, the curly mat of hair abrading her skin with an erotic caress.

As aroused as they both were, it took him only a few strokes before they both exploded in a fierce orgasm. Bodies slick with sweat crashed against each other. He held her tight against him as he emptied into her before collapsing on top of her. Their lungs begging for air, little pulsations still gripping their bodies.

When they could both breathe again, he rolled onto his back, taking her with him, holding her against his body. "Jesus, Cassie. I think we might kill ourselves."

"I...do things with you I never thought I'd do with anyone."

Suddenly shy, she turned her face away from him.

"Good, sugar." He kissed her shoulder. "Because I'd hate to have to go out and *really* kill someone." He bit her shoulder, a tiny love nip. "I love you, Cassie. There should be no boundaries between us."

"Will you keep teaching me?" She was surprised she could get any words out. Every muscle, every nerve in her body was wrung dry.

"You bet. We've just begun, darlin'."

"Griff?"

"What, honey?"

"I think you made today all better."

He chuckled, rolled onto his side, and molded her against him. The outside world might conspire against them, but what they had no one could destroy.

Chapter Twenty-Six

Griff left the house before sunup, planning to go by his house to check it out and pack before he started his first job of the day. Cassie rose with him, anxious to get started on her own project.

"I have mixed feelings about taking this trip with you, Dewdrop," he told her. "But I'm not about to let you do it alone."

"I can handle it if you need to be here," she reminded him.

"That's not the point. I'd never have a peaceful moment with you driving back from Tampa by yourself, being on the highway for two days."

When she opened the front door for him she saw a car cruising slowly down the street.

"Fuck," he growled. "They're out before dawn now."

"We've sure had our share of traffic in this neighborhood alright."

They were both aware of the chattering tongues in town and the parade of cars past her house, hoping for a titillating glimpse of the two of them together. Cassie would have thrown up the window shades and told them to take a look. Griff, however, insisted on protecting her from prying eyes as much as possible, the hot and heavy scene in the backyard the other night notwithstanding. He promised them both that would never happen again.

While Griff was off trimming shrubs and shoveling mulch, Cassie again worked her way through the house room by room. She decided to start with one more look in Diane's room, in case they had missed anything. All of her sister's clothes were stacked in a corner, ready for packing in cartons when Cassie got back from Tampa. There were plenty of places to donate them. However, they hadn't yielded anything.

She stripped the sheets from the bed, tossing them in the washer and folding away the blanket, leaving the mattress to air out for the time being. Then she scoured every inch of the room, even checking to see if the carpet had been pulled up anywhere, but found nothing. If Diane had hidden something in the house, she had hidden it well enough that Cassie was having a difficult time finding it.

Going through her mother's room, where her parents had slept together until her father's fall from reality was equally as difficult. The stale air of sickness hung in the air, along with something more. Neglect? Failure? Retreat? Cassie found it very depressing.

She followed the same process with the clothes and the bedding. Then she dumped everything from the nightstand drawer into a sack and put it in her room along with her mother's jewelry box.

By the time she'd finished with the upstairs, she was hot and dusty and still had no answers. She drank almost a whole pitcher of iced tea with her lunch then began with the downstairs.

By four o'clock, she'd accumulated a lot of trash to haul to the curb, another sack of papers to go through, and every inch of the house had been dusted and vacuumed. She was still, however, empty-handed as well as discouraged. She felt in her bones that Diane's secret was hiding somewhere close at hand, but no clue jumped out at her.

She decided to use some of the food she'd bought to make spaghetti sauce for dinner. A salad, French bread, and the bottle of red wine she'd picked up rounded out the menu. Not quite the gourmet meal she had in mind, but, for once, they wouldn't be eating takeout.

Griff ate everything she put before him with obvious gusto, complimenting her with each bite. After dinner they sat out on the patio again, in the fading light, discussing their options. Cassie reported on the fruitlessness of her search.

"We just need to drop everything until we get back," he told her. "Whatever our unwelcome visitor is looking for, if you couldn't find it today, as much as you tore the house apart, he or she won't either."

"I thought for sure I'd have better luck." She rubbed her forehead. "But I'm trying not to get discouraged."

"You shouldn't leave that jewelry and all those papers lying around, though," Griff told her. "I wouldn't put it past dear sweet Carol Markham to do a little snooping while we're gone, either."

Cassie chuckled. "We do have nasty suspicious minds, don't we? You'll be happy to know tomorrow morning I'm going to run by the bank and rent a big enough safety deposit box to dump everything into."

"I asked Phil to check on things every once in a while till we get back." Griff saw her open her mouth to object. "I know, I know, Phil's just Phil. But maybe he'll see something that will help us."

Phil was not the person she would have picked to keep an eye on the house. She wouldn't put it past him to do a little light burglary himself if given the chance, but she decided if Griff trusted him, she should, too.

After they finished their wine, they made one more sweep of the house and discovered some old cartons stacked any old way in one corner of the garage.

Cassie dumped all the clothes into them for the time being. "I'll make things neater when we get back. I just wanted the closets and dressers emptied in case Carol troops people through here this weekend. She's putting the For Sale sign up tomorrow, and I'm sure it will attract plenty of snoops."

"Don't you have to be a serious buyer to have someone show you a house?" Griffin wrinkled his forehead with curiosity.

"Sure." She mimed dialing the phone. "Hello, Markham Realty? I'm a serious buyer. You have a house listed I want to see."

He shook his head. "Maybe there's a lot to be said for being out of the mainstream. People sound less appealing to me all the time."

She laughed. "Try being a reporter. You get to see a side of people you wish they'd shipped on the Titanic."

When they dropped Griffin's truck at his house the next day, Cassie waited while he double-checked the locks on the doors.

"You surprise me every day," she told him, watching him reset his alarm system. "I'd never have thought you were the kind for such fancy gadgetry."

He grinned, but with a touch of bitterness. "When you're as popular in town as I am, you need to cover all your bases."

"You mean people might try to break in and damage your things?" She was aghast.

He shrugged. "They make me uneasy enough I wouldn't put anything past them. Especially with Diane's murder still unsolved."

"My God, Griff, what a way to live. With these people treating you the way they do, why didn't you leave here long ago?"

He slid into the driver's seat of her rental car, leaned over, and kissed her. "Maybe I was waiting for you to come back, sugar."

Warmth spread through her that always came with his touch. *Heaven help me, I'm becoming a sex maniac.* She giggled.

"My kisses are funny now?" he asked.

"No. Just a little private joke. I'll tell you tonight if you're real,

real nice to me."

Chapter Twenty-Seven

The flight was on time, smooth and easy. In Tampa, they retrieved their luggage and went outside to the cabstand.

"You didn't leave your car here?" Griffin asked.

"No." Cassie shook her head. "It's at my place. My friend Claire chauffeured me. She thinks all airport parking lots are treasure chests for thieves."

"My guess is she's right."

They snagged a cab, and, in less than thirty minutes, Cassie was unlocking the door to her apartment. Griffin carried their bags inside then stopped in the living room, looking around.

"Something wrong?" She opened drapes, letting in the light.

"No, just interested in how you live. How come the place looks so temporary? It's almost like a hotel room."

Cassie glanced about, trying to see things through his eyes. She was struck by the fact he saw what she hadn't—everything appeared as if she'd bought it from a discount showroom and plunked it down without thought or scheme. Which was pretty much what she'd done. She'd always promised herself to fix it up the way she wanted, but, somehow, the urge had never quite stirred within her.

Is that how Griff sees it? She nibbled her lip as he took in every inch.

At last, he came up behind her and hugged her. "You weren't planning on staying here forever, were you, sugar." It was a statement more than a question.

She shook her head. "I guess not. Claire always told me I should make more of a home out of this place, and I see now what she meant." She turned in his arms. "Maybe you were right. Maybe I was just waiting to get back to you, to have you in my life again."

They stood, just holding each other for a moment, until she broke the contact.

"Okay. We'll open the suitcases on the floor in the bedroom and take out what we need. Shower, fresh clothes, food and drink. In that order."

She didn't want to go to any of her usual places to eat. They'd be bound to run into people she knew, and she wasn't yet ready to share Griff with anyone. Besides, Claire would kill her if she didn't get the first look. They went, instead, to a little pub in a strip center near her apartment where they had thick steaks and aged bourbon.

"So, this is Tampa," he said, polishing off the last of his dinner. "This is where you've been hiding from me?"

"Maybe hiding from myself."

"You came here that summer after...."

"Yes. After. I called Claire and told her I needed emotional first aid. She never blinked, just told me to pack my bags and come on down. I'd spent vacations with her before, so it wasn't like I was a stranger. Her folks were very welcoming and gave me the space I needed."

"Just out of curiosity, what did you do all that summer? You had a long time before classes started again."

"I got a job as a summer intern at the newspaper. They had just fired the one they had. I walked in, looking to find anything at all, and they hired me on the spot. That's how I met Mike Rivard, my editor at the sports publication."

"So, you worked there the next summer, too?"

She nodded, sipping at her drink. "Semester breaks and vacations I just hung out with Claire and her family."

"Didn't your folks ever want you to come home?" He raised an eyebrow. "I can't believe they were happy to let you just opt out of seeing them at all."

Cassie stirred her drink with the tip of her finger, weighing her words. *How to explain this to someone and not have it come out wrong?* "When Diane was killed, I always had the feeling my folks would have been happier if it had been me. It didn't make me anxious to hurry back to the bosom of my family."

"Shit, Cassie. That's an awful way to live."

"You get used to it. They never stinted on money. Until my dad began drinking after Diane's death and just sort of faded away, finances weren't a problem. They paid all my college expenses and sent me a check every month."

He reached across the table and took both of her hands in his, rubbing his fingers over the knuckles, caressing the skin. "Life hasn't been much better for you than it has for me, has it, sugar?"

"Oh, don't get me wrong," she told him. "I didn't spend my time wallowing in self-pity. I went to work full-time at the paper here right after graduation, then went with Mike to this new publication. I'd saved a lot of the money my folks sent me, so I was able to get my own apartment, buy a car, things like that."

"What do you say we get out of here? We'll be a long time making up for what we lost, and I don't want to waste a minute."

Chapter Twenty-Eight

As soon as they were up in the morning, Cassie took care of her apartment situation. Next, she called Claire and arranged for them to meet her for lunch.

"I want to stop and get some moving cartons." She stood in front of her open closet. "Tonight, we're going to pack my clothes and the few things I want shipped to Texas. I'll hire a mover and ask Claire to be here for the pickup."

"What about the rest of your stuff? You don't plan to just walk out on it, do you?"

"Nope. I'll talk to Claire about that, too. She'll have some ideas."

And she did, but not before the woman had given Griff a thorough once over. Cassie knew he had dressed with care, wanting to make a good impression for her. The blue polo shirt was almost the exact color of his eyes, and his black slacks fit his body as if he'd had them custom made. His deep tan set off his sun-bleached hair that just brushed the collar of his shirt.

"Wow!" Claire let her eyes travel the length of his lean body. "So, you're the guy who broke her heart."

Cassie's face heated, and she kicked Claire under the table.

Griff smiled his sexy smile. "I'm also the guy who gave her his to hold—and would never break her heart again." He placed his hand over Cassie's and rubbed his thumb over her knuckles.

Claire grinned. "Well, I can see what the fuss is all about. Cassie, my dear, you didn't half do him justice. I'd give my soul to have some guy look at me this way."

"Hands off," Cassie laughed. "He's all mine."

Claire smiled at her. "Oh, I can see that. I just have one favor to ask. If there's another one back there like this one, crate him up and ship him right to my front door."

Throughout lunch, Griffin found every opportunity to touch her, rubbing the nape of her neck, brushing his fingers against her cheek. He was advertising ownership, sending the silent message to Claire to spread the word, and Cassie had to admit it made her feel good. When they rose to leave, Claire reached out and hugged her hard, blinking back tears.

"Take care, my wonderful friend. Don't let him get away no matter what you have to do. But remember. I'm always here if you need me, though."

"I know you are. And thanks for agreeing to take care of things for me."

Cassie promised to call the next week so they could check in with each other. Then Claire was gone, not looking back.

"She really is a good friend, isn't she?" Griff said.

"The best," Cassie replied. "The very best."

After picking up cartons at the U-Haul place, their last stop before returning to the apartment, was to say good-bye to Mike. That was almost as hard for Cassie as lunch with Claire.

Mike was his usual gruff self, helping her clear out her desk, handing her a final paycheck. "Something happens to her, you'll answer to me," he told Griff, taking a hard look at him.

Griff rested a proprietary hand at Cassie's waist, giving Mike the same look back. "I'll be taking good care of her." His voice was firm.

Mike just grunted then gave her an uncharacteristic hug. "Anything at all, you call me." Then he waved them both away.

"You made quite a life for yourself without me," Griffin commented when they were back in the car.

"Jealous?" she teased.

"Damn straight. I hate it that we missed all that time together."

"Did you think I wouldn't move on? If so, then you don't know me at all."

He shook his head. "No, you did just what I was afraid you'd do. You locked me away and moved ahead." He leaned close and kissed her ear, teasing it with his tongue.

She almost ran the car off the road. "God. Don't do that when I'm driving."

"But not quite completely away, right, sugar?" His words caressed her like warm honey.

"No. Not completely." She smiled to herself. "I think you know that by now."

"It's nice to see how everyone respects you, though. You're a complex person, Cassie. People appreciate you. But so do I. Just don't forget that."

Dinner was sandwiches from the deli, eaten while they took a break from packing and cleaning. Afterward, she emptied the drawers in her bedroom.

"Well, well," he said. "What have we here?"

She turned to see him holding a narrow black case from her nightstand drawer.

"Give it here." She'd forgotten her vibrator was stashed there. She should have snuck it into her suitcase when he wasn't looking.

"Uh-uh." He held it above his head. "Was this your substitute for me, sugar?"

Her cheeks heated, and she lowered her gaze. "Yes. Now, come on. Give it back."

"Under one condition." He tilted her face up, forcing her to look at him. "Let me watch you use it. One time, here in this place. Okay?"

She couldn't believe how embarrassed she was, after all the intimate things they'd done together. "I...don't think I can."

"Sure you can. I'll help you. Come on. We can finish this other stuff in the morning. We're almost done anyway." He pulled her against him, his lips brushing her temple, his hand smoothing her hair. "Cassie, I love you. I would never do anything to make you uncomfortable. Whatever we do together is good and right. It would please me to see the pleasure on your face when you make yourself feel good, knowing that you're thinking of me when you're doing it." He brushed his lips against her forehead. "But if you don't want to, it's okay."

"No, it's all right," she whispered on a shuddering breath.

He pressed soft kisses to her cheeks and eyelids. "Trust me. Please."

While they showered, he roamed his hands over her, murmuring in her ear what he wanted her to do and how he wanted her to do it. They'd picked up a bottle of wine, and he'd brought a glass of it into the shower with them, feeding her light sips as he whispered to her. She began to shake just from listening to him.

By the time he'd dried her off and led her to the bed, she was already flushed with the first heat of passion.

"All right, sugar. Like this." He lowered her to her back then bent her legs so her feet were flat on the sheet. With a gentle touch, he spread her legs as wide apart as he could get them. "Lick your fingers, Cassie. Just the tips. Yes, like that."

She ran her tongue over her fingertips, wetting them with her saliva, her eyes never leaving his face.

"Okay. Put your hands between your legs and pull those sweet lips apart. Let me see that beautiful cunt that I love so much. Do it, Cassie." As he talked, he'd shed his clothes, and he sat on the end bed, his eyes focused on the spot between her legs.

Still self-conscious but wanting to share her private pleasure with Griff, she slid her hands down through the nest of curls and separated her labia, already tingling with anticipation. She was wide open to him, and his eyes feasted on her in greedy appreciation.

"Good, honey. Very good. Oh, yes, I love that sweet place so much. Now, show me how you tease that little clit when you're by yourself and thinking of me. Yes, that's it. Pull back that tiny hood and let me see it all."

She closed her eyes, and in her mind she was in her bedroom alone, Griffin's face dancing beneath her eyelids, her body craving his. She used her fingertips to expose her swollen nub and, without any prompting, began moving one finger back and forth over its tip, the heat inside her escalating.

"Now inside, Cassie." The sound was a whisper, and his hands caressed the outside of her thighs. "Put your fingers inside."

She slid two fingers into her pussy and stroked herself as she'd done so many times before. Her body moved with the rhythm, onc fingertip still sliding in a steady rhythm on her clit, now so sensitive she could hardly stand to touch it. In and out, her hand moved, while the coil in her body wound tighter and tighter, and, like windswept clouds, any embarrassment fell away.

"Okay, sugar. Now, the big guy." He handed her the vibrator, already turned on. "God, Cassie, you don't know how it turns me on to know you did this imagining us together." He placed his hands on her knees, his thumbs drawing gentle circles.

She fell into her remembered pattern, stroking the instrument over her clitoris, into her channel, around and around the opening damp with the evidence of her desire. As her nerves caught fire, she slid the vibrator all the way inside her, holding it with one hand while she stroked herself with the other.

"Beautiful," Griff murmured. "Just beautiful." As he crooned to her, he rubbed the backs and insides of her thighs, ran his fingertips along the crease where her thighs joined her body, brushed over the curls now so wet they were plastered against her skin. "I'm going to give you an orgasm that will blow your mind, sugar. Just keep your eyes closed and feel."

She couldn't even think any more, she was so intent on reaching that elusive peak. Her body was one sensual flame, so aroused and so alive she felt as if her skin had been peeled back.

"I love this cream, darlin'." He held the little tube he'd found with the vibrator. "It smells like peaches. Just like you. Do you use this on the vibrator when you're fucking yourself? I've got a better use for it."

She was so lost in a sensual fog her brain wouldn't process what he was saying. But then she felt Griffin's hand slide into the cleft between her buttocks, massaging the cream heavy on her skin.

He moved his hand back and forth, rubbing the crevice, tickling at the entrance to the one place he hadn't yet plundered. And then, just as she pressed harder with the vibrator and her hand moved faster, he slipped one finger inside that hot, dark place. His thumb caressing the tender skin just below her pussy, and he pressed a second finger into her anus to join the first. She came, an orgasm so shattering she didn't think her body could stand it. She cried his name over and over, bucking, twisting, pushing, wanting it to last, wanting it to end.

When it did end, she fell back exhausted, panting for breath, her heart thundering, a fine layer of sweat coating her body. As she lay there trembling with aftershocks, he kissed his way down her body, nipping at her breasts, her navel, the soft hair between her legs. He slid the vibrator out and replaced it with his tongue, drinking the fluid she'd spilled for him. Heat rose in her again.

She reached for his shaft, feeling it so engorged she didn't know how he kept from going off.

"God, Cassie," he whispered, "I can't ever get enough of you. You turn me on like no other woman ever has. I worship you, baby."

With gentle hands, he turned her over and trailed kisses down her spine, just as he had the other night. No area was left untouched. His lips slid over her calves, the backs of her knees, her inner thighs. Then he was at her opening again, pressing the head of his cock against the tight opening.

"I've wanted to do this since that very first night six years ago." His voice was soft, loving. "I didn't think you trusted me enough then. You trust me now, though, don't you, Cassie?"

"Yes." The word hissed out between her teeth. She was so lost in an erotic fog she couldn't think. She only knew this was Griff, who could do whatever he wanted with her body and she'd take pleasure in it.

He leaned forward and licked her shoulder. "Good, darlin', because I want you so bad this way I can hardly see straight. I love you, Cassie, more than I ever thought I'd love another human being. I want to have you every way I can, to make you totally mine. Is that okay, sugar? Tell me, Cassie."

As he talked, he squeezed more cream from the tube he'd found, rubbing the globes of her buttocks, and slid his fingers along the separation. Then, one knuckle at a time, he eased his finger into that place he had yet to fill with his cock, the heat grabbing the cream from his skin until she was well-lubricated.

"It's all right, Griff. I love you." Then she jerked, tensing, as his finger intruded farther. "Griffin?"

"It's okay. Everything we do is okay, remember? I promise you'll love this. I promise I'll never do anything to hurt you. Any time you want me to stop, just say so." She heard the strain in his words as he fought to hold onto his control. "Cassie, I wouldn't do this with just anyone. It's too intimate. Trust me, all right?"

She lay there in a tense state of anticipation as he rolled on a condom. Then he was behind her, pulling her to her knees, separating her buttocks, and pushing inside her with steady pressure. When she cried out at the unexpected intrusion, he kissed her skin again, and pressed his hand against her mound to pull her tight against him.

"Just relax. You'll be fine in a minute. Breathe, Cassie."

Slipping the tip of one finger onto her clit and massaging it, he continued his invasion until the entire length of him was swallowed up by her hot, tight rectum. He began thrusting in and out of her, long, slow strokes.

She bit down against the first shock of invasion, but, in a moment, a feeling she could only call lust replaced it. Every nerve, every muscle in her body responded to this new assault. Before she even realized it, she was moving in rhythm with him, shoving her hips back against him, driving him deeper, her body wrapped in sharp, fierce pleasure. He filled the hollow of her body, his cock so large she didn't know how he got it in, yet it wasn't enough.

She felt his body against hers, his skin heated, and she wanted to wrap herself in him and stay there forever. He whispered in her ear, erotic words, sexy words, love words. Everything receded except herself and Griff in this time, this place.

It built with rapid speed, the tremors, the spasms, sensation piling on sensation, and she heard herself screaming. "Now, Griff. Now. Now." As she shouted, she forced herself hard against him.

They came in a simultaneous explosion that shook the bed, Cassie's screams loud, their bodies convulsing with such force she thought her heart would stop. When they collapsed, he slid out of her and pulled her tight against him for a moment, raining kisses on her spine and the cheeks of her ass, stroking her arms and her shoulder.

"I love you, Cassie." His words were filled with emotion. "You're mine. I will do anything in the world to make you happy. All that matters is that we're together."

"I love you, too, Griff. More than my life." That wasn't a lie. Never had she expected to have this kind of connection with someone, be so treasured and so worshiped.

He left the bed long enough to dispose of the condom. She heard the water running in the bathroom then he was stretched out beside her, pulling her tight to him. She snuggled with him, feeling the slow thud of his heart against her back.

Their bodies relaxed, sated, and they slept.

Chapter Twenty-Nine

They were ready to hit the highway as the sun was coming up, wanting to cover as much distance as they could.

"I hope the next residents living here enjoy it as much as we did." The corner of Griff's mouth turned up in a teasing grin as they took a last look around.

"Impossible." Cassie laughed and hugged him. "Just plain impossible."

The memory of the things they'd done the night before made her body glow. Her last vestige of self-consciousness had vanished, and she wanted to tell Griffin how eager she was to explore more uncharted sexual waters with him.

As they walked into the parking lot, a white convertible squealed in and stopped in front of them. Cassie was stunned to see Claire emerge.

"I can't believe you got up at this hour." Cassie gave her friend a tight hug.

"I wanted one last look at the gorgeous hunk," Claire whispered.

Griff leaned against the car, giving them some space. In his soft jeans, T-shirt, and aviator shades, with the wind riffling his wheat-colored hair, he could have stepped from the pages of a romance novel.

"Don't let him get away," she told Cassie. "He loves you. It's there in his eyes and the way he touches you. If you ask me, he always did."

"Don't worry. I'm hanging onto him this time." She gave Claire a lingering look. "I'll call you when we get to Stoneham. Thanks again for taking care of everything. And you'd better start planning a trip out west."

"If there are any more like him back there, I'll be hard on your heels."

One more stop at a drive-through for coffee and they said good-bye to Tampa. They followed U.S. 19 north almost to Jacksonville where they picked up Interstate 10 heading west. Cassie tried to find a comfortable place to put her body, but the activities of the night before had left her tender in places she didn't even know she had.

Griffin reached over and squeezed her knee, trying to hide the self-satisfied smile teasing at his mouth. "A little sore today, are we?"

"Get that smug look off your face, buster." She grimaced, but said, "I'm fine."

He laughed, a rich, full sound. "Can I tell you that making love with you is a most extraordinary experience?"

She laced her fingers through his where they still rested on her knee. "For me, too, Griff."

She started to say something more when his cell phone rang. He spoke briefly then snapped the phone shut, his jaw clenching.

"What?" She tensed, knowing the call hadn't been about anything good. "What is it?"

"That was Phil. He's been cruising by your house like I asked, checking things out."

"And?" she prompted.

"It seems that sometime last night our mysterious visitor decided to show up again and got inside."

"What do you mean?" She was stunned, her heart racing. "Are you saying someone broke into my house?"

"Got it in one. It happened sometime between about ten last

night, when Phil went by the first time, and four this morning, when he checked it on his way home from a late night out. He decided for some reason to walk around the house, just in case, and found the glass in the back door broken."

"Did he go inside?" Her mouth went dry. "Was anything taken?"

He shook his head. "He didn't go through the whole house. He said it was obvious from what little he could see that someone had been in there searching, but he didn't spend much time checking it out."

"What should I do? Should I call Dangler?" She looked over at Griff, trying to think. "You were afraid something like this might happen."

"Don't call anyone yet." A muscle twitched in his jaw. "First of all, I don't want to put Phil in a spot. Second, I don't think whoever it was will be back, at least for the moment. They don't know when we're supposed to return. Plus, people are around more on the weekends, and the intruder won't want to take any more chances than he or she has already taken."

"I need to call Carol. What if she's showing the house while we're gone?"

Cassie swallowed against the nausea rising in her throat. Someone had actually broken into her house. She felt violated, defenseless. Griff reached over again and took both her hands in one of his. The warmth from his body seeped into hers and chased the away the cold creeping over her.

"Don't sweat it. As a matter of fact, it might even be good if she were the one who found the break in."

"But—"

"I know it will be hard," he said, "but you've got to put it out of your mind till we get back. Besides, this is good, in a way. It means we were right. Someone's looking for something. We just have to figure out what it is."

Before either of them could say anything else, Cassie's cell rang.

"This is Carol," the breathless voice said. "Something awful has happened. Where are you?"

"Passing Mobile." Cassie made herself found as calm as possible. "Why?"

"I have a showing already, believe it or not. I went by to check on your house and it's a disaster."

When Griff glanced at her, she mouthed *Carol*. "What do you mean by a disaster?" she asked. "The showing or the house? What's wrong?"

"Honey, someone's broken into your house. It's just awful!" Carol's tone was a mixture of horror and excitement.

Cassie could almost hear her drooling at the thought of the gossip she'd have to pass around. "I-I don't know what to say. Did they do much damage?"

"Luckily no. I called Barry Dangler, and he said he'd send someone by to take a look, but I couldn't wait. I did make arrangements to get the back door fixed, though, since someone broke the glass in order to get in." She paused. "But I don't think I can show it again until you come back and figure out what's going on. My client won't want to buy a house that's a target for robbery."

"I think someone just saw an empty house and tried their luck." Cassie rubbed her forehead. "I'll call Barry and see what's going on. Can you hold onto your client a little bit?"

There was a long pause. "Did you say 'we'?" Carol said at last.

Cassie wanted to laugh. Her house had been burglarized, she had a jittery buyer, and Carol was looking for dirt. "Yes, I did. Griffin Hunter is with me."

"I see." More silence. "I know it's none of my business, but—"

"I don't mean to be rude, but you're right, Carol," she interrupted. "It *is* none of your business. Anyway, we should be back very late tomorrow night. I'll call you first thing Monday."

"Carol giving you advice?" Griff grinned when she hung up.

"What do you think? Let me tell you something. She may be holier than thou, but she and every other woman in that town would give their household treasures to trade places with me."

"You don't know what you're talking about." His hands on the wheel tightened in anger. "All those *nice* ladies would run me out of town in a hot flash if they could."

"All those *nice* ladies would rip their clothes off for you if you gave them half a chance," she contradicted. "It's all about forbidden fruit, Griff. When the town bad boy is wickedly sexy, it makes the forbidden fruit that much more tempting. You were every female's guilty pleasure. They might point fingers at me now, but every one of them wishes they were in my shoes—or bed."

He threw back his head and laughed, the sound breaking the tension the calls had generated. "Well, damn, Cassie. If I'd known that, I'd have figured out how to take advantage of all the free flesh long before this."

She thumped him on the thigh again.

"You'd better quit that or we'll have an accident," he teased, then sobered. "That was just a joke, sugar, although I must say, it was good for my ego." He reached his arm over and slid his hand between her thighs. "They're nothing. This is where my heart is." He gave her a slight squeeze that made her squeal before he pulled his hand back.

"And don't go thinking it's just sex again because you have to know it isn't. Sure, we're great in bed. But that's because of how we feel about each other. You're the one good thing that's ever come into my life. Like I keep telling you, this is real."

She slid over as close to him as the seat belt would allow. "It is real," she told him. "I can't tell you how free I feel when we make love. That's because I do know it's more than sex."

"For me, too, darlin'. I do things with you that with anyone else would just be physical exercise. Every time we make love, every way, I feel as if our souls are mating."

Her throat tightened. Griffin was not a man given to poetic declarations, so his words had all the more meaning for her. She touched the locket around her neck where the tiny heart was enclosed. "I'll always keep your heart safe, Griff. Always."

Chapter Thirty

They pushed themselves hard for two days, pulling into Cassie's driveway late Sunday night. She sat staring at the house.

"I'm not even sure I want to deal with this now." She was tired, depressed, dreading what they'd find, and angry at the violation of her privacy.

"Tell you what." Griff opened his door. "Let me go take a quick look and I'll tell you if we need to do something tonight. My guess is no."

"Uh-uh." She shook her head. "I need to go in and see for myself what the damage is. Then we can make a decision."

He made her give him her keys, though, insisting he should go in the front door ahead of her. What she found when she stepped inside wasn't as bad as she'd imagined. Things were moved around a bit. Some drawers in the old-fashioned desk were still pulled out a little, and the kitchen cupboards hung open. She could tell where furniture had been repositioned .

Griff went through the upstairs and came back to report it appeared to be the same up there. "No real damage," he told her. "But you can tell someone's been through here."

"I checked the back door. I guess Carol had them replace the entire door with one that doesn't have glass panes."

"Probably a good idea." He pulled her against his side and gave her a reassuring squeeze. "I say leave it for tonight, and, in the morning, you can call Dangler and get him out here. You at least need to make a report, and Carol's alerted him."

She sighed. "You're right. At this moment, I want a shower and bed more than you can imagine."

"Come on, then." He hustled her out to the car, locking the door behind him.

"Where are we going?"

"My house." He backed out of the driveway. "I can pull your car into the garage, and I have an alarm system."

"Griff, I don't think...."

He reached over and brushed his fingers over her cheek. "I know what's on your mind, and I understand. But our only other option is going to a motel, and you know everyone in town would be parked outside our room come morning."

"I hate this." She pounded a fist on her knee.

He pulled over to the curb and put the car in Park. "Listen, Cassie. Diane and I slept in that room, but it was a long, long time ago, if that's what's on your mind. I've lived in it by myself for most of my life. It's my personality, not hers in there." He grinned. "I even bought a new bed and sheets."

"Oh, Griff." She leaned over and laid her head on his shoulder. She was too worn out even to cry. "All right. I guess if you can do it, I can. Maybe it's just one more thing to get past."

It seemed just a few minutes before they were at his house. He opened the garage door with the remote control he'd taken with him and pulled her car into the space. After disarming the alarm panel, he led her inside, carrying the overnight bag they'd used the night before at the motel.

She stopped in the living room and stared. Whatever she'd expected, it wasn't what she found.

The house was spotless. The kitchen they came through gleamed as if it had just been polished, and the living room, although threadbare, was neat as a pin. When she followed Griffin upstairs, she got another shock. There was no mistake that his bedroom had been furnished for a man. A navy and tan quilt covered a king-sized bed. Book shelves lined two walls. And everything, not just the bed, looked almost new.

Griffin chuckled. "Were you imagining one step up from the homeless shelter?"

"I didn't know what to expect," she said. "I'm amazed."

"Bad boys don't have to live like slobs, you know." Pain flashed across his face. "After my father died, I was determined never to let the house go the way he did."

In the bathroom, he handed her towels and soap, and gave her privacy to shower.

"I'll use the one that's off what was my folks' bedroom."

"But—"

"Listen, Dewdrop." He gave her a tired smile. "I know you need time to adjust to being here. But I promise you there's no trace of Diane left anywhere."

Tears clouded her eyes at his thoughtfulness, and she hurried into the bathroom before she embarrassed herself and slobbered all over him.

She sat in his bedroom, waiting for him, when he walked in still damp from his shower, a towel wrapped around his hips.

"It's okay to get in the bed, sugar," he told her. "No one's ever slept in it but me. Come on. Let me show you." He led her to the bed, turned back the covers, and gently nudged her into it.

She laid back, her eyes never leaving his face. Then he was next to her, cradling her in his arms, soothing her with his hands and his voice. She was strung tighter than telephone wire, grateful when he began rubbing her back, her shoulders, her neck, his hands warm against her.

He put his lips next to her ear. "Shall we chase some ghosts, Cassie?"

Then his mouth came down on hers.

Tired as they were, it was what they both needed. A door needed to slam shut for them, and this was the time to do it.

It wasn't the frantic lovemaking of that first night, or the sensual, exploratory kind they'd indulged in since then. It was more a blending of soul and mind and heart, a recognition that while the past might always be with them, they wouldn't let it hurt them.

Griff's mouth and hands were everywhere, kissing and licking, teasing first her nipples, then her throbbing clit. He penetrated her first with his fingers and then with his mouth, building the pleasure in her body.

Panting, she pushed hard and shoved him onto his back. Rising to her knees, she took his shaft into her mouth, probing the slit in the head with her tongue and stroking his balls with teasing fingers. When she squeezed them, his whole body tightened next to her, and he pulled her head away then flipped her over.

"Inside you," he whispered. "I want to be inside you when I come."

Remembering in the nick of time to sheath himself, he pushed her knees back against her chest to open her wide to him and slid inside. She gripped him with the muscles of her cunt, milking him, knowing they were both close. So very close.

The climax this time was like the gentle rolling of a heavy tide, the spasms like whitecaps beating against a shore. Griff dropped the condom into the wastebasket beside the bed and pulled her against him. She could feel the rhythmic beat of his heart at her back, feel his breath against her skin.

"I love you," she whispered.

"I love you more."

And strange as it seemed, in this place where the specter of Diane should have been the strongest she no longer felt her sister hovering over her. Mocking her.

Chapter Thirty-One

Cassie stood in her living room, listening to Barry Dangler and getting angrier by the minute.

"This was a real break-in, Barry," she snapped, her words laced with venom. "Don't try to make out it's nothing."

"Well, why in the hell would anyone want to break in here?" he demanded. "What could they want?"

"That's what I'm trying to find out, and that's what I'm asking you to check into." She was furious. "Why is it you just want to sweep it under the table the way you did with Diane's death?"

"Whoa, there." Now *he* was angry. "Back off there, Cassie. Nobody's sweeping anything under the rug. I'm still convinced that somehow, some way, Griffin Hunter engineered what happened with your sister."

"Well, he didn't break into my house." She planted her hands on her hips. "He was with me in Florida when it happened."

"There's always his friend, Phil," Dangler reminded her. "We noticed him cruising by here a few times."

"Is that so?" Cassie wanted to stamp her foot or throw something. She was beyond frustrated. "Just how did you notice that? You checking up on my house for your own reasons?"

His face reddened. "Just doing regular night patrols."

"Which increased 1,000 percent since Griff came into the picture." She drew in a deep breath and let it out slowly. "We asked Phil to keep an eye on the house because we were afraid something like this would happen. Phil wouldn't have to break in like that. He's a locksmith. He could have done it without any trace. Besides, what would be his motive?"

Dangler glanced around the room. "Lots of valuable stuff here, you know. Mighty tempting."

"Oh, please. Now, you're reaching. First, you tell me there's no reason for a robbery, now you tell me I've got stuff anyone would want to steal. You can't have it both ways, Chief. What's going on here, anyway? Why are you giving me such a bad time?"

Dangler gave her a hard look. "When you run with the wrong people, Cassie, most anything can happen."

Just like that, it was clear to her. As long as Griffin Hunter slept in her bed and was a part of her life, she'd be tarred with the same brush the town had used on him. This was the very thing he'd warned her about, but she hadn't realized just how bad it could be.

With a supreme effort, she controlled the anger raging in her. "Fine." She turned away from him. "Just write up some kind of report so I'll have it for the insurance company. I won't bother you again. If I have a problem, I'll take care of it myself. Just remember, I still have a sister whose murder hasn't ever been solved. I won't stop poking my nose around until I get some answers."

"You might not like what you find," the chief said in a flat voice.

Cassie gritted her teeth. She was tired of hearing this from everyone. "At least I'll be the one to find it since you and everyone else seems to think we're not worth bothering about."

"Cassie, I didn't mean—"

"Yes, you did. You can show yourself out."

She spent the morning putting the house back in order, dusting and vacuuming as she went along. She needed to keep it in shape for any prospective buyers.

At noon, she called Carol, thanked her for everything she'd done, and told her the place was ready to show again.

"I know I shouldn't be saying this, Cassie—"

"Then don't. Do you want the listing or not, Carol? It's no problem for me to call someone else."

"Who on earth would you call?"

Carol sounded so astonished, Cassie almost laughed.

"Strange as this may seem to you, there are other real estate agents in Texas."

"But we're the experts in this area." Carol's disbelief was evident. "We're the best you can get."

"Then I suggest you do your job and leave my personal business out of this. Let me know when your client wants a showing again." She disconnected the call, wishing she could slam it into Carol Markham's smug face.

She finished unpacking her car and putting things away. The cartons coming from Tampa on the moving van would be stored in Griff's garage on a temporary basis.

She called the bank, relieved to learn all the papers for the annuities had been processed and the appropriate checks transmitted electronically. She realized she still hadn't told Griff about the windfall and made a mental note to do so.

That done, she decided to go through all the clothes in the garage. Family Services always needed clothing so after checking everything with great care, she would send it all to them. But before she could get started, Neil called.

"I just wanted to make sure you were all right," he told her.

"I'm fine, Neil." God, she just wanted to slap his patronizing self. "Why wouldn't I be? Is there something I should not be fine about?"

"Not at all, not at all." She could visualize him thinking of how to rephrase his words. "I heard about the break-in, and I just felt a responsibility to check on you."

She bit down on her temper but failed to keep the sarcasm from her voice. "I didn't realize the break-in was in the paper so soon. News sure gets around this place in a hurry."

"Stoneham is a small town," he reminded her. "We all look out for each other."

"If that's true, how come Barry Dangler is trying to blow off what happened?" she demanded. "If Griffin hadn't been with me, I'm sure he'd have him in jail for it. And if everyone is so very concerned about the Fitzgerald family, how come Diane's murder is still unsolved?"

There was a long silence at the other end of the line. She could almost hear Neil turning sentences over in his mind.

"Cassie, you need to leave Diane alone," he said at last. "She's dead, and that's unfortunate, but your sister lived a life where some kind of violence was the only possible ending. You need to get on with yours. Away from Stoneham. Away from Griffin Hunter. Maybe coming back here wasn't such a good idea for you after all."

"Is that a threat?" she asked, her tone quiet desire her boiling anger. "Or do you know something you'd rather I didn't find out?"

"That's totally unfair," he protested. "I'm just saying, let sleeping dogs lie. If you hadn't gotten yourself mixed up with Hunter, you wouldn't be on this kick."

"You are so wrong." *What an insufferable ass.* "Diane was my sister, no matter what you think of her. And she's not just dead, she was murdered. I'm entitled to some answers."

"Fine. But don't blame me if you don't like the ones you get."

They terminated the conversation without either of them saying good-bye.

Cassie's rage, which had been receding, threatened to erupt again. The best thing would be to attack the project out in the garage.

Chapter Thirty-Two

Despite the heat of the day, the garage wasn't too unbearable. Cassie found an old fan in the corner, which she plugged in, and opened the back door to get some circulation. Sitting cross-legged on the floor, she pulled the first box toward her and began lifting things out. Her mother's things.

Faint traces of the familiar scent of the rose sachet her mother had used for as long as she could remember still clung to the garments. On impulse, she held a blouse to her cheek, the material soft against her skin. Tears welled up for all the hugs she'd never received, and for the last six years when she might as well have had no mother.

One by one, she lifted each garment, examined it for usability, and folded it, stacking everything in piles around her. Then she attacked the next carton and the next. In an hour, she had gone through several cartons, rejecting only a few items. When she was almost finished, she was startled to find one that contained her father's clothes. It must have been in the garage all this time.

Out of habit, she checked each of the pockets, not expecting to find anything. But then, in the back pocket of one pair of slacks, her fingers encountered a slip of paper. She withdrew it with great care and unfolded it. Something was written on it, the letters faded with age. She had to walk to the open door to get better light. When she read what was written, her heart thumped with an erratic beat.

You'd better rein in that bitch daughter of yours or you and she are both dead. Ten o'clock tonight.

Cassie's hand shook. Did this mean her father knew what had
been going on with Diane? And what would that have been? How did
her father figure into it? Who had he been meeting? The questions
bombarded her so fast she got dizzy.

Pulling herself together, she fished her cell phone from her
pocket and dialed the chief's office. She was sure she'd get precious
little from him, but she still had to try.

"What is it now, Cassie?" He sounded tired—of her, more than
anything. "Haven't you stirred things up enough already?"

She forced herself to swallow a quick retort. "I was going through
some things in the house, and it just occurred to me I never saw a
hard copy of the report of my father's suicide. Do you have one?"

"Shit, Cassie, now you're seeing problems where none exist.
Maybe if you'd come home for the funeral, you'd have found out
then."

"I didn't call for a lecture, just to ask a simple question. Can you
answer it for me or not?"

"I guess so." His sigh carried through the connection. "Otherwise,
you'll be down here driving me crazy again. Yes, there's a report. Cut
and dried. Nothing funny."

"All I ever knew was he became depressed after Diane's death,"
she told him. "Six months later, someone found him in the park in his
car. He'd shot himself with that old gun he kept around."

"That's correct. That's all there was to it." Dangler cleared his
throat. "I suppose you want a copy of that report, too?"

"Yes, if you don't mind. I'd like to come by and pick it up now."

"I do mind, but I don't guess there's any getting around it." He sighed. "But you need to give me a day or two, just like with Diane. All those old files are in storage."

Cassie blew out her breath in exasperation. "Fine. Wednesday afternoon, then. But don't put me off."

"I'll have it for you." She could tell he was irritated. "But I'm getting real pissed off at all the cans of worms you want to keep opening. Go back to Florida, Cassie. You don't belong here."

"You won't get rid of me that fast," she snapped. "For your information—and everyone else you'll share it with—I quit my job and gave up my apartment. I'm back to stay." She waited for him to say something. To show some reaction. There was such a long silence, she didn't know if he was still there. "Chief?"

"I think that's a big mistake," he murmured. "You're making yourself pretty unpopular around here, you know."

"I didn't know I had to win a popularity contest to stay in this town." She was getting madder by the minute.

"Go away, Cassie. Anywhere. And take that damned Griffin Hunter with you. Good riddance to you both."

She poked the disconnect button as hard as she could. She was glad she and Griff had already decided to move when this was all over. Stoneham was making her sicker by the day.

Her hand was still on the telephone when it rang again.

"Hello, Cassie." Harley, warm and familiar. "Just checking in on you since you got back."

Cassie exhaled. "Hello, Harley. I'm fine, thank you. And it seems still sticking my nose in where it isn't wanted."

"Cassie, honey." His words were couched in his best bedside manner. "We're just looking after your welfare, you know. You're stirring up a lot of things best left untouched. If you plan to stay in this town, you don't want to be raising everyone's hackles. Especially over nothing."

"You call my sister's murder nothing?" Anger kept battering at her. "Harley, I thought you were a friend to my family."

His sigh traveled through the connection. "I am, sweetheart. I'm still trying to be one."

"Duly noted." Then a thought occurred to her. "Who says we're staying in Stoneham, anyway?"

"I don't understand."

"And you don't have to. Thanks for the call. Good-bye, Harley."

Neil had to have called him the minute he had hung up from her, but why? Was there some kind of conspiracy? What would it be about? It was hard to believe any of these people had anything to do with Diane. Or did they?

There was one unopened box left, the one containing all the papers from her father's desk. After finding the slip of paper, she couldn't bring herself to face any more discoveries at the moment. She'd need Griffin beside her to do that.

By seven, when Griff got home, she had showered, changed into fresh shorts and shirt, and lay on the couch, letting aspirin work on her headache. He held up two white paper sacks.

"I figured you'd be too busy today to cook," he told her, dropping a kiss on her forehead. "And it's too hot for anything heavy. I got sandwiches from the deli. Okay?"

"That's wonderful," she said. "You're wonderful. Come here and let me show you how wonderful."

"Wait until I shower," he said. "I'm sweaty and dirty. I'll just be a minute."

She waited until they had finished eating and drinking the last of the iced tea before she pulled the slip of paper out of her pocket and handed it to him.

"I found this today." She watched his face for a reaction.

"What the hell is this about?" He studied it, obviously as puzzled as she was. He turned the paper over, looking at both sides.

"I guess that's what I'm asking you. Does this mean anything to you?"

"No." He smoothed it out with his fingers. "But let's see if we can figure it out."

Cassie nibbled on her thumbnail. "I know this is a terrible thing to ask you, but could Diane have known who the real father of her baby was and been blackmailing him?"

"Anything is possible where Diane was concerned." Bitterness tinged his words. "I think there's a lot none of us knew about her."

"How does my father fit into all of this? Who could he have been meeting? I'm more confused than ever." She closed her eyes for a moment then snapped them open. "I almost forgot. I called the chief today to ask about a report on my father's suicide, and he was none too happy with my request."

"I'm sure he wasn't." Griffin snorted. "You're giving him the biggest headache he's had in a long time."

"Something's not right here." She swallowed the last of her iced tea then rolled the glass against her forehead. "There are just too many unanswered questions floating around. Like, was my father's death an actual suicide?"

"Don't get carried away, Cassie, seeing bogeymen where there aren't any."

"I'm not," she insisted. "I know my father was very depressed after...what happened...but I never could see him killing himself. It just didn't make sense, no matter what my mother said. I told the chief I'd pick up the report on Wednesday. I'm sure he wanted to object, but he couldn't very well refuse me."

"We have a lot to check out," he agreed, "and we need to do it carefully and quietly. You can't charge around anymore with a big sign on your forehead. If someone out there killed your father as well as Diane, he won't hesitate to get rid of you, too."

Cassie shivered as a sudden chill raced over her. "You know, everyone seems to want you and me to leave town. Do you have that feeling?"

He laughed. "Hell, they've been wanting me to leave for years. That's nothing new."

"I want to talk to you about something else, too," she said, being careful with her words, "and I don't know if this is the right time or not."

"You look like I might bite you. Why don't we go sit outside?" He stood up and took her hand. "It's always easier to talk in the dark."

When they were sitting in the lounge chairs, hands linked in the space between them, she asked, "Were you serious when you asked me to marry you?"

His fingers tensed on hers. "I thought I made it pretty clear I want the whole ball of wax. You, a home, kids. I thought you understood that."

"I needed you to say that again," she told him. "Because that means we're partners in everything, right?"

In a moment, he was beside her on the edge of her chair, his hands on her shoulders, his mouth hard on hers. "Damn straight. But I remind you I have precious little to offer you," he told her after he raised his head. "I have plans but haven't quite figured out how to make them all happen yet. As long as you're with me, you'll be an outcast here. But I love you, and I want to marry you." He moved back to his own chair. "So, what's this all about?"

She drew a deep breath and let it out. "If we sell both houses and you sell your business, we'll have a nice little bundle of cash. I told you my mother had two good-sized annuities my father left her. I cashed them out, and the money's already in the bank." She watched him with intensity, gauging his reaction. "I want us to buy the land you showed me and the nursery. You know how much is there. We've got enough cash that, by the time we combine everything, we'll be free and clear of debt."

She sat very still, waiting for him to say something. Anything. For a long moment, she thought he might get up and leave. Had she offered too much, too soon? Hurt his pride in some way?

"I can't take your money," he told her at last. "I'd feel bought and paid for."

"That is just so ridiculous," she exploded. "Why did you take me out there if you didn't think it was something we could share? Answer that for me."

When he just sat in the dark, saying nothing, she sat up, spitting fire. "You aren't *taking* anything. This is for both of us. Let me be part of this, please. Knowing we're doing this together will make everything else we have to do that much easier. Please, Griffin." She clenched her teeth so hard, waiting for him to speak again, she thought her jaw would break. "We're either together or we're not. Here's your chance to show me you meant what you said. We can do this. Together."

He rubbed his forehead. "I do want us to have a life together. I'm just not used to this. You know that." He pinned her with an intense look in his eyes. "But your name goes on everything, too. Whatever we do is for both of us."

"If we're getting married, I guess *so*." She moved to his chair, leaning close to him, and hugged him. All of a sudden, she felt more lighthearted than she had since they'd gotten back. "It will make leaving this town a reality."

"But I have something I want to do first," he told her.

"What?" She scrunched her eyebrows, puzzled.

"You'll see. Tomorrow." And that was all he told her.

Chapter Thirty-Three

The moving van arrived at Griffin's house the next day, and the men stacked all of Cassie's cartons in the garage. *Not much to show for six years.* She shook herself. Her life wasn't in the past but in the future with Griffin.

Carol called to tell her she had two showings she'd like to schedule. When would be good for her? Two possibles. Cassie crossed her fingers. They settled on Wednesday afternoon while she would be out.

"I'd be ecstatic if we got rid of this place that soon," she told Griff that night. "Some people have fond memories of the house they grew up in. Not me. Good riddance, I say. So. How was your day?"

He grasped one of her hands and rubbed his thumb over her knuckles in a gesture rapidly becoming both familiar and comforting. "I took you at your word," he told her. "I called the owner of the nursery and asked if we could come by and talk to him. I also called the agent listing that property."

"And?" she prompted.

"We can go by and see both of them Saturday." He looked hard at her. "You sure we're not rushing this? I feel like we're on a roller coaster."

"It's time to move fast. We spent the last six years standing still. We need to list your house and go about finding temporary quarters while we build our dream house." She laughed. "That'll give the town something to talk about."

"Like they don't have enough already."

"Maybe if they talk enough," she pointed out, "we'll find out something no one wants to tell us."

"Don't hold your breath." He snorted then reached into the pocket of his jeans. "But I have a requirement."

"Oh? Does this have to do with the business you wouldn't tell me about?"

"Everything to do with it. Close your eyes."

"Why?"

He blew out a breath of exasperation. "Cassie, just for once, don't ask questions and do as I say."

She closed her eyes and, in a moment, felt him taking her hand and doing something with her fingers.

"Okay, open."

Her eyes almost popped out of head at the sight of the solitaire diamond he had slipped onto her finger. "My God, this must have cost the earth."

"I told you I had some money put away. I want to advertise what we're doing to all of Stoneham. It's very important to me that everyone know I love you and we're making a life together."

Cassie laughed. "This is better than an ad in the paper. But you shouldn't have—"

His mouth closed over hers. "Yes, I should. I should have done it six years ago." He searched her eyes. "Do you like it? If not—"

"Are you kidding? I love it." She held her hand out so the moonlight could catch the sparkle.

"Maybe we should go upstairs and make this official." His grin was wicked.

She was already ahead of him, stripping off her clothes as she moved through the house.

"Impatient, are we?" he asked, as he caught up with her.

"You bet."

By the time they reached the bedroom, they were both naked. Tonight, they were too eager to take their time. The moment he lay down next to her, Cassie reached for his engorged shaft, stroking and pulling, the tip of her nail seeking the familiar slit in the velvety head. Thick moisture was already seeping from it. She loved the feel of the soft skin over the hard rod it covered and the heaviness of his balls as she reached down farther to cradle the sac in her hand.

"I'll go off in a second if you keep doing that, sugar." His voice was husky, strained with the effort at control.

"Good. That's what I want."

"But not until I'm inside you." He lifted her legs over his shoulders and, as he had done the other night, spread the petal-soft lips of her labia as wide as he could. "Damn, Cassie, you're cream is already so thick I can almost taste it. Your little puss is so pink and perfect. I could look at you forever, but right now I have to be inside you."

His hands trembled as he rolled on the condom. Then, with one hard thrust, he filled her, the tip of his cock touching her womb. "Look at me, Cassie," he commanded.

She opened her eyes, but they were so fogged with desire, he was a blurry image.

He pulled her tight against him, reaching down and exposing her clit, pinching it between thumb and forefinger. As he began the familiar dance, in and out, in and out, he rubbed the hot little bud faster and faster.

She writhed, unintelligible cries escaping her throat, her hands gripping the sheet. When her orgasm rolled through her, he let himself go, jetting every bit of his semen high up into her vaginal vault, tilting her to take all of it.

"Will we live to make it to the wedding?" she asked in a weak voice, all she could manage.

"I don't know, sugar." He still gasped for air. "But what a way to go."

***

Wednesday, Cassie picked up the report on her father's death from a reluctant and very irritated Barry Dangler.

"Cassie." He wore a stern expression on his face. "I'll tell you one more time. There's nothing here you can do except stir up more trouble. This is a quiet town, just like when you grew up here. You make a mess here, people won't forgive you."

"As if I'd care," she retorted. "All I've gotten from anyone in this town since I got back is grief of one kind or another. Well, everyone can go to hell. Someone's covering up something, and I'm going to find out what it is. If you won't do your job, I guess I'll do it for you."

Dangler threw up his hands. "Have it your own way. Just don't forget, I warned you."

She stomped out of his office, seething.

At home, she found a note Carol had left for her on the kitchen counter.

"I may have some good news. Both women want to see the house again, with their husbands. Saturday's convenient for them, if it's okay with you. Call me."

Good. Maybe someone will make an offer. She called Carol and told her Saturday would be fine.

"I'm keeping my fingers crossed," she told Griff when they met at his house later. "We can go take care of business that morning."

He kissed her forehead. "Let's hope."

After dinner, she took the box with all the papers from her father's desk, the folder with the police reports, and her laptop and set everything on the kitchen table.

"What's that?" He looked at the sheet of paper she was studying.

"The report on my dad. I want you to read the one on Diane. Can you do it?"

His mouth tightened, but he nodded.

The information on her father's death was just a single page. James Fitzgerald had been found in his car at Stoneham Municipal Park about eleven o'clock at night, reeking of scotch, with a revolver still in his hand, and a bullet hole in his head. Everyone knew he had been very depressed over Diane's murder.

They had found no bloodstains except his. There was gunshot residue on his hands plus a bullet hole in the window on the driver's side. The police on the scene, however, had surmised that on his first try her father had lost his nerve and jerked the gun away. Case closed.

"You know, there's another explanation for this scene." She leaned back and pushed her hair away from her face. "Someone else could have shot him then fired a bullet through the window to get the residue on his skin."

Griffin scratched his head. "Wouldn't they have opened the window first?"

"Maybe." Cassie shrugged. "Or maybe they were just sloppy."

"But I ask again. Six years later, where do you start?"

She looked at the report, brows drawn together. "I don't know. I have to think about that. But my reporter's nose tells me there's something rumbling underneath all this."

"Reporter's nose, huh?" He chuckled. "If it's half as nice as the rest of your body, I'll follow it anywhere."

She threw a pencil at him, grinning. "Did you get anything from the sheet on Diane?"

He scowled. "Not anything new." Then he snapped his fingers. "Wait. Remember I told you she had this kind of purse she always kept with her? The one that wasn't with the things Dangler has? That nobody found in the park, or anywhere else?"

Cassie nodded, waiting.

"Just now I remembered how she looked when she left. She grabbed her keys off the hall table, but Cassie?" he leaned forward, intent. "She didn't have that purse with her."

"Are you sure?" A tendril of excitement curled through her. "You're not mistaken? Think again. It's important."

"I'm sure. Positive." He described again everything she'd been wearing, the keys in her hand, but *no purse*.

"What about her driver's license?" Cassie persisted. "Money? Anything like that?"

He shook his head. "I don't know. I'll have to think again. But she didn't have that purse with her. That's for sure." He sat up suddenly. "You know what that means, don't you?"

"It's still in your house," she whispered. "Hidden somewhere. We've been going about this all wrong."

"What do you mean?"

"I mean, I don't think what we're looking for is in my parents' house." She stood up, dumping everything into the box on the table. "Come on. Let's go see what we can find."

Once at his house, they stood in the foyer just looking around.

"Where do we even start?" she asked him.

"We need to do this in methodical fashion," he said. "Go through one room at a time. Cover every inch of it. We can't do all the rooms tonight, so let's take the logical ones first."

They began with the living room, seldom used so an obvious place to stash something. With no results there, they moved on to the dining room, and, last, the little room Griff used as an office. Nothing.

"She wouldn't put it in my office, anyway," he said. "Too much chance I'd find it." He pulled Cassie against him, rubbing her back. "Let's go to bed, sugar. We're both too tired to do any more good tonight."

"I guess." But she couldn't shake the feeling of dejection.

He moved her a couple of inches away from him and looked down at her. "Why don't you spend the day here tomorrow while I'm working, instead of going back to the other house? You've done all you can there, anyway. Tomorrow night, we'll go through that box of papers."

She nodded, knowing he was right. At the moment, she just wanted to lie down and close her eyes and forget about everything. She was tired of the town, tired of looking for a needle in a haystack, tired of everyone's attitude. The problem was, her anger kept her going.

"Okay. Just point me to a bed, and I'll try to keep my eyes open till we get there."

But her mind was already focused on the next day.

Chapter Thirty-Four

Griff was already out of the house when Cassie awoke the next morning, but he'd left a note on the pillow next to her.

Back in a minute with breakfast. Extra toothbrush in bathroom. Love, G.

She smiled and stretched like a lazy cat. A satisfied cat. She liked having someone watch over her. By the time she was showered and dressed again, albeit in yesterday's clothes, Griff was back with two bags from McDonald's.

"McMuffins and coffee." He held up the goodies. "Hope that's okay."

"An excellent choice. Thank you." She kissed his cheek. "You spoil me,"

They munched breakfast in an easy silence, each preoccupied with their own thoughts.

"Okay," Griff said when they finished and he'd thrown away their trash. "I'm off. All my fans are eagerly waiting for me. I have a longer break than usual in the middle of the day, so I'll be here at lunch. Since there's not much food in the house at the moment, I'll pick something up. You can give me an update then."

"Let's hope I'll have something to talk about." She had mixed feelings of anticipation and dread. "Something we can deal with."

"Dewdrop." He smiled and placed a kiss on her nose. "As long as we're in this together, we can deal with anything."

Cassie watched him drive away then went back to work, searching the house. But as the morning wore on, and she had little success, she was afraid she wouldn't have much at all to tell him. But as she started up the stairs, she noticed a tiny closet wedged under the stairway. The door was locked, but she'd faced that problem before. Many times as a reporter she'd been confronted with locked spaces and managed to get into them. As long as she didn't get arrested, her bosses looked the other way.

In the kitchen junk drawer, she found a small screwdriver. It took her less than five minutes to jimmy the lock and drag the door open. When she looked inside, she found an odd collection of old and dusty suitcases of every size and shape. She guessed after Griff's mother died, no one did any traveling. She pulled them out into the hall then sat down to open them one by one.

The first two were duds, containing nothing of value. The third one, however, yielded a real treasure, a small packet of papers held together with a rubber band. Hands shaking, Cassie pulled them out to look at them and discovered they were notes written on scraps of paper.

Cassie's hands shook as she read first one then another.

Meet me tonight, same place. All I have is an hour, though.

I can take a long lunch today. You know where.

You were fantastic the other night. I can't wait any longer to be with you again.

And on and on and on.

The notes were printed, not written, an obvious attempt to disguise the handwriting. However, she knew an expert could make a match with something to use as comparison. Some of the notes were explicit, suggestive, even erotic at times. Whoever wrote them was meeting on a regular basis with Diane. Put these together with the note she'd found in her father's slacks, and a picture began to emerge.

Cassie didn't know why her sister had risked keeping the notes, except that, even at twenty-four, she'd still had a teenager's perspective. Having a secret lover would have been romantic to her. The danger in keeping the notes and hiding them would have appealed to her.

She set the bundle aside and resumed her search, checking the rest of the luggage.

By the time noon rolled around, she'd added two expensive-looking bracelets and two notes Diane had written to herself. She was reading those when she heard Griff come in.

He shook his head when she pointed to the space under the stairs.

"You know, I'd forgotten all about that little cubbyhole. We sure never had any use for suitcases after my mother died. What did you find?"

"After lunch." She got up and walked into the kitchen.

"Is it that good or that bad?" he asked with apprehension, following her.

"After lunch," she repeated. "Go wash up."

She kept the conversation light while they ate. They talked again about the possible buyers for her house and what she would do if one of them made an offer. Griffin told her he'd called both the nursery and the agent for the land and made appointments for Saturday.

After she cleared away the debris from lunch, Cassie retrieved her morning's treasures and set everything on the table. "Look at these and I think you'll see a picture emerging."

"Quite a haul," he commented when he was finished.

"Do you recognize the bracelets?"

He shook his head. "No. Not at all."

"She never wore them?" Cassie thought how unbelievable it was that her sister had taken this jewelry from someone and never worn it.

"Not around me. They look pretty expensive. I could never have bought anything like that for her. Not then." He picked up the papers and scanned them again.

"I'm not showing these to Dangler," she told him.

"No?"

She shook her head. "First of all, he's still determined to prove it was you. Second, I think if he gets this stuff in his hands, it will disappear. He's much more interested in protecting the reputations of the upright citizens of Stoneham than yours or mine or Diane's." She swept everything into a pile.

"That's no lie."

"No," she continued. "I think we're going to have to do this ourselves. Also, these two sheets of paper lead me to believe Diane kept a diary. I'm assuming for whatever reason she couldn't get to it when she wrote these notes. I'll just bet she's got some names in there nobody wants made public."

"That has to be what someone's looking for."

"I'm going back to my house later." She cleared everything away. "I want to take one more look around. So come there after work, okay?"

"Okay. Watch yourself, though." He kissed her and was gone.

She refused to go through the room Griffin's parents had shared without him there, so she forced herself to go into his room. Closet first, she thought. But nothing remained of Diane, not the smallest trace.

She dragged a chair in from the guest room, stood on it, and searched around the closet shelf. Again nothing. She even tested the ceiling to see if there were any panels that might lift but no luck there, either. As little as the closet revealed, Diane might never have been in the room.

She figured the rest of the furniture would be a waste; Griffin had told her he bought everything new after Diane's death. If there was anything to find, it would have turned up then. Curiosity got the better of her, though, and she couldn't resist peeking in his drawers.

Like the rest of the house, everything was precise and neat. Nothing unusual. Underwear, socks, T-shirts. She lifted one of his T-shirts out and held it to her face, wishing it held his male scent. As she did so, the pile shifted and found a wallet hidden under the pile. It wasn't the one he carried now, and it piqued her curiosity.

It appeared old, the leather worn and faded. When she opened it, there was only one thing in it, something that made her catch her breath. She stared at a picture of herself that had to be ten years old. She stood with two of her friends in her cheerleading uniform in front of the high school. Someone must have said something funny because her head was thrown back and she was laughing.

She hadn't even known the picture was taken, or who had snapped it. Or how Griff had gotten hold of it. He would have been twenty at the time, not given to hanging out with high school students, virgins or not, so he must have had a reason for wanting this. It amazed her he'd kept it all this time.

She replaced it in the drawer and laid the T-shirts back in their neat stack. All of a sudden, a dull headache throbbed behind her eyes. It was time for her to get out of this house until Griff could help her finish up.

The rest of the afternoon was not just fruitless, it was also depressing. Cassie returned to her house knowing she wouldn't find anything new. When Griff showed up after work, he bullied her into her car and made her follow him home. Over pizza, they dragged up every detail of everything they'd learned so far, but still no clue as to the whereabouts of the diary.

"It has to be somewhere we haven't thought of." She gathered their trash and dumped it in the wastebasket. "I'm certain whoever killed Diane killed my father. It just fits too well."

"We'll finish going through this house tomorrow night," he promised, "but we also need to think of other places she might have picked to stash it." He raked his fingers through his hair. "We're missing something. I just wish I knew what."

"Whatever it is, we want to find it before our mysterious stranger steps up his activities."

Chapter Thirty-Five

Cassie had just finished dressing the next morning when Neil McLeod called her cell phone to give her what she'd taken to calling his Griffin Hunter speech.

"I see you've already moved into Hunter's house," he began.

"Leave it alone, Neil." She closed her eyes and tried to imagine herself stabbing him with his letter opener.

"In good conscience, I feel I have to make one more attempt to talk sense into you," he went on. "You don't know what a big mistake you're making here."

"The truth, Neil?" She took great pleasure in her words, "I think for the first time in my life I'm *not* making a mistake. I know exactly what I'm doing, and I'm enjoying it."

"I'm just worried about your inheritance. I feel a proprietary interest in it and you."

God, can he sound any more pompous and full of himself?

"My inheritance?" She bit back her irritation. "What does that have to do with anything?"

"I understand Griffin is planning on buying a business and some property over in Marble Hill," he related. "Is it your money he's using, Cassie? Has he already got his hooks into you?"

She was so furious she was almost speechless and had to swallow twice to control herself. *Okay, no more being polite.* "First of all, I don't know how you found out about Marble Hill, but it's none of your damn business. Neither is my money. It's mine, and I can do what I want with it."

"So, that's the way he plays it." Neil was nasty. "Well, it's no less than I expected from him."

"Damn it, Neil." She gripped her cell phone, imagining it was his neck. "I'm getting really tired of this song. Stay out of my business. *Our* business. If I had wanted your advice, I would have asked for it."

"Your mother always took my advice."

"Well, my mother isn't here anymore," she pointed out, "and I'm a little better prepared to make my own decisions."

"You know, the chief still thinks Griffin's the one who killed Diane." His tone was harsh and filled with irritation he couldn't quite conceal.

"Is that so?" *God, what an ass.* "Well, I may be digging up a few surprises on that score."

There was dead silence on the other end of the line. "Don't let Griffin Hunter sell you a bill of goods." His anger vibrated across the connection.

"For your information, Griffin and I are planning to be married. So, save your breath from now on."

"Walk away from this, Cassie." He hung up without even a good-bye.

She stood there, holding the phone, wondering how and why she'd ever thought these were nice people. Then she shoved the phone in her pocket and set the coffee to brewing. She had just filled a mug when her cell rang again.

Now what? She dug it out to answer.

"I wanted to touch base with you and make sure you were doing all right." Donald Brandon's oily words slid over the phone wires. "I know this has been a sad and trying time for you, Cassie."

Had they all decided to tag team her?

"No offense, Donald," she said, biting off each word, "but it would be a lot less trying if all of you would just leave me alone."

"Why, Cassie, no offense taken," he said, his tone changing, "but I'm sorry you feel that way. The thing we all want is to make this time of grief easier for you and help you settle things here."

And get out of town. "I'm fine, Donald. I'm handling things well. You can tell all the rest of your friends I can do without the calls and warnings. I'm not an idiot. I know what I'm doing."

Silence hung between them for a moment. "I see Griffin Hunter is still hanging around, sucking up to you. I hope you're on your guard with him."

"For God's sake, Donald," she snapped. "That's insulting. As a matter fact, Griff and I are engaged."

Dead silence filled the other end of the call. Cassie chuckled to herself as she pictured Donald at an uncharacteristic loss for words.

"I would feel derelict in my duty," he said at last, "if I didn't remind you the chief still believes Griffin is Diane's killer."

"You know," she said, "the chief would do a lot better to stop pointing the finger at Griffin and try to find the real killer."

"Go away, Cassie. Leave Stoneham, and we'll leave you alone." When he hung up the harsh sound of the receiver being slammed down echoed in her ears.

The next one on the tag team was Cyrus McLeod, and she made short shrift of him. His professed paternal concern sounded like so much garbage to her, and she told him so.

"You're burning a lot of bridges," he pointed out. "The sooner you finish up here and leave, the better for everyone."

"Well, chew on this, Cyrus." Anger built inside her again. "When I came here, my plan was to get out as fast as I could. Maybe if you all had left me alone or not been so adamant about making Griff a murderer, I might have done so. But now, I find there are still so many questions about Diane's death—and my father's—there's no way I'm leaving until I have all the answers and know the truth."

"Cassie," he began again, "I just—"

"Maybe if everyone hadn't been so quick to hustle me out of town," she snapped, "and cover everything over, I'd be long gone. You can pass that along to all your very good friends."

"Your father?" A different tone came through as he picked up on that reference. "Your father committed suicide. Don't go making problems where there aren't any."

This time it was Cassie who hung up first. She couldn't wait to get away from these people who refused to leave her alone. A headache was building again so she dumped the coffee and poured a fresh cup. She went out in the backyard to lie on one of the lounges when a thought popped into her brain.

Was there something more to this besides Griff's reputation and her unwillingness to be led around by her nose? Was she missing something here that should be obvious? Surely none of them could have anything to do with what happened, but did they know something they didn't want her to find out?

"You didn't answer the bell, so I thought I'd check out here." Harley Graham's voice behind her almost startled her out of her skin.

She jumped. "Oh, my God." She bolted upright and clapped a hand to her chest. "Damn, Harley. You scared me half to death."

"Sorry, honey." He smiled down at her. "I didn't mean to surprise you. Okay if I sit down?"

"As long as you're not here to lecture me about Griffin Hunter or tell me I need to get out of town."

Harley chuckled. "That bad, is it?"

"Worse," she groaned. "I'm just so sick of everyone telling me what they think is good for me."

"I guess that's what some people consider the charm of this town. What they like to call closeness."

She snorted. "Too damned close for me. Excuse my language."

"No problem. I'd bet by this time you've got plenty to swear about." His eyes dropped to her hand. "Nice ring, by the way. I guess that means you and Griffin are serious."

She nodded. "Serious about getting out of here, too."

"Okay, let's hear it all."

He leaned back in the other lounge chair and listened while she described the day's phone calls. He was the least judgmental person she'd ever known and easy to talk to. Just being in his presence cheered her up.

"Cassie, not much has changed here since you left," he reminded her. "Griffin Hunter isn't ever going to live down his reputation. Barry Dangler isn't going to stop trying to hang Diane's death on him. The upright folks around here aren't going to stop giving anyone who'll listen a piece of their mind, either. You just do what you need to do and forget about them."

"Hah! Forget about them? That would be a neat trick." Sitting up again, she looked over at him. "Harley, I need to tell you about some things I've found out, strange things, and some stuff that's happened, and ask you some questions. Is that okay?"

"Fire away, kiddo. I'm all ears."

Trying to remember all the details, she told him what she and Griffin had found out about Diane, about the things that hadn't been in the police report, and the surprises that had been, such as the baby's parentage. She told him about the notes she'd found, and the jewelry. Last, she told him about the report on her father's so-called suicide and the note she'd found in his clothes.

"So, what do you think?" she asked, when at last she wound down.

Harley shook his head. "That's some story, Cassie. Have you talked to Barry Dangler about it?"

"That idiot?" she spat out. "All he wants to do is find one piece of proof to lock Griffin up and throw away the key. He's not interested in anything else."

Harley sighed. "Still singing the same song, it seems."

She leaned toward him. "But this is evidence of something. Harley, I didn't mention this to anyone else, but Diane was seeing someone, a person who needed to keep his identity secret. I'd guess the baby's father. And the jewelry? It sure looks like she was trying to get money out of him. That's what the warning note to my father was all about."

"You know, I signed your father's death certificate," he told her.

"Did you examine him yourself?" she demanded.

"I guess I took what Barry said and didn't bother looking for anything else." He sighed. "I had no reason to. Everything seemed so cut and dried." He paused. "Did you know I had been treating him for clinical depression?"

"No, I didn't." She tried to get past the shock of the news. "But I do know my father was not a person who would take his own life. Diane's death may have upset him, but he would never have just left my mother alone like that. I'm positive about that."

"You may be chasing shadows," he pointed out. "Diane had a vivid imagination and loved to conjure things up. Did you ever think she might have written those notes herself?"

"No." Cassie shook her head. "She wouldn't go that far. Someone killed her, Harley, and it wasn't Griff."

"Forgive me, honey, but I can't see any decent person getting involved with her. She was your sister, and I'm sorry to have to tell you, but she was trouble walking. If there is someone lurking in the shadows, it would more likely be one of that wild bunch she ran with."

"But they wouldn't have any money," she protested. "Someone was giving her expensive gifts. Keep in mind, none of the men Diane ran with would have much that she could blackmail them about. Also, it had to be someone who'd kill my father to keep his secret. Griff had no reason to do that. Neither did anyone else in that crowd."

"You never can tell what someone will kill to protect. Be careful," he warned her. "If you're right, that means there's a dangerous person out there who thinks he's safe. He won't like having things disturbed after all these years."

"Don't worry. Griff's taking very good care of me." She narrowed her eyes. "You aren't going to give me grief about that like everyone else has, are you?"

He sat up and grinned at her. "Not a chance. I figure you're old enough to know what you're doing, and if you don't, it's your problem. That doesn't mean I don't care, but I'm not your self-appointed keeper."

Cassie leaned over and hugged him. "Thank you for that. At least I have one person I can count on."

"Just call me if you need me," he told her, and headed off to his car.

Chapter Thirty-Six

Deciding she needed to cook again and give Griff some real food, Cassie made a quick trip to the grocery store, picking up three bottles of wine along with everything else. When he got home, she was in the kitchen, basting a roast and halfway through one of the bottles.

He raised an eyebrow at the wine. "Having a tough day, are we?"

"You don't know the half of it," she told him.

He sniffed the air. "Dinner sure smells good. I didn't know you were such a good cook."

"It's pretty basic, but I decided I'm letting you eat way too much takeout."

He came up behind her, wrapping his arms around her and resting his chin on the top of her head. She leaned back against him, thankful for the feel of him.

"I'm dirty and sweaty and I need a shower, but I can't wait to do this." He turned her around and kissed her with such tenderness she almost cried. Ignoring his disheveled condition, she reached up and wrapped her arms around him, pressing her body to him.

"I love you, Cassie," he murmured. "I don't think I'll ever get tired of telling you that."

"Love you, too."

Then he was gone up the stairs, and, soon, she heard the shower running. It felt so good to be with him like this, at last. She hummed happily as she finished dinner.

He came into the kitchen as she served the food, scrubbed clean and carrying the delicious scent of spicy aftershave. He stooped and kissed her again.

"So, did the news get out today?" He lifted her hand with the ring on it."

"Enough so they won't have to print a paper this week." She grinned.

"Good. I just wish I'd been able to tell everyone myself."

They ate slowly, talking about this and that but avoiding the topic that was the elephant in the room. After they finished cleaning up, they took a bottle of the wine out to the yard and sat in the lounge chairs. Cassie gave him chapter and verse on the telephone calls and on Harley's visit.

"Whatever campaign's going on," she said, "it seems to be stepping up in intensity." She paused to take a sip of her wine. "I'm curious as to why everyone is trying so hard to get me to drop what I'm doing and get out of town. I'd hate to think there's some big conspiracy going on, but it sure seems like someone's pulling some strings."

"No one knows about the notes we found, or the jewelry," Griff reminded her. "They think you're just looking for someone to pin everything on because of what's going on with you and me. Remember, it would make everyone sleep better at night if I just confessed and Dangler could close the file."

"The notes aren't quite the secret they were," she apologized. "I told Harley about them when he was here, but he's the only one." She chewed her thumbnail. "I'm trying to attack this as if I were after a story, but it's a lot different when it's personal. When I mentioned there might be something suspicious about my father's death, you would have thought I'd cursed the pastor."

"If they discount the suicide decision," Griff pointed out, "that means they have to look at Diane's death again because they might be connected, and that's not going to happen. Your questions are making people nervous, so they want you to go away."

"We'll just have to keep searching for the diary." She sighed.

"I agree. That could be the key to everything."

They batted ideas back and forth, dissecting every conversation she'd had and going over the notes again. The sun disappeared, and, soon, bright stars twinkled in a clear sky overhead. For a change, a faint night breeze stirred the sultry air.

Griff stood up and reached for Cassie. "I think we need to discuss this with fewer clothes on." He grinned. "We've given the neighbors enough to think about for the year. Let's go upstairs and see what comes up."

He leered at her and wiggled his eyebrows. She burst out laughing then followed him into the house.

Chapter Thirty-Seven

They left the house before nine Saturday morning. Cassie wanted to be long gone before Carol showed up with her clients.

"I don't think we have to worry about another break-in," Griff told her. "Too much commotion over the last one. If someone still wants to get in here, they'll figure something else out."

"What a comforting thought." Cassie bit her cheek. "Maybe I should just buy a gun."

"You'd probably shoot yourself instead. No, I think what we need to do instead is try to see if anyone follows us around. Whoever it is may have decided it would just be easier to let us find what they're looking for and go from there."

"And what, kill us, too?" She was incredulous. "You don't think we'd be two deaths too many? Suicide wouldn't work this time."

His eyes darkened, and his jaw tightened. "No, but they could make it look like I'd killed you, just like Diane, then killed myself in a sudden fit of remorse."

"My God!" Her jaw dropped. "But that's unbelievable."

"Whoever we're looking for has managed to kill twice and get away with it," he reminded her. "By this time, they'd have great confidence in their ability to get away with anything."

She shivered and reached across the seat for Griff's hand. She remembered when all that that bothered her was her dark, erotic dreams about him.

They still hadn't gone through the carton of papers from her father's desk. Griff suggested bringing them along and looking at them over a picnic lunch. But first things first. They spent most of the morning at the nursery, talking to the owner. Cassie was impressed with Griff's knowledge and business sense, and she could tell the owner was, too.

Griff shook hands with the man. "Thanks for all the information. I think my fiancée and I need to discuss this, but we won't waste any time. I'll give you a call Monday or Tuesday, okay?"

The owner nodded, although he seemed reluctant to let them get away.

"What do you think?" Cassie asked when they were back in the truck.

"I think tomorrow we should sit down and do a financial projection. Then, Monday we can call him with a formal offer."

"How soon could we close?" Suddenly, she was eager to get this taken care of.

"I'd say no more than ninety days, which gives us time to wind up everything else."

In Marble Hill, they found a deli where they could buy sandwiches and drinks for lunch then drove out to the property Griff had taken her to the other day. They had an hour before the agent was to meet them, so they let down the tailgate on the truck and spread out their food. Over lunch, they took their first good look at the papers from the desk. Most of them were run-of-the-mill, but, underneath the jumble, they found a tiny envelope with a key in it.

"Griff, this is a key to a safety deposit box." She held it up, staring at it, hardly able to contain her excitement.

"You're right. You think it's just been in here all this time?"

She nodded. "It could have belonged to my father, but I have an itchy feeling Diane stuck it in here. She wanted a safe place for it, figuring no one would open this envelope. She was right."

"Your mother wouldn't have found it?"

She shook her head. "No. I'm guessing that after Dad died, all my mother did was shove papers in the drawer and forget them. She left everything for Neil to deal with."

Griff studied the items on the truck bed, forehead creased. "Why do you suppose he never asked her what she kept at home, or where she kept personal papers? I'd have thought he'd want to get his hands on them."

Cassie shrugged. "I'm guessing he never gave it a thought. He was too sure my father had given him everything important. Unless he's the one looking for the diary, why would it even occur to him?"

"Monday, you need to call that idiot at the bank and see if either of your folks had a safety deposit box he conveniently forgot to mention to you." He bit into a sandwich as if it was Howard Cook's head.

She giggled then turned sober. "But Neil or Howard would have told me when we went over all the paperwork. Wouldn't they?"

"Not necessarily. If one of them is our killer, they'd just as soon not have you find out. If it's not at dimwit Howard's bank, you could try Bank of America where you have your account. Or maybe we need to start checking the banks in San Antonio."

Cassie blew out her breath and grimaced. "That's a job and a half." She snapped her fingers. "But, if we need to do it, I think I know someone who can help us. She's very good at sneaking into computer records."

"You can't go hacking into the banks' records, sugar." He grinned. "I think they put you in jail for that."

"First they have to find out," she reminded him.

"I didn't know I was marrying a potential felon," Griff joked. He leaned over and kissed her.

She ran her tongue over his lips, tasting the special blend of ham, potato salad, and the special essence that was Griff. She'd already concluded kissing him was one of the most pleasurable experiences of her life.

They had just finished bagging their trash when the real estate agent drove up. He handed Griffin a folder with all the information on the property then suggested they walk at least part of it. When they reached the crest of the hill, Cassie drew in her breath in awe and amazement. The ground sloped away to a creek below, and everywhere she looked, the area was guarded by old oak trees and sycamore. Wildflowers grew in abundant profusion, coloring the landscape with their brilliant reds and blues and yellows.

She reached for Griff's hand and squeezed it, hard. His answering pressure told her he knew what she wanted and he did, too. In another hour, they were done, signing a contract to purchase and giving the agent a deposit check for escrow. They were filled with excitement and yes, optimism on the ride home.

"Our very own piece of property," Cassie crowed. "We need to start thinking about plans and getting an architect."

"In a hurry, are we, darlin?" He smiled at her.

"You bet. I feel like we're in a different world out here."

"We are. And a lot closer to Austin than San Antonio, so even our city trips will be different."

"Oh, Griff." She hugged his arm. "I'm having a hard time believing our good luck."

That same luck continued to hold because, as they neared Stoneham, Cassie's cell phone rang.

"Carol Markham," she told him as she glanced at the Caller ID.

"Cassie, you won't believe this," the woman gushed. "I just have to pat myself on the back."

She rolled her eyes. "What is it, Carol?"

"We have a buyer. And almost the full price you want." She giggled. "Am I good or what!"

"Yes, Carol. You're terrific." She forced herself to sound enthusiastic. In truth, she was very happy. She would be more than glad to at last be rid of the house that carried so much pain and unhappiness.

"I've got a signed agreement to purchase," Carol continued, "and a good faith check. If you're okay with this, I'd like to drop by tonight so I can get your signature and we can proceed to closing."

"That's fine. I'm staying at Griff's, so why don't you come by there?" She should have been used to the long silences she always received any time she paired herself with Griffin.

"I see. Well. All right, if that's what you want. Is seven okay?"

Cassie stifled a laugh. "Yes, that'll be fine." She disconnected the call and let the laugh bubble out. "We won't have to worry if someone hasn't heard the news anymore. Oh Lordy, Griff, I'd give a month's pay to have seen her face."

"Tonight should be interesting, sugar. Very interesting." He squeezed her hand. "Now, if we can just find that safety deposit box, we'll be in clover."

Chapter Thirty-Eight

When Carol walked into Griff's house that night, the air was thick with tension. Cassie refused to let him hide in another room, reminding him that, after all, it was his home. Carol pointedly ignored him while they all sat at the kitchen table, but it was hard for her not to notice the engagement ring, which Cassie took every opportunity to flash.

"Yes," Cassie said, noticing Carol's avid glances, "Griffin and I are getting married. Just as soon as we can."

Carol's gaze slid from one to the other. "I see. Isn't that interesting."

Cassie wished she'd had a camera to take a picture of the woman's face at that moment. The careful mask disintegrated, and her eyes bulged. Her mouth looked like that of a gaping fish. With visible effort, she pulled herself together and gathered up her materials. At last, everything was signed. Carol handed a copy of the agreement to Cassie and put everything else back into her folder.

"The buyers are a very nice couple," she said. "Older. Retired. They want to close and take possession in three weeks, if possible. Is that going to be a problem for you?"

Cassie shook her head. "My biggest problem is going to be getting rid of the furniture. Otherwise, I'm okay."

"I'm guessing you'll have a place to stay." It was a statement, not a question, and tinged with more than a little sarcasm.

"Yes, that's not a problem." Cassie stood and moved closer to Griff.

"I guess you know what you're doing, but if you ask me, you're making a huge mistake."

"Then I guess it's a good thing I didn't ask you." Cassie's voice was sweeter than sugar. "Thanks for coming by. Just let me know when the closing is."

Carol ran from the house.

Griff and Cassie looked at each other and burst out laughing.

"Well," he said, "you're right. We won't have to worry about telling anyone our news."

"Good." She hugged him. "I'd put it on the front page of the paper if they'd take my ad."

"If you think people bothered you before," Griff warned, "just wait until tomorrow."

"By the time church is over, it will be better than an ad," she agreed.

She was right. They had just finished a late breakfast before they heard a car in the driveway followed by the ring of the doorbell.

"Here it comes," Griff told her.

"I'm ready for them, and then some."

She opened the door to the McLeod triad—Neil, Cyrus, and Leslie.

"Wow," she said. "The big guns, huh? To what do I owe the pleasure?"

"Hello, Cassie." Leslie stepped forward, the picture of poise and elegance. "We thought we'd stop by after church. May we come in for just a minute?"

"I think you should ask Griffin. This is his house, after all."

Three pairs of icy eyes swept over Griff who stood behind Cassie, his hands on her shoulders in a protective gesture.

"By all means," he drawled. "Welcome to my home."

They trooped with military precision into the living room, arranging themselves on the furniture.

"We're a little busy," Cassie told them, "so I hope this won't take too long. I'm right in assuming this isn't just a nice Welcome Wagon visit?"

It appeared Leslie was taking the lead today. "Cassie, you know how fond we all are of you, and how fond we were of your parents," she began.

"No, Leslie. Tell me. I don't seem to remember being invited to any of your parties. Diane, either. And when did your parents ever socialize with mine?"

"I think you're being deliberately obtuse," she snapped. "You have to know that everyone has your best interests at heart. We're concerned about what's happening to you. We may not have been close friends, but that doesn't mean Neil and I aren't very concerned about what you're doing."

"After yesterday's phone calls and Carol's visit, I wondered how long it would take for you all to show up. If you're here to ask me if the rumors are true and I'm going to marry Griffin Hunter, the answer is yes." She flashed her ring at them. "It's official."

"Now listen, Cassie," Cyrus began.

Cassie went on as smoothly as if no one had spoken. "If you want to know if I'm going to quit poking into Diane's death, or my father's so-called suicide, the answer is no. You can save yourselves any more visits and phone calls. My answers won't change. Does that about cover it?"

Cyrus scowled. "Funny. I don't remember you as being this headstrong."

"I think determined is more like it," she told him. "I'd sure like to know why everyone is so hell bent on sweeping Diane's murder under the rug. Don't you want to find the real killer?" She studied each face in turn. "Isn't anyone worried it could happen again?"

Neil's mouth was set in an angry line. "No, I don't think it will happen again. Unless it happens to you."

White heat consumed her, a rage so great she wasn't sure she could control it. "Do you want to explain that to me?"

"You may be blind, Cassie, but I think we all know who's the culprit here." He glanced at Griff. "It's just a matter of proving it. But if you want to put yourself in harm's way, I guess that's your choice."

She clenched her fists so tight her nails dug into her palms. Behind her, she felt the tension radiating from Griff's body like a solid mass. "You come into a man's home and insult him that way? Who the hell do you think you are? And why, after all these years, are any of you interested in the Fitzgerald family?"

Cyrus rose and took a step forward, restraining Neil with a hand on his arm. "Cassie, you were always the good girl in your family. The one with bright promise. You've made a good life for yourself. Why are you throwing it away and putting yourself in jeopardy?"

"Everyone's just concerned for you, Cassie," Neil added.

Cassie snorted. "Yeah, right. If you're that concerned, you can help me get at the real truth here."

"Don't you see, Cassie?" All eyes turned to Leslie. "All you're doing is bringing up unpleasant memories that everyone would just as soon forget. Poor Diane's murder was the single violent crime in Stoneham for fifty years."

"And my father's. Let's not forget about him."

"Your father's death was ruled a suicide, and that's what it was."

Cyrus used his stern legal manner. He gave her a definite look of disapproval. "Everyone knew how depressed he was. If you'd been here, you would have known that, too."

"We'd all be a lot better," Neil said to Griff, "if you'd get your hooks out of this girl. Own up to Diane's death and stop filling Cassie's head with crazy ideas."

"Well," he drawled, "I think that's up to Cassie."

She went to stand next to him, purposely wrapping her arms around him and moving as close to him as she could. The trio rose as one.

"You're making a big mistake, Cassie." This from Cyrus. It seemed they each had specific lines in this little drama. "You don't know this man as well as you think you do."

"Maybe not, but I'm having a lot of fun getting to know him better." She smiled up at Griffin.

The McLeods filed toward the door.

Leslie turned before they left. "I thought we could give you some good advice but it seems you're not interested. When you get hurt, don't come crying to any of us. Your house has already been broken into. Who knows what could happen next."

"Is that a threat?" Griffin's voice was deceptively calm.

"Of course not." Leslie glared at him as if she smelled something bad. "We just don't want any harm to come to Cassie. I'd say you're the one threat she has to worry about."

"By the way, Neil," Cassie called out. "Did you forget to tell me about the safety deposit box my folks had at the bank?"

They all stopped dead.

Neil turned in slow motion to face her. "I have no idea what you're talking about."

"You know, a box in the bank for important papers? I believe my folks had one. Did you deliberately leave out that little piece of information?"

"You must be mistaken," he said, his body rigid. "I gave you everything of theirs I had. You should stop making crazy accusations."

"Well, you can pass the word that I'm going to keep stirring the pot until I get the answers I want. The sooner I get them, the faster I'll be out of everyone's hair." She had to restrain herself from slamming the door as they filed out.

They got into Neil's car and backed out of the driveway. She held onto her temper by a slender thread.

Griff sensed it and came to stand behind her, his hands resting on her shoulders. "Let it go, sugar. They have their own agenda, and nothing you say will change it."

"Don't you think it's very interesting that every time I get a little closer or a little more aggressive, someone jumps all over me about it? My telephone calls the other day must have stirred up more of a hornet's nest than I thought."

"You might have gotten a little more than you bargained for," he warned. "I don't trust any of these people. Someone out there is dangerous. I've about decided that whoever Diane's mysterious lover was, a lot of people know about it and aren't anxious for it to come out. And I'm not so sure she wasn't involved with more men than him."

"Oh?" She raised an eyebrow at him. "What do you mean?"

"Money meant everything to Diane." Bitterness laced his words. "It was a huge shock to her when she discovered the money I threw around was all I had. There wasn't some big pot of gold hidden away.

I wouldn't be surprised if she was pushing more than one person. I'd sure like to find proof of that."

"Me, too." She pressed herself against his chest. "Do you really think someone will try to hurt me?"

"I hope not, but we're getting into some murky waters here. Malicious mischief may be more their style at the moment, though." He tucked a finger beneath her chin and tilted up her face. "You should call Carol Markham and get her to put a *Sold* sign out today. You don't want any more damage to that house. They might leave it alone if they know it's sold. "

"On the other hand," she countered, "if someone's in a real panic, they might want to break in to search it one more time."

"I still think the sign's a good idea, but we'll keep an eye on the house. Asking Dangler to watch it is like spitting in the wind."

"Okay." She let go of him with great reluctance and moved toward the kitchen. "I'll call Carol right now."

They spent the rest of the afternoon going over the information on the nursery and preparing a counteroffer. She realized Griff had done his homework with great thoroughness. He had a thick file of information from other nurseries he'd talked to, so they had some idea of where to start.

"I'll call the guy in the morning," he told her when they finished, stacking everything together. "I think what we're offering is a fair price and close to what he's asking."

Cassie poured herself a glass of iced tea and sat at the kitchen table with a pad of paper, trying to make a list of anyone Diane might have been involved with. She threw the pen down, shoved the pad away from her, and looked at Griffin. "This is impossible."

"No, just difficult. But I have a feeling we're getting close, so don't give up now."

Chapter Thirty-Nine

Monday, Cassie drove to the Bank of America office and met with the manager. She presented her probate papers, explained what she was looking for, and the manager scrolled through her computer.

"I don't see a box here for either your mother or father," she said. "Are you sure they'd have come here? I don't believe this is where they did their banking."

"For this, I think they'd have wanted some anonymity," Cassie explained. "Can you see if there's a box under Diane Fitzgerald or Diane Hunter?"

Again Janet searched her database, and again she came up empty.

"Thanks, anyway." She tried to hide her disappointment."

"Hold on a second," Janet said. "Let me go into the main data base and see if there's one at another branch."

Cassie sat, crossing her fingers while the woman's computer did its thing.

"All right, Miss Fitzgerald." Janet looked up at her. "I have a box listed for a Diane Hunter at a branch in San Antonio. Is that where she's living now?"

Cassie was shocked. *San Antonio?* "My sister died six years ago! I don't understand. Who would even be paying for it now? Doesn't it have to be paid for each year?"

"Yes, but according to my records, when Mrs. Hunter rented the box, she paid for ten years in advance."

Planning. Covering her bases.

She left the bank in a daze then sat in her car with the air conditioner on and called Griff on his cell phone.

"Hunter," he answered.

"It's me. You'll never believe what I found out. Can you talk?"

"Hold on a sec."

She heard a door slam and assumed he had climbed into his truck.

"That's better. I can crank up the A/C for a minute and have some privacy. What's up, sugar?"

She gave him all the details of her meeting with the bank manager. "I'm stunned, but not as much as I thought I'd be."

"But that's too weird," he said. "Why did she pick that location? And pay for so many years in advance?"

"I'd say she wanted it to be as far away from Stoneham as possible. She picked a place where it would be lost in the records of a big bank but close enough for her to access when she wanted. As to paying for it, I think she wanted to hedge her bets. Life was pretty unstable for Diane."

"Tell me about it." He snorted. "So, what can we do next? You said they wouldn't give you access to the box, right?"

"Yes, but you could get into it. You were her husband. I think all you'd need is a copy of the marriage license and her death certificate."

"All right." He thought a minute. "We'll do it tomorrow afternoon. Can you call and find out how late they're open?"

"Sure, but what about your jobs tomorrow? You can't keep blowing people off."

"I'll just start earlier than usual. Anyway, don't worry about me. These people may hate my guts, but, right now, I'm the only game in town. Besides, I'm hoping we won't have to worry about this much longer."

"I just don't want you to have any more hassles than you've already got."

He laughed. "Honey, that's my middle name. I'll see you later at home."

The rest of the day brought them good news, more than enough to counterbalance the moments of dread that had hovered over them. The owner of the land accepted their offer and wanted to close as soon as possible. The nursery owner was happy with Griff's price and asked when he could come over to sign papers and bring a deposit check. And Carol called with a firm closing date for the house.

"This is all good luck." Cassie hugged Griff when he got home. "Everything's going to work out the way we want. I just know it. I feel so sure we'll find what we're looking for in that deposit box."

"I told the guy in Marble Falls we'd be able to drive over tomorrow evening," he told her. "Does that work out for us?"

"Sure. The bank's open until five. If we leave here at four, we can get there before closing. If we're lucky we can get to open the box with no trouble. That way we can be in Marble Hills before eight."

"All right. Can you call the real estate agent and set up a date to close on the land? Maybe we can sign the final papers for the nursery then, too."

"No problem," she assured him. "All I'm doing tomorrow is getting rid of those boxes of clothes."

"Okay. I'll be home early enough to shower and change."

Cassie was surprised at how easy it was to run through her tasks the next day. *Too bad every day isn't this simple*, she mused. Family Services was happy to get the clothes and anything else she wanted to give them. A used furniture dealer in Kerrville said he'd come by

Thursday to see what she had, and, if it suited him, he'd take everything off her hands.

Confirming a closing date on the land was the last thing she did before heading off to shower and change and wait for Griff. She sat in the kitchen, reading the police and autopsy reports one more time on both Diane and her father, when he came in the back door.

"I thought you'd have those memorized by now." He kissed the top of her head. "You know, sometimes I have to pinch myself to be sure everything is real. How could someone whose life has been so messed up have caught the brass ring?"

"It was always there waiting for us." She smiled up at him. "We just had to reach for it."

He chuckled. "Before long, we'll even be like normal people, owning a business, building a new house, starting a new life together." He brushed light stands of hair back from her hair. "I wake up sometimes in the middle of the night in a sweat, wondering if I dreamed it all. Then I touch you, and I know it's all real."

"It's real alright." She rested her head against his chest for a moment. "If only I didn't keep thinking we're missing something. My reporter's nose is twitching."

"It'll come to you." He set her away from his sweaty body. "Give me ten and I'll be ready."

They were silent, driving into the city, both expectant at what they might find, both worried about the process of opening the box. But that, too, followed the rest of the day, and everything went more with greater ease than they could have hoped. Griff's documents were examined and copied along with his personal ID. He pulled out the key, and in short order they were in a small room with the box sitting on the table between them.

Cassie and Griff stared at each other, neither of them making a move.

"You open it," she said. "You were her husband."

"Yeah, right." He reached for the box and flipped open the lid.

They both stared.

In one side of the box were neat stacks of hundred dollar bills, each with a rubber band around it. Next to the money sat a soft velvet pouch. Griff opened it, and a bracelet studded with precious gems fell out into his hands. He looked at Cassie, bewildered.

"Blackmail," she murmured. "It has to be."

Last, tucked in the other corner of the box, a small red-leather book that couldn't be anything but a diary.

"You take it," Griff said. "I don't know if I can stand to open it."

Cassie lifted it out with trembling hands. Holding her breath, she thumbed the lock and opened the book. Almost every page was filled with writing that she recognized as Diane's. Would they find the answers to their questions at last?

She pushed the book toward Griffin. "You should read this."

He shook his head. "I don't think I can. In fact, I don't think I can sit here another minute. Dump all that in your purse and let's get out of here. I feel like I'm choking."

Once they were on the way to Marble Hills, they relaxed a little.

"I can't read that book." Griff gritted his teeth. "I know it probably has clues in it, but I'm asking you to be the one to do it. When Diane told me about the baby, I was willing to make an effort to shape up. That bitch had no intention of being straight with me. She must have been on the prowl before the ink was dry on the marriage license." There was more anger than pain in his voice.

Cassie didn't ever remember hearing him sound like this. "Don't let her keep reaching for you from the grave. We'll get the answers and be done with it. We have a life together now. Don't let her ruin that, too."

The muscles in his jaw worked as he tried to calm himself. After a moment, he reached over and took one of her hands. "I love you, Cassie. That's the one good thing that's come out of this."

She let out the breath she didn't even know she'd been holding. "Then everything else is a piece of cake." She squeezed his hand then brought it to her lips and kissed his fingers. "Let's go buy a business. When we get home, I'll look through the diary. Right now, let's just concentrate on us."

Chapter Forty

The whole time they were at the nursery, signing papers, writing checks, making arrangements, the diary was a hot coal in her purse. Cassie could almost feel its heat. Not to mention the money, shoved into an envelope the bank manager had provided. What in God's name would she do with it? She was thankful when, at last, they were back in the truck and headed for Stoneham.

Griff reached over and gave her hand one of his reassuring squeezes. "Even with all the distractions, we did good, honey."

"Did we?"

"You bet. We got him down to an acceptable price, and we've got ninety days before we have to close and take possession."

"Can we do that?" she asked. "I mean, I'll be done with my house in another week, but you still have yours to get rid of, not to mention your business. Where will we live while we're building our new house?"

"Don't sweat it. I'm putting an ad in the paper tomorrow for the landscaping service, and I guess I'll go ahead and get Carol to list my house. Maybe we'll get lucky there, too."

"But where will we live?" she repeated.

"We'll rent. The guy in the nursery said there are several small houses in town that are available. Tomorrow, you can call the agent handling the land and get him to e-mail you some listings to look at."

"I can't say I'll be sorry to see the last of Stoneham," she said with resentment. "Good riddance."

"Are you hungry?" he asked, when they were finally home. "We haven't eaten at all."

"Yes, but I want to look at this diary. I can't wait any longer."

"Then I'll make sandwiches while you read, okay? You can tell me what I need to know."

When they entered Griff's house, she took the book into the living room, kicked off her shoes, and curled up on the couch, the diary in her hands. She looked at the cover for a long time, knowing the minute she opened it there'd be no turning back. At last, she released the catch and turned to the beginning.

The first several pages yielded nothing, just musings about Griff, about parties, words about nothing in particular. She sat up when she came to another page.

No one can know. It has to be our secret, but I don't care. The secrecy is part of the fun. And I know I can get him to buy me presents. He just wants me to keep my mouth shut.

The page was dated three months before Griff and Diane's wedding. So, this was where it began. No name yet, but it was the first indication of the dangerous game Diane was about to play.

The next entry was dated a week later.

He certainly knows more than the guys I've been hanging out with. I guess sex is all about what you know after all. Too bad I can't teach some of this stuff to Griffin or any of the other guys, but they'd wonder how I learned everything all of a sudden. Oh, well. I guess once a week will hold me. For now.

A week later, she wrote more.

I told him I love the bracelet. He gave me cash, too, lots of it, to buy stuff to wear for him. Also, I think he knows if he gives me money, I'll keep my mouth shut. He doesn't have to worry. I don't want to upset his applecart or mine.

The next few pages were more of the same, then a new entry.

If it's good with one, it's great with two. Little did I know there were so many frustrated men in this tiny town. Their wives must sleep in an icebox. Although my Cookie has worse problems than that. But he's a nice addition to my collection. He doesn't mind paying, either.

Cassie felt as if a lead weight had dropped into her body and taken up residence, her stomach roiling with nausea. She knew her sister had been wild, but this was beyond even her imaginings.

"Find anything yet?" Griff carried in a tray with two drinks and a plate of sandwiches, setting it on the coffee table.

She looked at him, trying to find the words to describe what she was reading.

His face took on a closed look. "That bad, huh?"

"Griffin, I—"

"Never mind." He shook his head. "That's why I wanted you to read it. Here. Eat something."

"I can't." She waved the food away. "I don't think I can swallow anything."

"Cassie, you are not responsible for what she did. You have to eat or you'll be sick for sure. Come on." He handed her half a sandwich on a napkin, which she took reluctantly. "That's right. Now chew and swallow."

In spite of herself, she had to smile, and she forced herself to take a bite. She scanned through a few more pages of the diary then stopped on another page where the words leaped out at her.

This is getting harder than I thought. I can't ditch the crowd too many nights a week or they'll start asking questions, but now I have three wonderful admirers who can't wait to give me presents and money. Well, a smart person like me will just have to figure it out.

She looked up at Griff, hating the things she would have to tell him. *Well, just blurt it out.* "She was seeing three men on the side, three no doubt married men, who gave her gifts and money. Diane wasn't much better than a prostitute."

"Ask me if I'm surprised," he growled.

Cassie hated the look of pain on his face. He hadn't loved Diane, but he had tried to do the right thing for her. She had repaid him with her self-destructive behavior. Without much thought Cassie kept turning the pages, hoping for a clue to a name. She stopped, however, when she came to a page that had the words *The baby* at the top, underlined.

I will not have an abortion. I've heard too many scary stories. No, I'll find someone to marry me, have it, then go back to the way things were. But they're all going to pay for this mistake, you can bet on it. Or I'll set this town on its ear.

There was a lot more of the same, including the notes on her marriage to Griffin. Cassie hurried over them, not wanting to read the mean things her sister had written. Then, a week before her death, an entry was written with anger.

None of them want to take responsibility. Fine. Then I'll make them all pay. I told them each to meet me next week at our usual time and place or they'll see their names on the front page of the paper. If I have to have this kid, I want money to hightail it away from here when it's done. Griffin says he always wanted a family. Well, now he can have one.

Underneath the entry was a string of letters that at first glance made no sense at all to Cassie. She needed to figure out what they meant, but, for a moment, she needed to close the book. She felt as if she'd been wading through slime and would never be clean.

Griff stared at her, questions burning in his eyes, his face set in grim lines. "Well?"

"All right." She sat up and took a swallow of her drink. "Here's the bare outline. Diane was blackmailing three men. Any one of them could have killed her. She never identified which one actually fathered the baby, but she was heading for a showdown with all of them." She opened the book again to the last entry. "Maybe if I could figure out what all these letters mean, we'd know who she was meeting."

She held the book so he could see the page, but he sat like a statue, eyes averted, not saying a word. She got up and sat on his lap, curling her arms around him and laying her head in his shoulder.

"Think of this as an abstract puzzle," she told him. "The one thing that's real is us. We've put a down payment on our dreams, Griff.

Let's not lose sight of that."

"You're right." He held her against him, arms banded tight around her. They stood like that for long moments before took a deep breath and released it. "But the sooner we find the answers to this, the sooner we can close the book on Diane and this town altogether."

"Meanwhile, let's get some sleep." She cuddled against him. "We can tackle this tomorrow."

But as tired and emotionally spent as they were, tonight the need to lose themselves in each other was stronger than ever. They made such gentle love Cassie thought her heart would burst from the sensations she felt. She had not believed Griff could be such a needy lover in a quiet way, his emotions greater than his physical needs.

He suckled her breasts, pulling at her nipples with his mouth until they throbbed from his touch. His teeth nipped at the underside of her breasts then his tongue soothed them, while his warm hands massaged their fullness. Then he did it again. And again, until she thought she would come just from his attention to her breasts.

He licked every inch of her soft abdomen, teasing her navel with the tip of his tongue until every nerve was inflamed. With a gentle touch he tugged at her pubic curls with his teeth before opening her legs wide. With the same easy touch, so light it sent shivers through her, he slid his tongue from her clit down the length of her slit to the very soft, very tender, very sensitive flesh just below her opening. Searing heat flashed through her, every nerve sizzling.

"I could taste you forever," he told her, his words ramping up the heat even more.

He gripped her knees and pressed them back toward her chest, opening her wide for whatever he chose to do. She'd learned it was his favorite position, except when he had her on her hands and knees.

With his fingers inside her, he sucked her entire clit into his mouth and Cassie almost levitated off the bed.

"Get ready, darlin'," he said in low tones. "My fingers are good and soaked with your cream now, so this will feel so very good. Remember how good it is?"

He slid one then two into the opening between the cheeks of her buttocks, his mouth still fastened on the swollen bud of her sex, his arm holding her in place while she bucked under his touch. He stroked in and out of her hot rectum, touching every sensitive place inside, driving her higher and higher. But he never allowed her to peak. Every time she neared the crest, he backed off, soothed her then started again.

Then there was no talking, only touching and feeling.

At the moment she was ready to scream with frustration, he rolled over onto his back, took her hand, and placed it on his thick erection.

Giving him the same careful attention, Cassie licked the length of his cock until it was wet with her saliva, probing the tip of the soft head with her tongue until he begged her to stop. She stroked her hand up and down his shaft while her other hand caressed the heavy sac between his legs.

When she felt his balls tighten, she moved over and straddled him. Taking his shaft in her hand, she positioned it at her vaginal entrance then slid down so he was completely inside her.

Tonight, she set the rhythm, moving in the slow cadence he had set, not wanting to rush, feeling him stroke every inch of her sex he could reach. Her fingers found his flat, hard nipples and rasped them with her nails until he cried out. And then, almost in slow motion, a shuddering orgasm rolled over them. Cassie could feel Griff's body shaking in tempo with hers as they were caught up in wave after wave of sexual ecstasy.

Finally, finally it ebbed and abated, leaving them spent and exhausted.

Cassie leaned forward and rested her head on Griffin's chest. His heartbeat thudded in time with hers. As much as he'd teased her tonight, plundered her, sent flames of scorching passion through her body, there was none of the usual frenzy or intensity. With every touch tonight, he was telling her what an important part of his life she was.

She wanted to weep with the love she felt for him. She kissed his warm lips then rested her palm on his cheek and slept.

***

Carol Markham called in the morning to tell Cassie she had a client with rental properties who would take all her furniture if she made him a good price.

"Get whatever you can," she said. "I just want to be rid of it."

"You know I'll bargain well for you," Carol promised.

Cassie could almost see the other woman setting her shoulders back. "Of course. Thank you." It would save hassling with the man from Kerrville and leave one less thing for her to attend to.

When she was finished, Griff took the phone and Cassie listened while he explained he wanted to list his place, also. The conversation was brief. After he hung up, he told Cassie, "She had a hard time concealing her surprise. I'm guessing she assumed like everyone else will that we'd be living here."

"Not anywhere in this town," she said with emphasis. "So, when is she coming by with a listing agreement?"

"Maybe later today but she'll call my cell to let me know." His mouth curled in a wry grin. "I think the gossip line will be heating up again in a very short time. Think how much excitement we've brought into their lives."

Cassie giggled. "Think how bored they'll be when we move away from here."

She called the real estate agent in Marble Hills to inquire about rentals. Then Griff placed an ad in the Stoneham newspaper as well as San Antonio and Austin to sell his business. Then they sat for a minute and looked at each other.

"We're really doing it," he said at last.

"Yes, we are." Cassie smiled. "Any second thoughts?"

"You're kidding, right? I'm kicking myself because I didn't come looking for you a long time ago."

"Tonight, we need to take a good look at what we want from your house and start packing," she pointed out. "I know we've got some time, but maybe we'll get lucky and your house will sell as fast as mine did."

Carol came by late in the afternoon, trying to balance her distaste for Griff with her greed for a commission. She kept up a running chatter about nothing in particular while she took inventory of the rooms and the yard. The tension in the air was like thick wet cotton. Her gaze kept straying to the ring on Cassie's finger. The expression on Carol's face said plainly she wanted to ask a million questions, but couldn't figure out a way to do it gracefully.

Griff conducted his business with her then he and Cassie sat back and waited for her to leave.

"Well, I'll get a photographer out to take pictures and this listing in the computer as fast as I can," she told them, fussing with the signed contracts. "I'll call as soon as I get a nibble."

"Thank you." He opened the door and ushered her out onto the porch.

"Bye, then."

"Good-bye." Griff smiled as Carol hustled to her car then he turned to Cassie. "She had her cell phone out of her purse before she even cranked the ignition. Can't wait to spread the word, I'd say."

"Let's order a pizza and go to sleep," Cassie said. "You've got a lot of work to make up tomorrow. You've got to start telling your clients what you're doing. My morning project is going to be trying to solve the puzzle of the diary."

Good luck with that, she thought.

Chapter Forty-One

In the morning, Cassie stopped by the police station to turn over the money and jewelry from the safety deposit box to Dangler as evidence of Diane's blackmail. The one request she made was after the case was settled it be used for some community purpose. The chief nodded, his eyes troubled. When he took the envelope from her, he touched it as if it burned his fingers. In a way, it was possible it did.

"Maybe this will give you the urge to open the case again," Cassie taunted. "That money didn't come from Griff, and you know it."

"We'll see," was all Dangler said, but he looked uncomfortable.

She picked up a few things at the grocery store then went home and made herself a sandwich. Then, with her laptop booted up, she opened the diary. She tried every type of code she could think of, but nothing seemed to work. By the time Griffin came home, her head was throbbing and she felt physically ill.

"Bad day, sugar?" He dropped a kiss on her lips.

"Frustrating. I'm not getting anywhere." She threw down her pencil. "Go take your shower. I bought some thick steaks today for you to grill while I throw a salad together."

He gave her another quick kiss. "Sounds good to me. Give me ten."

She splashed cold water on her face at the kitchen sink then took two bottles of beer from the refrigerator. She opened them and drank from one as she looked at the diary again. At the moment, she was about to close it and toss it down again, something clicked in her brain. She opened a clean document on her laptop and constructed an alpha code. By the time Griff came downstairs, she was both excited and dismayed.

"Got something?" he asked.

"Yes." She took another swallow of beer. "I think I know who the three men were that Diane was sleeping with and blackmailing. And it isn't pretty." She turned the laptop so he could see the screen. "I don't know why I didn't remember this before. Diane and I made this up as kids to write notes to each other our parents couldn't read."

"Yeah?" He cocked an eyebrow. "How does it work?"

"Much too easy. We split the alphabet, then substituted letters. See? A equals N, B equals O, and so on. I used that to decipher the three lines at the end of the diary." She bit her bottom lip. "Look what I came up with."

They both stared at the names. In the end, the answer to the riddle had been simple, staring them in the face if they had just looked beneath the surface of the town.

"This isn't proof, though." Her shoulders slumped in discouragement. "There's nothing in here to identify them except what I've figured out. If I took it to Dangler or any cop, they'd laugh in my face. We need to set some kind of trap for them."

Griff shook his head. "I am not letting you put yourself in any kind of danger. It isn't worth it."

"But we have to do something," she protested. "I refuse to let these people get away with this. No way will I let this town continue to lay two murders at your doorstep."

"Cassie, they've already got blood on their hands," he reminded her. "A little more won't make a difference. I say we go to Dangler."

She glared at him. "You don't think he knows this already and has been covering up for them?"

"I think, when we show him the diary, he'll cave."

She wished she had as much confidence as Griff did. Of course, she wasn't anxious to put herself in a dangerous situation, either. "Fine. I guess that's the smartest thing to do. But we can't wait to do it."

"Just until the morning, okay?" He stroked her cheek with the backs of his fingers, and she leaned her head into them.

"Okay. I guess."

"No one's going to do anything tonight, anyway."

Cassie nodded and went to take out the stuff for dinner.

Later, in bed with Griff sleeping beside her, she thought again of the men involved. She would never have imagined any of them being part of something this sordid. But then she thought, did you ever know all about anyone or know what they would do under certain circumstances?

At last she fell asleep, but she dreamt of a faceless man pushing her over a cliff, his hollow laugh echoing in her head.

***

"You knew about this all the time, didn't you?" Cassie stood in front of Barry Dangler's desk, her tone accusing, her face tight with anger.

Beside her, Griff's body was rigid with tension.

"Cassie, I —"

"You're the police chief, for God's sake," Griffin exploded. "You would have been just as happy to see me rot in jail for a crime someone else committed. What kind of man are you, anyway?"

"Try to understand," he pleaded, his face stamped with defeat, his shoulders slumped, his body posture one of resignation. "These men are my friends. My backers. They put me in this office."

"So, that gives you the right to cover up a murder?" Cassie wanted to spit fire.

Dangler held out his hands, palms up. "An apology is useless now. What do you want me to do?"

"I want to set a trap for them," she proposed, "and I want you to catch them."

He shook his head. "Too dangerous. Besides, it's police business."

"Oh, right." She slammed her purse down on her desk. "I don't think that excuse will fly. There hasn't been much police business conducted on this case until now. Why ruin a good thing, right?"

Dangler lowered his gaze but not before she could see they were filled with shame. "I deserve whatever you say, Cassie. I just...I guess none of us thought you'd ever come back here. Or if you did, that you'd even care about what happened."

"I've wasted six years of my life because of this mess and what Diane and all of you did." She pounded her fist on the desk. "I'd like to see it finished. Over and done with. Either you do this with us, or I'll go to the media with my speculations. You'd be amazed at the damage innuendo can do."

He threw up his hands. "All right. What choice do I have? Tell me your plan."

***

I have the diary, and I know everything. I want something out of this, or the police will have it. I will contact you with further details. Be ready.

That was the first message she sent to three fax machines that afternoon. Dangler had agreed that was the best method of contacting all the men. While Griff followed his usual routine, Cassie drove into San Antonio and used fax machines at three different office supply stores. Then she found three more to send the second message. That way, no one could pinpoint a single source for them.

From the moment she sent the last fax, she was tense and anxious. Driving home, she convinced herself all over again this was a good plan, but there was real danger involved with it. She glanced at her watch. Right about now, they should all be sweating over their faxes. It would be interesting to know if they were all involved, or just one or two of them. And did they each know about the others?

Diane, you played too close to the fire, and now other people are getting burned. How could you do this?

She would have given a lot to know how fast all the men got in contact with each other and what they had to say. She hoped they were plenty scared and damned unhappy. Their perfect lives were about to unravel, and she was glad to be the one pulling the strings.

She looked at her watch for perhaps the tenth time. It would be hours before Griff came home. She needed to find something to occupy herself or she'd go crazy.

Chapter Forty-Two

"Cassie?" Griff dropped his keys in the dish on the hall table. "You here, baby?"

She ran from the kitchen and launched herself into his arms. She locked her hands behind his head as if she'd never let go and pulled his face down to hers.

"It's nice to be missed." He grinned when they broke the kiss. "Unfortunately, I don't think this has to do with my masculine charms. Right?"

She leaned her head against his chest, her arms still wrapped around him.

"Honey?" He tilted her face up to him. She was trembling, and her heart beat hard against his chest. "What is it? Did something happen? Damn. I knew this was a bad idea. I never should have let you talk me into it."

"No, nothing happened." She stood on tiptoe to kiss him again. "Just my nerves, is all."

"Did you see anyone today? Did someone do something?"

"No. Nothing like that." She shook her head. "I stayed inside all day. I was afraid I'd run into one of them and give myself away."

"All right. Come on. Let's go in the kitchen and get something cold to drink. Do we have any beer left?"

She nodded.

"Good. I think you could use something to settle your nerves." He insisted she come out on the patio with him after he'd opened the bottles. "What could be more natural? We do it almost every evening.

If you hide in the house, they'll know something's up."

"You're right. I just...I'm glad you're home."

He reached across the space between them and took her hand in his, linking their fingers together and planting gentle kisses. "I've done a lot of thinking about this today, Cassie. I have to say again I'm not real crazy about putting you in any kind of danger. I don't think I could handle it if anything happened to you."

"Chief Dangler said if they agree to the meet, he'll be there with plenty of backup. And you'll be there. I'll be fine."

"You sent the second fax written just as we agreed?"

"I did." She nodded and recited, "Tonight. In the park where Diane died. One hundred thousand dollars and the diary is yours. Otherwise, I go to the police."

"Okay." He took another swallow of beer, trying to calm his nerves. If anything happened to her....

No. He wouldn't even think that way. She'd be safe. He'd do whatever it took to make sure of that.

***

Barry Dangler arrived at Griff's not too long after dark, with electronic equipment and his techie.

"I'm going out in the back, so we can test this thing and see if it works." He made sure his earpiece was set while his officer who handled most of their technical stuff set up the wireless microphone kit. "Count to twenty then say something."

Cassie finished buttoning her blouse, her hands trembling just a little. This had to work.

Griff slid one arm around her waist, his touch reassuring. "You'll be well covered," he reminded her. "I don't think any of these guys will do anything. I think they've had their fill of killing, but we still need to be careful. Desperation does funny things to people."

The most interesting part of the preparation, as far as Cassie was concerned, had been the noticeable decrease in hostility on Dangler's part toward Griff. The chief wasn't cutting him any slack, but something in his attitude had changed. A new Griffin had emerged when the chief wasn't looking, one they could see the other man was having trouble reconciling with the bad boy image.

"Go ahead and try it now, Miss Fitzgerald," the young deputy said.

"All right." She cleared her throat. "Can you hear me, Chief?"

"Loud and clear, Cassie." He came back into the house. "Okay, then. I'd say we're ready to go."

"I still think I should be right there with you," Griff said.

She could see from his body language he wasn't too keen on leaving her by herself, even though he'd agreed to the plan.

"We've already discussed this," she reminded him. "This won't work unless they see just me. Besides, you'll be just a few feet away behind the restrooms with everyone else."

It was obvious he still didn't like it, but he was just as obvious he was through arguing. Ignoring the presence of everyone else in the room, he pulled her close and kissed her hard and deep. "That's for luck," he whispered. "You get the rest of it later." He hugged her then let her go. "All right, Chief. Let's do it."

They all left and got into the two cars in the driveway. They would arrive at the park far enough in advance not to be observed. She checked her watch. One more hour. She could do this. She could confront them, and it would all be over. When she and Griffin left town, they'd have nothing they needed to look back on.

***

From where she waited, Cassie could see the three men approach. They did their best to keep out of the halos thrown by the park lights as they trudged into the park's interior. She could hear the faint sound of their voices, loud enough that she could make out what they were saying.

"I don't see anyone." Neil McCloud looked around. "What if this is all a hoax?"

"It's not a hoax," Harley Graham snapped. "Get serious. Whoever it is, they'll be here. No one is going to walk away from this much money."

"That's right, no one is. I'm over here, gentlemen." Cassie stepped out from behind a giant oak next to the public restrooms.

"Cassie?" Harley Graham's jaw dropped.

"Yes, Harley, it's me." She stopped several feet away from them. "Surprised?"

"I have to say, I am. I think all of us are." He rubbed his forehead. "You're the last person we'd expect to try this kind of thing."

"What kind of thing is that?" she taunted. "Making the people who murdered my sister and my father pay for it?"

"Blackmail." Cyrus McLeod's tone was sharp. "It doesn't seem quite your style."

"We were all good to you, Cassie," Neil told her. "Very good. Why are you doing this?"

"Oh, yes," she sneered. "You were all very good to me. You killed

279

most of my family and shortstopped every effort I made to get the facts. Thanks to you, Griffin Hunter's been walking around town all this time with people speculating behind his back. Is that fair?"

"I can't imagine Griffin's reputation is anything for you to defend." Neil's jaw worked, a sign of his growing anger. "This is more his type of thing anyway. He had to put you up to it. We all told you to stay away from him. He's bad news."

"As a matter of fact, Griff tried to talk me out of this. We're leaving town as soon as his house sells, and he wanted to just walk away. I couldn't do that. His name needs to be cleared, and my father and Diane deserve justice."

"If you wanted justice," Cyrus growled, "you'd give this book to the chief. All you want is the money. That makes you no better than the rest of us."

"So far we haven't admitted anything," Cyrus pointed out in his lawyer voice.

"But you did do it, didn't you?" She was so disgusted with all of them.

"Diane was an accident," Harley blurted out.

"Shut up, you old fool," Cyrus hissed. "All she's doing is guessing right now."

"An accident?" She studied him. "Then why didn't you come forward at the time?"

"We had our own reputations to think about." Harley shook off Cyrus's restraining hand.

"Then none of you should have started fooling around with my sister," she pointed out. "And what about my father? What was the problem with him?"

"Your father stuck his nose in where it didn't belong," Cyrus said.

"So, you admit you killed him?" she pushed. "I want to hear you say it."

"We're sorry about that." Harley mopped his sweating brow. "Diane, too. But neither of them would listen to reason."

Cassie moved one step closer. "But I will. Three hundred thousand of them. Do you have the money?"

"It's right here." Neil held up the briefcase. "Where's the diary?"

Cassie held up the package in her left hand. "I'll put it down right here. You toss the briefcase over. I'll check inside, and if the money's there, I'll just walk away."

"You don't think we're going to stand here and let you have both the money and the diary, do you?" Neil's tone was vicious. "Toss the diary over here."

"Uh-uh. I don't trust any of you. Look here. I'm putting it down. Toss the briefcase."

"You think we're going to stand still for this, you little bitch?" Neil's self-control had snapped. In three long strides, he was at Cassie's side. Before she could back away, he had an iron grip on her arm and tried to wrench away the diary."

"Let go of me." She struggled, but he was too strong for her.

"Give it to me, or you'll get what your tramp sister got."

The sound of a gunshot stunned everyone. Barry Dangler and two of his deputies stepped out from behind the restrooms. Griff was with them, moving with speed to Cassie's side.

"The next one won't be in the air." Dangler's disgust was evident. "Step away from the girl. And don't even think about running," he added, as Harley tried to back away. "I have deputies at your cars and two more here with me."

As he spoke, the two men he indicated stepped up, guns drawn, and forced the men to kneeling positions. The only sound that broke the night was the clink of handcuffs.

"You'll regret this, Barry," Cyrus threatened.

"I already have too much to regret," Dangler said, his tone sad. "I'd like to get a little of my self-respect back."

"You still have to prove this." Neil was in a rage. "I want to see what that diary says."

"Whatever it says doesn't matter." He held up a small tape recorder, pushed a button, and the entire conversation began to play back. "I've covered for you all long enough, and I have to say, I'm ashamed of myself. But I have a chance to correct things, and I'm doing it."

The three men were led away, swearing and protesting. Cassie watched the little tableau play out, hoping she wasn't going to be sick to her stomach.

"Are you all right?" Griff wrapped his arms around her. "I swear my heart stopped beating when I heard that shot. Tell me you're okay."

"I am now." She shook in his embrace. "I just want to get away from them. Take me home, please."

He held her tight against his body and looked at Dangler, who watched them.

The chief nodded. "Go on. I've got a busy night ahead of me." He held up the briefcase and the diary. "Cassie, I'll need to take your statement, but it can wait until tomorrow." He paused. "I just want to say I'm sorry. About a lot of things." Then he was gone.

Griff placed a soft kiss on her lips. "Okay, sugar. Let's blow this pop stand."

Chapter Forty-Three

Time dragged in the month since the McLeods and Harley had been arrested. Cassie gave a detailed statement to Barry Dangler, and they'd been shocked when he actually reached out his hand to Griffin. He didn't say anything—that was as much of an apology as he was giving to the town's bad boy, but they shook hands, banishing the past.

The story made every newspaper in Texas and some on the national scene. After all, three upstanding citizens arrested on double homicide charges was fodder for gossip everywhere. Especially in Stoneham. Cassie and Griff had to shut off their cells, checking with regularity in case there were calls they needed to return. After a couple days, they also stopped answering the door. Everyone, it seemed, wanted a firsthand account.

"They don't deserve anything at all," Cassie spat. "Not after the way everyone in this town has treated you."

"We can forget about them now," he told her. "We'll be gone soon enough."

His words turned out to be prophetic. His business sold faster than they'd expected. A man who read the lurid story in the *Dallas Morning News* saw the item about Griff selling out and called. He and his wife wanted to leave "the big bad city," as he called it, and regroup in a small town.

"At least the notoriety served one useful purpose." Cassie laughed.

Carol had paraded a steady stream of potential buyers through the house, most of them just satisfying their avid curiosity. But then the couple who'd bought the landscaping business asked if they might get a better price if they made it a package deal. Preliminary contracts were signed, the Marble Hills agent found a rental house for them, and they concluded the transaction on the purchase of the nursery. The movers arrived and carted away their belongings to the rental house, although much of what they had would go into storage until the new house was ready.

That afternoon, they drove into San Antonio, and Griff took Cassie shopping for wedding rings first then stopped at a florist to buy a rose. Afterward, they paid for their marriage license at the courthouse and emerged as Mr. and Mrs. Griffin Hunter. Barry Dangler, in his effort to make amends, had arranged for a judge who was a friend of his to perform the ceremony quickly.

"One perfect rose, Dewdrop. Just like before. That's you. My perfect flower." He tucked it in her hair then bought her a bridal bouquet of roses and mums and baby's breath. All in white. "For fidelity," he told her. "Just in case there's any question on your part."

He grinned when he said it, but Cassie knew the message he was giving her. The past was finished and done with. There was no one for either of them now or ever again. When he kissed her at the end of the ceremony and told her she'd always hold his heart for safekeeping, even the judge got a little teary-eyed.

In two days, they'd leave for a week in Hawaii, but tonight, they were spending the first night as man and wife in their rented house in Marble Hills. As soon as they returned, construction on their new home would begin, one with plenty of bedrooms for the family they planned to have.

On the way home from the city, they teased each other with

words and touches, so, by the time they reached the bedroom, they were both at fever pitch, frantic as they removed their clothes. Griff pulled back the covers on the bed and placed her on the cool sheets, lying down next to her. She moved in a restless rhythm against him, urging him, small whimpers escaping from her mouth. She was already so aroused, as much from relief at having everything behind them, that she was sure she could climax by herself.

"Easy, sugar," he crooned, as she shifted beneath his languid stroking. "We've got all the time in the world."

His thumbs brushed against her nipples, which were already in tight peaks, and stroked down the soft slope of her breasts. Wherever he touched with his hands, he followed with his mouth.

She wanted to pull him tight to her, but he took her wrists in a firm grip, pinning her hands over her head. He used his tongue to draw feathery circles at her navel while he drifted his other hand lower, parting her thighs with a gentle nudge and stroking the dampness between them.

"More," she moaned, and jerked as his fingers found her clit and massaged it.

"More what?" He watched her with heavy-lidded eyes.

She licked her lips, gaze locked with his. It still amazed her the erotic words they exchanged no longer embarrassed her or made her uncomfortable. They were so attuned to each other, so comfortable in what they did, that talking to him this way had become second nature for her. The words excited her as much as they did Griff.

"Rub my clit more. Rub my slit more." She shifted, trying to urge him to action with her body.

"And what else, sugar?"

"Fuck me with your fingers. Slide them into me. You know." As if for emphasis, she arched her body, pushing against his hand.

"Into you where, darlin'?"

"Into my pussy," she panted. "Way...in. Farther. Farther. Touch me way inside."

Sliding one long finger into her hot sheath, he felt her wet heat enveloping him.

"And what else? What else do you want me to do?"

"Suck me." She writhed under his touch. "Suck me, lick me, stick your tongue in me. Do it, Griffin. Now."

When he replaced his hand with his mouth, shivers raced over her entire body. His erection was hard and throbbing, testing his self-control, but he was determined to draw out her pleasure.

Separating her folds to plunge his tongue deeper inside, he felt her convulse, twisting, clenching at him as shudders overtook her. Her liquid poured like a waterfall into his mouth. He continued to touch and stroke as the storm subsided, just the aftershocks still producing light quivers.

"Good, sugar?" he whispered.

"Yes, but I want it all. I want to feel you inside me. Fill me, Griffin."

"You want my cock inside you, sugar?"

"Yes. Yes. Now. Oh, God, now."

Releasing her hands and bracing himself on his forearms, he entered her in one smooth stroke. This was the first time they'd fucked without the thin barrier of latex between them since that insane night on the lawn, and the sensation consumed him with heat. Skin to skin. He could hardly stand it.

Cassie let out a low moan as he filled her. He kept his tempo even, watching her face for signs she was reaching her peak again. When her body surged against him, he plunged hard—once, twice, then a final hard thrust as he poured into her. Her legs wrapped around him and her hands clutched at his straining muscles.

At last, they were quiet again, stretched out with their arms around each other, the lazily turning ceiling fan cooling their sweat-soaked bodies.

"I love you." She reached up and brushed her hand over his cheek.

"I love you, too, Cassie." He cradled her head to him. "God, I thought this day would never get here."

"I know what you mean."

She lifted her hand and looked at her wedding ring nestled with her engagement ring. The diamonds caught the light filtering in from outside. She wore both of them even when she was naked, insisting they were her talismans.

"Any regrets?" Griff asked as they lay naked on the bed, his hands continuing to touch her with learned familiarity.

"Not a one." She wrinkled her forehead at him. "You?"

"Are you kidding? I feel like the kid who woke up and found out there really is a Santa Claus." He kissed her, letting his lips linger over hers. "Tomorrow's a fresh start, sugar."

"I know. I never thought we'd get to this point."

"Are you still okay about going back to testify?" He still worried about how she'd handle it.

"As long as you're with me, nothing bothers me." She snuggled tighter to him. "And I'm glad that after all this time everyone will know the truth about my sister and my father."

"Dangler's been more than polite and accommodating to us."

"He should be, damn him." She sat up. "None of this might have happened if he hadn't had it in for you from the beginning."

"Let it go." He pulled her down again. "Tomorrow is the first day of the rest of our lives."

"Yes, it is, isn't it?"

"And I know just how to start it." He turned her toward him, his mouth coming down on hers. Cassie moaned under him, little bursts of pleasure that told him how heated her blood was becoming. Their bodies were finely tuned with each other, their give and take natural.

When they again lay gasping, side by side, Griffin pulled her to him the way he liked to, stroking her satiny skin, dropping little kisses here and there.

"I think it's against the law to be this happy." Cassie smiled, running a fingertip along the arm wrapped around her. "But we deserve it."

"I don't know how I got so lucky," Griffin murmured, "but I'll spend the rest of my life treasuring you. And our children, when they come."

"Mmm. Yes. Children. I can't wait."

He looked into her eyes and saw everything there he'd wanted for so long—love, desire, caring, and a future. The past six years had been hard on both of them. Seeing each other again could have been a painful ending rather than a new beginning. Whenever he looked at Cassie, he saw complete love and acceptance in her eyes, a love she was eager and happy to surround him with.

He wasn't a praying sort of man, but he gave thanks every day that circumstances had brought Cassie back into his life and given them a second chance. For the first time, he knew peace. Real peace, after years of torment and uncertainty.

The long journey was over. He and Cassie had each other, and the lies and deceit had been washed away. Cassie was where she belonged, and at last Griffin Hunter was content.

Sexy Designs by Desiree Holt

Chapter One

"Grace, you've done a fabulous job."

Ben Randall stood in the living room of a Paradise Ranch model townhouse and took in the exquisite décor. Blues and greens blended with subtle earth tones for a feeling of warmth without being overbearing. The furniture was inviting, especially bathed as it was by the sun spilling in from the large picture window.

"I'm glad you like everything."

"You promised me warm, sexy designs, and that's exactly what you gave me."

Grace Traynor slid folders and her iPad into her briefcase and snapped the lock. "Thanks, Ben. I'm happy we got just the look you wanted to achieve."

What he really wanted to achieve was Grace across a dinner table from him. Lying on the grass in warm sunshine. *Naked and in my bed.* From the day he met her, he'd been strongly attracted to her, an attraction that only increased over time. At sixty-five, his sex drive might be a little lower, but he hadn't lost any of the nuances of touch. And he'd learned long ago that a lot more than the physical made a relationship spark. He wasn't slow where women were concerned, but, for months, he'd been searching for the right opportunity to move forward with Grace, and each time it seemed he hit a wall.

In the months they'd been working together, he had made a giant number of casual overtures. She'd politely rebuffed every one of them. At first, he'd figured maybe she just didn't feel the same physical pull, the same interest in taking this out of the business arena. That would be disappointing, but he'd make himself deal with it. However, the more time they spent together, the more frequently he caught her looking at him with banked hunger in her eyes.

No, Grace was just as attracted to him as he was to her. Over time, he'd noticed whenever he came too close or invaded what he assumed was her personal space, she became as tense as a stretched rubber band. He'd love to know what that was all about. He just had to be smart enough to figure out what the problem was.

"Yes," he said now. "I agree."

"You know," she told him, "when you first brought me out here to look at this place and tried to share your vision with me, I thought you might be crazy."

He laughed. "Fourteen hundred empty acres with nothing but trees and deer? I might have felt the same way."

"No." She shook her head. "You had the vision. And the more you talked, the more I could see it."

He smiled and lifted her hand, brushing his lips across her knuckles then dropping it before she could tug it away. "But the credit for this goes to you."

He looked at the view from the sliding patio doors.

Selling the Crooked R ranch had been hard for him. Generations of Randalls had raised cattle on it, very successfully. But, somehow, the cowboy gene hadn't passed down to any of his three sons so he'd looked for a buyer, one who knew the business. And he'd kept fourteen hundred acres for himself.

It wasn't just that he needed something to do, although that was part of it. At sixty, he was far from ready to retire. He had visited friends who'd moved to one of the many Sun City developments or The Villages in Florida and been struck with the idea of creating a community for people fifty-five and over. A place where they could begin a new phase of their lives, with every amenity and convenience he could contrive. The community would have a definite Texas theme and be called Paradise Ranch because, as he told his sons, "It's for people entering a new phase of paradise."

Working with McMann Brothers Development, seeing his ideas

actually come to life, had revitalized him. Paradise Ranch showed him life had a lot of excitement still waiting for him. Meeting Grace Traynor had kicked it up another notch.

Alex McMann had recommended her as someone they often worked with, so he'd made an appointment. When he walked into her office, his heart did a little drum beat and his cock, which hadn't been interested in a lot lately, stood up and demanded attention. A silk blouse the same blue as her eyes, and navy slacks outlined a lush, mature figure. Highlighted sable hair fell in soft waves to just above her collar, and the wide smile she greeted him with made him want to taste those plump lips.

The first thing he'd thought was, *Holy shit!* He hadn't exactly been a hermit since his wife passed away, but he also hadn't met a woman who turned him on like this in more years than he wanted to count. The more time he spent with her, the more he was attracted to her. Not just her body, either. He wasn't a horny teenager anymore. Grace was smart, funny, easy to be with. Someone he wanted to spend time with outside the work environment.

A goal he knew would not be easy to achieve.

"Let's do one more walkthrough," she said to him. "Make sure we've got the feel you want for the townhouses before we start on the first detached villa."

Ben was sure she'd nailed it, but it gave him a chance to spend more time in her company. "Sounds good. Lead the way."

He had to concentrate on what she was saying as they moved from room to room, mesmerized as he was by the musical lilt to her voice and the tempting sway of her hips.

"Ben?"

He stopped, almost bumping into her as he realized she had

paused and turned to him.

"Sorry. Did I miss something? I was just enjoying the feel you've created here."

She laughed. "I don't think you've heard a word I said. We've spent a lot of time on this today. I think you need a break."

"What I think I need is a cup of coffee," he told her. "Or, better yet, a glass of wine. Thistle Creek Winery wants to open a retail outlet in the first town center we're building, and they sent over some bottles for us to try. Let's see what they gave us."

She took a step back, holding her briefcase tightly. "Oh, I don't think so." She made a show of looking at her watch. "It's actually later than I thought. I should get going."

"One glass of wine won't hurt." He winked. "To celebrate what we've done so far. Come on. I won't take no for an answer."

She stood there, frowning.

"Come on," he urged again. "You've done a terrific job with the model townhouses. Kept right to the theme without being excessive in your designs. And I want to see what you have in store for the villas and the first clubhouse. The wine is locked up in the model we're using as an office. We can sit outside and enjoy the late afternoon sunshine."

He considered it a major accomplishment that when he took her elbow to guide her along, she didn't protest. By the time they reached the offices and he'd taken down a bottle of cab, she actually appeared slightly less tense. He urged her outside where a small café table and chairs were set upon the patio. The air was heavy with the scent of new shrubbery and flowers and freshly mowed grass. There was no one else behind the row of townhouses, but in the distance he could hear the sounds of construction. The signs of the ongoing development always excited him.

Ben couldn't take his eyes away from her graceful neck or the smooth movement of her throat muscles as she swallowed some of the wine. *Jesus!* He was besotted with the woman. That was the only explanation for it. Probably had been since the day he'd met her.

"To a long and successful relationship," he said, touching his glass to hers.

"I'll drink to that."

"Based on our most recent conversations, I've been working on the sketches for the first clubhouse," Grace told him, setting her glass on the table. "Done some refining. Added a few things. And I have four new interior design plans for the villas. Ideas for accessories and new color schemes. I think you'll like them."

"I like everything you've done so far, Grace. You managed to capture the exact feel I was looking for and blend it with the architecture. That's not an easy task."

"Actually, it's turning out to be one. I love your concept, especially since I'm Texas born and bred." She grinned. "And I've looked at a lot of Texas art lately for inspiration."

"Oh?"

"Mmhmm. Visited some museums. Even talked my way into a few private collections."

Ben studied her face as she spoke. She looked relaxed for the first time since he'd met her. The air was heavy with late spring warmth, and when Grace settled into her chair, she'd taken off her jacket. The late afternoon sun picked up the highlights in her hair and bathed her face in an amber glow. A gentle breeze kissed the soft fabric of her blouse so it outlined her breasts. And was that just the hint of her nipples barely discernible? Was she reacting to him, despite her *Keep*

Away attitude?

God, he hoped so. She was like a luscious plum, ripe for the picking.

As they chatted, very casually he lifted the wine bottle and topped off their drinks. Intent on what she was saying, Grace picked up the glass and sipped from it. He loved seeing her like this, less on guard, not quite so controlled. Could he possibly take this opportunity to move things along a little?

"You know," he said slowly, "in all the time we've sent together, you've never really told me much about yourself."

She tilted her head slightly. "What is it you want to know? I'm sure Josh gave you all my credentials. I've worked with them on a lot of projects. And you have my brochure."

"But I know nothing about Grace Traynor, the woman." He stroked the tip of one finger over her arm, just a brief touch. He felt a slight tremor and wondered if it was anxiety at his touch or, hopefully, controlled desire. If it was anxiety, what could possibly be the cause of it? He'd done his best not to crowd her.

"She's really very boring." She picked up her glass again and, this time, took a healthy swallow.

"I'll bet she's not." He took a chance and stroked her arm again. Maybe the wine was mellowing her, but she didn't jerk away. Instead, he noticed her nipples had become even more prominent beneath the thin fabric of her shirt. "For example, you never talk about your family. I'm sure I've bored you to tears about mine."

"Not at all. I love hearing about your ranch. It's too bad none of your sons wanted to take it over."

He shrugged. "It is what it is. I came to terms with it a long time ago. And Paradise Ranch is really filling my life in a way I never thought it would. But there we go, talking about me again. I want to know about you. Let's start with something simple. I know you have a degree from Rhode Island School of Design, but what made you start your own business?"

"I wanted my independence."

She said it very simply but in a way that told Ben there was a lot of meaning beneath that one sentence.

"And you certainly have it. You've done very well for yourself. I'm surprised, though, that you never wanted to marry. Have children."

The muscles in her face tightened, and her glance slid away. "I'm happy by myself."

"So no special man in your life? No one to celebrate holidays and successes with?"

She turned and looked at him, and he was startled by the pain in her eyes. "What exactly is it you want from me, Ben? You must have better things to do than playing Twenty Questions with me."

"What do I want from you?" Here was his opening. "I want to take you out to dinner. Maybe dancing. Spend a little time with you when we're not discussing business."

"Why?"

The question surprised him. "Why? Because you are an incredibly attractive, appealing woman, and I'd like to get to know you better."

She lifted her hand, breaking his contact with her arm, and took another swallow of wine. "I'm not all that. I guarantee you'd be disappointed."

What in hell? There was something going on here he didn't quite understand.

"Since I have no expectations, that wouldn't happen. But I think we'd enjoy each other's company. When was the last time you went out for an evening that wasn't related to business?"

She laughed. "If I went out with you, it would be."

"No. I'd make sure it was nothing but pleasure."

She paused, nibbled on her bottom lip in a way that made his cock swell and his balls ache. Unexpected desire flushed through him, stronger than he'd felt in years. All of a sudden, it became very important to convince her to do this.

"I don't think—"

"Right," he interrupted. "Don't think. Let's just do it. Tonight," he said on impulse. "And I know just the place."

She lifted an eyebrow, her expression skeptical. "And where would that be?"

He shook his head. "It's a surprise. But I promise you'll like it. No pressure. Just an evening out with a friend."

He held his breath, waiting for her answer. Maybe it was the wine she'd had, or maybe it was the relaxed environment. Whatever the trigger was, she finally nodded her head.

"All right. Tonight." She gave a breathy laugh. "Before I change my mind."

"Excellent." He wanted to pump his fist in the air. Instead, he looked at his watch. "It's almost five. Why don't you go home, change into something that's not your work clothes, and I'll pick you up at seven."

"I'm afraid everything I have looks like work clothes."

"Then just something different. Give me your address, and I'll see you at seven."

***

I have to be crazy. That's the only answer for this.

Grace repeated it to herself over and over again as she drove home from the Paradise Ranch site. What would Ben Randall think if she told him she hadn't been out on a date in twenty years? Oh, she didn't count the public events she'd attended for business where she'd been able to snag some business associate as an escort. She usually asked someone on the back end of a bad divorce who was happy to have someone's shoulder to cry on for an evening. Less danger for her that way.

Grace could have given them all chapter and verse on a bad divorce. More than that, on a bad marriage. Or what happens when you choose unwisely. Been there, done that, got more than one T-shirt to show for it.

For a brief moment, Alan Vaughan's face flashed across her mind, lips twisted in that supercilious smile he always had, eyes flashing with contempt. She had been so swept off her feet by him, thrilled at the age of twenty-two that an older man, handsome and rich, seemed to be so besotted with her. By the time she hit her twenty-fifth birthday, she had realized her appeal to him—she was young and malleable and easy to get under his thumb.

Finding her own spirit and grit had been an arduous journey, and painful. Three more years had passed, years that almost destroyed her, before she had arranged things so she could walk out and leave him. But her confidence in herself as a woman had taken a big hit that she'd never recovered from. She had also made a vow that no man would ever have an impact on her life again.

She had her work to stimulate her mentally and her trusty toys to satisfy herself sexually. By the time she hit her fiftieth birthday, she had firmly entrenched her life in a pattern she had no desire to break.

Then along came Ben Randall, six feet of physically fit man, with thick, steel-gray hair, a deep tan, and brown eyes like melted chocolate. She could almost see the pheromones floating in the room whenever she was around him. After every meeting, her toy box got a strenuous workout because it required a lot to take the edge off the desire Ben aroused in her.

Desire!

Hell, she hadn't felt sexual vibes for a man in so long, she'd begun think she'd buried them for good. Then Ben walked into her office, and arousal slammed into her like a speeding car. She had even taken to wearing a tailored jacket when they were together, to hide her hardened nipples that stood at attention at the sound of his voice. Today, she'd just been so warm she'd had to take it off. Had he noticed her reaction to him?

She had done her best to hide her reactions from him, to send her *Keep Off* signals. Although he'd respected them, it wasn't hard to spot the latent hunger that flared in his eyes whenever they were together. What stunned her was how tempted she was. No man had excited her even a little bit in all these years. After Alan, she'd shut that door so firmly no one had been able to open it.

So what was she doing, going on a date with Ben Randall? A date, for god's sake! Did she even know how to behave on one anymore?

The whole situation rumbled through her mind as she drove home, pulled into her garage, and carried her briefcase into the house. It bedeviled her while she stripped off her clothes, tossing them in the laundry hamper or the one for dry cleaning. And as she turned on the shower in her bathroom and prepared to step under the spray.

Ben Randall. He'd set her nerves buzzing from the first moment she'd seen him. At the time she'd told herself to turn him down as a client, but the lure of decorating such a massive project was too strong to resist. The unexpected attraction had grown over the many weeks they'd worked together until, now, it lurked constantly at the back of her mind. And made her body hum with desire whenever they were together.

She was afraid, plain and simple. Afraid of her feelings, afraid history might repeat itself, no matter that he and Alan were totally different people. Afraid of letting herself get out of control. Yet, here she was, preparing to have dinner with him.

She paused for a moment and took a hard look at herself in the mirror over the sink. *Not too bad.* She did her treadmill almost every day and tried to fit in an exercise class once a week. Her skin didn't have quite the elasticity it once did, and her breasts, while round, were a little less firm. But, all in all, not too bad.

Wait! What am I doing? We're going out to dinner, not getting naked.

Damn straight. That part of her life was long over. But, as she stood under the water, her body humming with need, the image of Ben rose unbidden. A pulse throbbed in her pussy, and her nipples tingled. She poured body wash into one hand, worked it into a lather, and slid that hand along the slightly curved slope of her tummy to the folds of her sex. Nobody's hands except hers had explored her there in all these years. By now, she'd learned exactly how to touch and stroke to give herself satisfaction. How to tug and pinch her clitoris to push herself up the slope of need. Bracing one foot on the built-in shower bench, she slid two fingers inside her body, feeling the clasp of her wet inner walls.

What if these were Ben's fingers? What if he were in the shower here with me? What would he look like naked?

As soon as the thought intruded, she made a deliberate effort to banish it from her mind. The mind she was obviously losing. She should just stop this, finish her shower, and get dressed. But there was no way she could go out with Ben while still riding the edge of arousal. No, she needed to take care of this first so she could be her usual composed, together self. Gritting her teeth, she accelerated the rhythm of her fingers, dropping the other hand to play with her clit at the same time. Her climax uncoiled from deep in her womb until finally—finally!—her cunt clamped down on her fingers and her body shook with her release.

She withdrew her hand, slightly breathless and weak in the knees, and dropped her foot from the bench. Leaning against the wall, she waited for her pulse to slow, aware that she really hadn't taken the edge off at all. In fact, if she were truthful, she was more aroused than before. How was that possible?

She needed to get her act together, or she'd be a hot mess when Ben showed up. Finishing her shower quickly, she turned off the water, stepped out, and wrapped herself in a large bath towel. A glance at the tiny clock told her she had an hour before Ben arrived to fetch her. More than enough time to lock away all those unwanted impulses and ideas and put on her public face.

Letting out a slow breath, she set about her task.

www.ingramcontent.com/pod-product-compliance
Lightning Source LLC
Chambersburg PA
CBHW021458240626
47154CB00002B/431